I0546798

THE DARK TIMES

P. A. Douglas   Dane Hatchell

Copyright © 2014 by P. A. Douglas & Dane Hatchell
Copyright © 2014 by Severed Press
www.severedpress.com
All rights reserved. No part of this book may be
reproduced or transmitted in any form or by any
electronic or mechanical means, including
photocopying, recording or by any information and
retrieval system, without the written permission of
the publisher and author, except where permitted by
law.
This novel is a work of fiction. Names,
characters, places and incidents are the product of
the author's imagination, or are used fictitiously.
Any resemblance to actual events, locales or persons,
living or dead, is purely coincidental.
ISBN: 978-1-925225-45-7

All rights reserved.

Author's Note:

Everyone has a grand picture for what the zombie apocalypse will be like. In truth it is pretty exciting. The idea of getting to start over. A new utopian order to the world that lets us come together as equals for once. The sad true however is hard to swallow. The apocalypse will only draw you closer to who you really are. Looking in the mirror at the end of it all would be a very scary thing indeed.

Acknowledgements:

P. A. Douglas would like to thank his co-author and friend, Dane, for all the hard work on this project. To Sean Leonard for his valued contribution. To Severed Press for being a great press to work with over the years. And to August Burns Red. Listening to you while I write makes the words flow so much easier.

Prologue
The year 2018

Life can turn on a dime, and sometimes the turn has already come and gone before we even see it coming.

"Ron, I think I found a movie for us to watch. Hurry up. It looks like it's already started."

Leah put the remote control for the television down on the couch and took a sip of her Bloody Mary. The shaft of celery periscoped from the top and jabbed her cheek. The cocktail was the perfect complement to the bag of popcorn she had pulled from the microwave only minutes before. The saltiness of the popcorn brought out the richness of the spicy tomato blend that cracked the ice in her cup.

"Yeah? What is it?" Ron poked his head from the kitchen's entrance into the living room.

She put her feet on the coffee table and gazed above her blue toenail polish. "It's a zombie movie. I don't know the name of this one. I don't think we've seen it. You're missing it."

"I'm making a sandwich—be there in a minute." Ron hurried back to finish up before the guts started to fly. He tightened the lid on the mayo, gathered the provolone and ham, and stuck them in the fridge. Before he closed the door, he plucked out a bottle of Yellow Jacket Porter from the top shelf, but needed something to open it with. "What's happening?" He opened a drawer, fumbled through measuring spoons, and carefully parted knives until spotting the onyx handle of the bottle opener.

"The zombies are wandering out of a cemetery and are walking the streets."

"Zombies don't walk, honey. Zombies shamble, or lurch, or something." Ron opened the pantry door and scanned the choice of chips to go with his sandwich. After sampling a bag of corn chips and deciding they were stale, he opened a new bag of sour cream and green onion potato chips. "Are the zombies eating anybody yet?"

"No—hey, this looks like it was filmed downtown."

"Downtown, here in Killeen? Why would they come to this town to film a zombie movie? This is small town Texas. Zombies on the beach would've had more appeal. It can't be our downtown. Must be some other place. Downtowns in most cities look alike."

He opened the bag of chips and crunched one down, then popped open the beer and chased the chip with a gulp. He folded the top of the chip bag and clamped on a clothespin to keep it fresh before placing it back in the pantry.

"I can't hear you. I'm trying to listen. I don't think it's a movie."

Ron stepped into the living room with beer and plate in hand. He stopped next to Leah and took another chug of beer. "That's Channel Ten News. See, that's Meg Gallo. Did you change the station?"

"No. Those zombies are coming out of Memory Gardens Cemetery. You know, by that big Baptist church. There was some audio in the beginning but now it's out. Meg looks scared."

Ron sat on the couch next to Leah and set his beer on the coffee table.

So much for watching a good horror movie, he thought.

The camera panned away from Meg, the reporter.

"Hey look, some homeless guy just walked out of the alley and those zombies over there are about to get him." He took a bite from the sandwich. With his mouth half full, he said, "Wow, look at that. They're on him like a swarm of locusts."

The video feed abruptly stopped. The screen stared back with obsidian emptiness.

"Oh, my God. What's happening? Ron, what should we do?"

"Uh, find another channel to watch?" Ron drank more beer and belched.

Leah shoved his shoulder. "I'm serious. You just saw what happened. What's going on? What are we going to do?"

"You bought that? You thought that was real?" Ron chuckled.

"What else am I supposed to think? It was on the news."

"I'll give you a hint. What's today?"

"Tuesday."

"No, the date?"

"The first."

"And, what month is it?"

"April."

"Annnnnd, what is April first famous for?"

The tension gripping Leah's face relaxed. "Oh, April Fool's Day."

"That's right. The dead return to life—April Fool's." Ron made a victorious smirk.

"But that didn't look like a joke. It looked so real."

"Do you remember one year when the news did the fake story that the Liberty Bell was getting a sponsor and was going to be renamed the Taco Bell Liberty Bell? What we just watched was the same type of thing. That news story looked like a prank gone south. They were having audio problems and probably pulled the plug from the live feed and the station wasn't prepared for it. The zombies looked real enough, but when that guy conveniently stepped out of the alley to become dinner, it looked like a set up to me. They needed a better script." Ron picked up the remote and changed the channel. "Pulp Fiction. I love this movie. Let's watch it."

Leah mindlessly reached in the bag and picked out some popcorn. She mechanically chewed the kernels, seemingly oblivious to what was on the television screen.

Chapter 1

"Rico, don't you think you've had enough tonight? Why don't you go home to your wife?"

James Connors, better known as Pop, the owner of Pop's Lounge, leaned on an elbow and smiled with one eye half closed. He had a tint of genuine concern in his voice, like always. Running a bar for the last forty years in downtown Killeen had taught him many life lessons on the power of suggestion. Taking into account the customer's level of inebriation was essential.

Rico's expression didn't change as he continued to stare through the short, red haired proprietor. Four empty shot glasses set in a neat row on the bar in front of him as he held onto the last shot he had finished some five minutes before. The empty glass reminded him of how he felt as he gripped it tightly in one hand.

"Rico... Hey, big guy. Whatever's eating at you, let it go."

No response.

Rico looked away from the barkeep and stared into the distance.

"You're sitting here in your police uniform getting shit faced. What if this gets back to your chief? You don't want to jeopardize your job."

The officer's cheeks puffed out like a bullfrog, widening his mouth as whiskey from his stomach rose to irritate his throat. "I'm off duty. Give me another."

"You've had five shots in the last hour. I can't give you anymore. It's my legal duty as a bartender to stop serving a patron if I think they're showing signs of inebriation."

"Fuck the law."

"Can't do that, buddy. Now you're talking about my ass. I can't let you get snookered to the point you leave out of here and

4

hurt someone on the road. I'd get fined and shut down if that happens."

Rico closed his eyes, adrift on a skiff through time and space. The bar chatter and music blended into an eerie silence. He had been alone before in life, but he had never felt this alone. Each passing second bled out an ounce of his will to live. The whiskey didn't replace what he'd lost, as he hoped. His trusted friend that eased the pain had finally let him down. He shifted the glass to the other hand and mindlessly tapped the side with a finger.

"She's not home," he finally said.

"Who? Oh, your wife?"

"Not home. Says she can't live with me anymore. Blames it on my drinking." Rico turned his gaze to Pop for the first time since he sat down. It had been hard to look other people in the eye these days, thinking maybe if he didn't engage them personally, then they couldn't see him. Because if they saw him for whom he was, he would be forced to acknowledge the problem. Pop's Irish grin melted a dam of bitter emotions. "I blame my drinking on my job. Fuck my job. Fuck the law. Fuck life."

The old man nodded. His green eyes sparkled under time-marred eyelids. "You're not the first cop to sit at my bar and drown his sorrows. I get that the job is tough. Day after day dealing with the worst society has to offer. Long hours, low pay, not knowing if the next guy you pull over for running a red light will whip out a gun and blow your head off. It sounds to me that you've just lost focus."

"Focus?"

"Sure, think back to why you took the job some . . . how long ago was it?"

"I finished the Academy when I was twenty-two. That was eight years ago. Hmm," Rico grimaced. "Eight years sounds like such a long time. Right now, it feels more like it was yesterday. I wish it were yesterday. I'd have done things differently."

"You went into law enforcement because you knew the American dream couldn't continue without men and women like you. You saw people getting older, like your parents, and wanted them to live a safe, happy life. You wanted your children growing up in an environment where they could play outside and go to school and make something of themselves." Pop pointed to the officer's name badge. "Sergeant Rico J. Cruz. You didn't become a Sergeant by eating doughnuts and directing traffic. You've worked your way up from the bottom and hung in there. Showed yourself to be the cream of the crop. The drive inside that led to your promotion to Sergeant is still there. Sure, the job's tough, but I've been in this business long enough to know that finding refuge in the bottom of a glass isn't all related to work."

Pop leaned toward Rico. His gaze cut like a priest waiting for a confession.

Rico grimaced again as he squeezed the shot glass. His face reddened under the dim, yellow lights above the bar. He had promised himself he wouldn't cry over the matter. For God's sake, he was a grown man after all. Tears would be a sure sign of defeat—ultimate humiliation. A deep breath strengthened his resolve.

"The drinking didn't start until . . . until Mary Etta started losing interest in me. We were married pretty young. Not more than kids, really. We were so in love though." His expression softened as he placed the shot glass on the counter. "Things were great at first. We lived in an apartment for the first two years. Those were the best of times. We bought a house, and she went to work. It all kind of started then. She was working with a lot of women her age that weren't married. Sometimes she would go out with them to bars and clubs. You know, when I worked night shift. I guess I stopped paying her the special attention women need." Rico lifted his head and with glistening eyes gazed at Pop. "At some point, she got that special attention from other men." His voice broke, and he clenched his teeth to keep his angst from spilling out.

Pop reached over and placed his hand on Rico's shoulder. "That's a shame. I wish I could say things like that don't happen very often but that wouldn't be true. I hear a story like that so much in this line of work that I think it's become the norm. Sometimes I think marriage licenses should only be good for three years. It's just the way society has gone. You're about to enter a new phase in life, buddy. Don't worry, there are plenty of hot women in the world that's in the same situation as you. It'll take a little time. You'll get over it." Pop raised his eyebrows. "But you gotta take control of this thing. You're better than that. Accept it for what it is and move on. You've got your whole life ahead of you."

Despite the fact Rico looked like his mind was a thousand miles away, he had heard every word. Pop was a kind man, even though he was also the kind you didn't want to cross. Right now, Pop felt like his best friend. Hell, maybe even more like his own father used to be back when he was a kid. Before his sister Jennifer died.

Rico sighed, and then said, "I've been trying to convince myself to move on for some time. I didn't know how to do that. I still don't. But, I hear you, Pop. I hear you, and I know what you mean. Thanks for giving me hope."

"You see, you've got to get out of the trap in your mind and get back into the swing of things. Not that I don't appreciate the business... I really do. But push the bottle away. Get some rest. Buy some new clothes and maybe change your hairstyle. You might look good with one of them Mohawk cuts. Seems all the rage these days. Well, at least that's what my grandson says."

"I'd probably look like an iguana."

"Some women love iguanas," Pop chuckled.

Rico let out a rip of laughter that had half the bar turning his way. When he managed to regain control, he said, "Pop, you slay me. You're the best."

"I'm just glad to see you smile. How about I call you a cab?"

"Nah, I can call one of my men on patrol and get them to pick me up and take me home. Don't worry. You aren't going to read about me in the morning paper."

"Good deal. Go home and get some rest." Pop patted Rico on the shoulder just before turning to attend to the needs of another customer at the bar.

Pop's right. Mary Etta shouldn't ruin my life. She don't want me? Fuck it. I can't let her do this to me. I can't let her ruin my job. I've worked too hard to blow it all on that bitch. Rico surprised himself. He had taken the blame for everything until now. *She is a bitch. A lying, cheating, good for nothing cu—* He stopped himself as he had vowed never to disrespect any woman to that level. From now on, things were going to change. They had to.

Rico's stomach reminded him he hadn't eaten since noon. He looked at his watch and thought how a pizza sure would be good right now. It would be hard to get a pizza and not have beer with it. He didn't need any more alcohol and decided he'd hit the next fast food joint on the way out.

Pop was at the other end of the bar when Rico waved goodbye. Pop waved back, showing his new set of dentures. Before Rico could rise, someone shouted.

"Look by the window. What's that?"

A *thump* against the storefront window followed. Someone looking more dead than alive mashed their face against the glass, startling some of the patrons. From the looks of the guy, it was probably safe to assume he was a member of the growing homeless crowd. He looked to be as rough as rough could get.

Pop's lounge played a mixture of soft jazz and blues in the background. It was one of the quieter bars in the area where people could meet and actually hold a conversation. Most everyone in the bar had their attention on the homeless man at the front window. He kept pounding on the window as if he wanted in, but was too drunk to figure out he wasn't actually in front of the door. Not counting Pop and Rico, there were close to thirty people in all watching the strange scene. A few sat at the bar by Rico while others sat scattered about in chairs and at tables drinking and carrying on in conversation. This was, of course, before the show they watched now. Other homeless people must have been drawn to the commotion, because a few more came out of the shadows to join in the banging session outside.

A bloated hand slapped the glass and left a trail of wet ooze.

A woman shrieked. "Eww… Gross, what is that?"

Louis Armstrong's classic voice sang over the sound system:
'I see trees of green, red roses too'
'I see them bloom for me and you'
'And I think to myself, what a wonderful world.'

"What the hell? I just cleaned those windows." Pop reached under the bar and pulled out a shiny, maple baseball bat. "Those bums are bad for business!"

Rico held up his hand. "Let me get this, Pop. It's probably just some high school kids pulling a prank." Pop's talk and the alcohol worked together to stoke Rico's fire. He was an officer of the law, and he was about to prove to himself and others that the real Rico Cruz was back in control of his life.

The barstool squealed across the concrete floor when he stood. Whoever this was had picked the wrong place and wrong time to try the patience of a lawman not in the mood to put up with any shit.

"There are more out in the street. Something's wrong with them. They seem lost," a thin girl in a red pencil skirt said, looking out another window. She flipped her long blonde hair to the side and brought her martini to her lips while keeping her gaze toward the street.

Rico headed for the door and watched his own reflection pass over the pawing vagrant on the other side. The shirttail of his uniform hung over his pants, and his tie was crooked. He looked a mess.

What a slob. I'm going to change a lot of things in my life—starting tomorrow.

Rico straightened his tie and approached the bar entrance.

The background music grossly mismatched the scene.
I see skies of blue and clouds of white
The bright blessed day, the dark sacred night
And I think to myself, what a wonderful world

When he reached the door and opened it, a man in a dark suit waited just outside. The skin on the man's face looked like worn leather. His cheeks were sunken giving him a skeletal smile. Rico froze—stunned at the sight of the person's face. The man in the dark suit appeared to be dead, but that just couldn't be. That didn't make sense. In the years he had spent on the force, he had run into his fair share of vagrants. The homeless population was always a little beat up looking. A little rough around the edges. But this man took the cake. His skin looked decayed.

While trying to wrap his mind around what he saw, two other vagrants bum rushed from his peripheral, slamming him against the open door. Rico fell backward into the establishment, landing hard on his butt on the floor. One of the attackers had grabbed hold of him and landed on top. The vagrant tried to pin Rico's arms to his side during the fall.

Rico had been taken by such surprise that he was lost at what to do next. He had expected to flex his muscles and give a stern warning to the homeless person to end the situation. Maybe it was the booze, maybe the emotions. Whatever it was, he had trouble focusing. The man on top of him writhed and slobbered thick muck. Rico managed to bring his arms up for protection. A withered face peered back at him with teeth chomping into empty air. The officer forced his forearm against his attacker's throat holding the bites at bay.

The other two assailants had turned their attention to the crowded bar.

The blonde haired woman in the skirt jumped out of her booth, sloshing most of her drink onto the floor as the mayhem began. Several of the patrons screamed and ran by the walls for safety. A few of the younger men, on the other hand, stepped forward to confront the deranged interlopers.

The three men who stepped forward to do something were all very different. One guy was short, looked to be in his early twenties. Height didn't appear to be a hindrance. His wide frame made him a tank of a man. His pectorals bulged under his white shirt, and it was obvious he chose the tight fit as an intimidation tactic, or as a way to attract the ladies. Of the other two men at his side, one was tall and skinny and looked like he should be working as a tech support nerd at a computer store. He had thick framed glasses and wore a tie. The other man was not as notable. Aside from a small tribal tattoo that peeked out from the sleeve on his left arm, he was just a regular looking Joe. Really though, they were just ordinary people. Just guys at a bar trying to relax and have a good time. They probably were enjoying themselves before the crazy freaks busted into Pop's and attacked a police officer.

Rico was still on his back, wrestling with the one that had landed on him. Even though the thing didn't feel like it weighed much, its strength more than made up for it. How was that sick old man able to keep him down?

Shouts and screams echoed out from male and female voices alike.

Louis sang on:

'I hear babies cryin', I watch them grow'
'They'll learn much more than I'll ever know'
'And I think to myself, what a wonderful world'

"Hey, buddy, what the hell's the big idea?" The beefy short man shoved a finger into the chest of one of the vagrants. His attitude was a powerful as his punch.

The vagrant staggered back. Only these weren't normal vagrants. It was clear to everyone in the bar these weren't homeless people. Their body movements were all wrong—robotic—not natural, and that wasn't ordinary dirt and grime on their faces. The smell that preceded them was beyond sour body odor. It was a musty smell mingled with rot and decay. It was the smell of death. It lingered in the air so thick it burned at the back of the nostrils and found refuge in the throat.

The computer geek put a hand over his mouth. "God, they smell worse than feta cheese." He muffled a gag.

"That ain't no shit!" The man with the tribal tattoo agreed, sticking his tongue out like a dog trying to get a bad taste out of its mouth.

"Someone, help that policeman," a female voice shouted.

The two decaying vagrants continued their slow trek toward muscle man, computer nerd, and tattoo arm. Rico fought for his life, and right now, the odds favored the attacker.

The woman screamed again, "Do something!" The urgency in her cry slapped people out of the debilitating fear cementing them to the floor. It's been written, 'All the world's a stage, and all the men and women merely players.' Her command acted like a movie director calling *'Action'* for the scene to start, setting the would-be actors into their roles. This wasn't a play, or a script from some silly movie. This was real life. In real life, there is no script.

The beefy workout man shoved the smelly bum in front of him again, knocking him back just like before. It caught its balance, as if becoming more comfortable in its new life, and continued its approach with a snarl. Its lips parted, showing rotted yellow teeth. The stench that bellowed out could only be described as coming from the sewage pits of Hell.

"What's wrong with these people?" the muscle man said with his arms held out at the ready.

The computer nerd opened his mouth as if he was about to say something. Instead, he gasped as if it was his last breath.

The nerd's outburst distracted the muscle man enough for the bum kept at bay to lunge forward, sinking its teeth into his hand. Blood spurted from his callused palm as the creature mashed its jaws together and thrashed its head from side to side. The man yelled so loud that it hurt Rico's left ear. His cry ignited the crowd, throwing another wave of panic across the bar. Blood splattered to the floor, peppering the side of Rico's face.

The creature pulled away with a mouthful of human flesh, its teeth stained with crimson and stuck bits of meat.

Like a magic trick performed by the great Houdini, the muscle man's hand was missing three fingers. A river of red gushed from the wound down his arm. He held it in front of his face, staring in disbelief, and lost all control of rationality.

"What the fuck?" the tattooed man whispered, his gaze locked on the second ghoul shuffling toward him and the geek.

The zombie—although not described as such until later—continued to chew a bit of meaty fingers in momentary contentment.

"Get outta my bar!" Pop stepped out from around the counter with bat at the ready.

'Yes, I think to myself, what a wonderful world'
'Oh yeah!'

*

Rico, still suffering from the ill effects of the alcohol, kept his attacker at bay with one arm against the throat. The creature gnashed and thrashed on top of him, determined to sink its teeth into any parts Rico was dumb enough to place in its path.

In the few moments he had been on his back, he had come to accept an unbelievable possibility. The vagrants were people, but they were no longer alive. It wasn't the alcohol playing tricks on his mind either. These creatures were dead—zombies. How they were able to function was beyond his reasoning. God, Satan, or science was responsible. Either way, everyone was fucked.

Rico mustered up his strength and gave a hefty shove, hoping to dislodge the attacker off him. It wasn't enough to do the job. The creature's bony arms pushed back, tugging at his tie while keeping a firm grip. The officer grunted, and for a moment, thought he was going to shit on himself. His muscles throbbed as he waited to build enough strength for another try. A second shove and he felt the sweet relief of the dead thing finally lifting off him. He had managed to use his left knee and both arms to shift his assailant off balance and toss it onto the floor beside him.

Rico's body ached, and a slight numbing buzz in his head made it hard to rise to his feet without keeling over. The world steadied after a few seconds, and he saw the front door was still wide open. One look outside told him this fight was just beginning. A mob of reanimated dead slowly ambled toward the bar from the street. He reached up, slammed the door shut, and locked the deadbolt in one fluid motion. It was just in time. Seconds later, the dead lined up next to the windows. Grimy hands banged and clawed against the glass. How long would the glass hold out before shattering into a thousand pieces?

They wanted in, and if many more showed up, there would be no way to stop them.

"What's happening?" someone shouted.

When Rico looked up, he saw images that would forever be burned in his memory. Things that would still haunt him later at night when he tried to close his eyes. Pop was coming from behind the bar heading toward two men who looked like they were waiting to help. A third man, who looked like he ate steroids for dessert, sat on the floor with his back against the bar. Blood dotted his face and an arm was covered in blood from an injured hand. He was obviously suffering from shock from the frozen expression on his pale face. Most of the crowd kept its distance, keeping backs against the wall. They reminded Rico of cattle. And, unless more of the men grew a set, then all would be heading to the slaughter shortly.

The zombie that had apparently attacked the man on the floor was on its knees in the middle of the room, chewing away on something in its mouth. It didn't take much imagination to figure out what it was. The sight of blood on its hand and face brought further chills down Rico's spine.

Pop had nutted up and was ready for action. The old man showed no fear on his face as he poised the bat over his shoulder. For a second, Pop reminded Rico of a warrior from medieval times—a soldier on the battlefield where it's kill or be killed. He wanted to dash over and help his friend, but he was still faced with a problem of his own. The ghoul he had tossed off of himself managed to stagger to its feet. If it were possible, it looked angrier than it did before. It hissed an evil warning of its intentions. Drool dripped like thick slime from its dry, cracking lips.

The creature made its move, but this time, Rico was ready.

The officer weaved to the side and grabbed the creature's outstretched arm. It tumbled to the floor like the drunken vagrant Rico had assumed it was. He wished it was only a drunken vagrant. Hell, Rico would take ten bums on the street with only his bare hands if he could have made a trade. The smell of cheap alcohol and B. O. would be a welcomed relief from the death stench emanating from these things.

This man... this man is already dead, Rico thought, pulling the pistol from the holster on his hip. *I wonder how I'm going to write this up on the report?*

"Freeze!" Rico shouted, the barrel of his pistol leveled at the chest of the assailant.

The zombie had no reaction to the warning. It had one drive in life and nothing seemed to deter it. Its feet slapped against the floor, and it stepped forward with unexpected quickness.

"I said stand down, or I will fire!"

Its two hands were nearly on him before he knew it. Rico jerked the trigger, rather than squeeze, but at this distance, he had little fear that he'd miss. The .40 caliber report of Rico's Glock reverberated off the walls. The confinements of the bar made the discharge *boom* more like a small explosion than a handgun.

The bullet found its mark, striking the attacker directly in the chest.

The damn thing didn't stop. Rico's eyes went wide, and he froze for a brief second.

He had been a member of the police force for years. In that time, he had done his fair share of hard work. A few car chases. Stopping a robbery. Dodged a few bullets that flew his way. But he never was the one who pulled the trigger in an altercation. In recent years, the academy had upgraded some of the simulation exercises to house lifelike replicas of real people during a shooting scenario. Rico had put a bullet in those dummies countless times, sometimes choosing areas of the body to hit not known for stopping the enemy—just to make it more challenging. Head shots, shots to the gut and shoulder. He even managed to shoot one right in the eye once. An ear, a knee, and even below the belt, right in the twig and berries. Those shots didn't earn any points, but it was enough to gain his superior's respect. None of that training had prepared him for what had just happened—shooting into real flesh, even though this flesh wasn't alive. There was no way it could be, even though the damn thing moved.

The gun jolted his wrist when he fired. He expected to see a fist sized hole open in its chest when the 180 grain slug of lead slammed into it, followed by a gush of blood. The zombie should have dropped to the floor like a sack of potatoes, but there was no blood. The bastard briefly slowed on the bullet's impact but kept coming. When the bullet punctured the dry, decaying skin that lay beneath the burial suit, there was only a puff of rancid dust. The stench huffed out an assaulting funk that made Rico gag.

"Stay back, I said!" Rico aimed again.

"Shoot it!" Someone shouted.

That's what Rico did. He realized no amount of preparation could guarantee how an officer of the law would react in a high-risk situation. Rico reacted the exact way he had always thought he would, but the results were far different than he thought possible.

Panicked cries resonated off of the walls with the blast of his pistol. The ping of brass casings rang against the hard floor between booms. Rico was determined to keep firing until the thing walked no more.

Click, click, click...

At least the barrage of bullets had managed to knock the creature to the ground again, but that was all. It wasn't alive, it was dead. And in death, it was more dangerous than if alive. It rose to its feet to finish its prey.

Rico's hands trembled as he fumbled to find a full clip. He hit the release on the grip, and the spent clip clanged to the floor. Drunk, confused, and in mild shock, it took him three tries before the clip slipped in. He yanked back the slide and chambered the first   bullet.

Chapter 2

Pop swung the bat, pelting the walking dead man as hard as he could with the business end for a fifth time. The zombie went down, but didn't stay down. The sixth swing of the bat connected with a shoulder. The crack of bone rang in his ears as the bat came away in his hand. Even still, dislocated arm and several hits to the face, and the thing was still persistent as hell. It was like a living a nightmare.

The zombie reached out with the one arm that worked—albeit stiff jointed—and scratched at Pop as it staggered to its feet again. The other arm wiggled by its side, unable to pose any threat.

Screams, mostly from women, continued from all corners of the bar. Some women were so scared they hid their face in their hands, or buried it in a man's chest. By the expressions on most of the men's faces, they might as well have been crying for mommy. What had happened with this generation to make them such pussies? Pop remembered back in the day when people pushed into a corner would stand up for themselves. Times were tougher back then. Not every married couple had two cars. Some people had to walk or take a bus into town or to work. There was no air conditioning either. Now people expected someone else to do the fighting for them—even if their own lives were in danger.

There was blood on the floor. One of his customers was on his butt leaning against the bar. Would he bleed to death from that bite? The creature had taken off a few fingers and maybe part of his hand, too.

The living corpse responsible was content for the moment, occupied with the hand sandwich. It gnawed away at the bits of bone and flesh that had left the muscular man's now bloody hand. The stench of decay hovered like a fog throughout the entire bar.

The last time Pop saw Rico, he was having a hell of a time reloading his gun. A gun emptied into a man that should be dead. A man that had just taken more than a dozen bullets to the chest at close range and was still coming. That doesn't happen it real life. What was going on and how in the hell were they going to get out of it alive? The swarm of thoughts and the immediacy of the situation made him dizzy. Then, in the chaos, someone shouted what he was thinking.

"They're dead! You can't kill them because they're already dead."

Rico's gun fired a single shot. Pop didn't have time to look.

Pop felt sick. How do you kill a dead person? He wasn't sure but knew one thing. If he could disable an arm he could do it harm, and a bag of mashed up bones and pulpy mess on the floor wouldn't be able to hurt anyone. He hit it a few more times and wished he'd had an ax instead of a bat. Ignoring the arthritic pain tearing through his arms, Pop swung the bat again. It struck its target. He couldn't tell, though, if he'd hit a home run. It was the bottom of the 9th and he was down in the count. Strike three would bring death. Reality shifted. His mind felt like it had taken a ride down a slide at a waterpark. His knees went weak just as blackness threatened to cover him. Rico's gun fired again.

Bam!

A single shot.

Everything went still. The screams stopped—cut off as if someone threw a switch. The chaos, although still present, blurred into slow motion.

*

Rico felt the familiar recoil of his gun's salvo. This time, he chose a smaller target. It was going to make more of a mess, but that was the least of his worries now. His aim was true. The bullets struck his attacker in the head. The left eye burst in a cloud of dust and blackish gray gunk. The zombie fell to the floor, dead for the second time in its miserable existence.

He rewarded himself with a deep breath, relieved he'd finally won the battle. The war wasn't over, though. He couldn't dally, but he found his mind second guessing if the thing was truly dead. His gaze returned to the rotting corpse, searching for any signs of movement. There were none. Rico looked away to assess the situation. Terror marred the expressions on the once carefree patrons. All dressed up to look their best—to strut their stuff and land a partner in the bedroom. They might as well have been attending a funeral.

Rico spun around with the pistol at the ready. The sudden motion made his head swoon as if he was on a runaway carousel. His head throbbed with the regret of one too many drinks. He shifted his weight to keep balance and forced the double vision to right itself. When his vision cleared, he saw Pop still battling the monster. Blood and blackish gray grime covered the bat. A man with a tribal tattoo and a geeky looking computer nerd stood as a shield between the zombie Pop battled and the people by the wall. The third zombie was still on its knees, mechanically chewing. The muscular man bleeding by the bar was still alive. Had anyone in the bar called 911? How bad was the injury? Too little time and too many questions. It was up to him to end the madness and take control.

The computer geek turned his head from the fray and frantically cried, "Help us!"

Pop charged with the bat cocked over his shoulder and swung. The two men kept their distance to give Pop room. The blow missed the creature by inches, but Pop brought the bat back around and connected with its side.

Pop might as well be hitting a punching bag, Rico thought. "Step away from it!" Rico shouted, stepping forward with the pistol raised.

Pop was in the zone. He showed no sign that he had heard Rico. The one arm of the zombie hung limply by its side.

"Pop, back away. I got this!" Rico went to move closer but the bat came back to deliver another blow. The swing connected, but it was Pop whose knees wavered as if he was about to fall down.

The two men in the wait to help Pop scattered as Rico stepped up with raised pistol. The geek's attempt to flee was haphazard. The computer nerd stumbled against a bar stool when he tried to step away and fell to the floor right in front of the ghoul that had been chowing down on muscle man's fingers.

Rico fired a shot. The bullet burst through the back of the zombie's skull. It fell limp, landing on the separated shoulder that Pop had hit with the bat. Rico turned his aim toward the zombie on its knees, but he was too late. The mouth full of fingers must have not been enough to satisfy it. The zombie fell on the computer geek and sank its teeth into his face. Blood gushed out from the nerd's nose. The *crunch* of cartilage separating by teeth crackled in the air. It continued to gnaw on his face.

One guy by the wall bent over, heaving like a steam locomotive. He erupted over the floor and fell to his knees. The rank emesis wasn't enough to cover up the rotting stench of putrid flesh.

Rico lowered his pistol and pressed it against the side of the kneeling creature's head.

He pulled the trigger.

All three zombies were dead and motionless on the floor. Finally, it was over.

The man with the injured hand no longer leaned against the bar and slid down to the floor, still conscious, but had lost all color in his face. The computer geek lay on his back. His chest jerked. Blood spurted from his mouth, cascading his already crimson face. His nose was a caved in mess of nothingness. Blood bubbles formed where his nose should have been and popped the second his back jerked again. He turned his head and coughed. This time, the blood splashed across Rico's police issued boots.

Chapter 3

A mellow sax played over the music system at the bar. Pop had recovered from his dizziness and surveyed the damage while massaging his hands. A few of the women sobbed while others tried to comfort them. Two patrons hovered over the computer nerd, who was alive, in obvious shock, and bleeding from various bites on his face. His left ear half missing made him look elfish.

Rico leaned against a table, fearing his shaky legs might give out. He felt his blood pressure rise in his face and the mixture of alcohol and the hamburger from lunch rose from his stomach. A few steps to the right had him over a trash can filled with empty bottles and plastic cups. Thankfully, he had time to keep the up-chuck off the floor.

"You okay, Rico?" Pop said—his face had aged ten years.

Rico spat a few times. The sour odor of decay and Jim Beam trapped in his nostrils threatened for him to swear off whiskey forever. "I'm fine. Stomach's upset over these rank-ass bastards on the floor." He looked around the room. "Anybody call for an ambulance?"

A voice from the crowd huddled together by the bar said, "I called 911."

As if right on cue, the wail of a siren sped past the tavern with lights flashing. The ambulance didn't even slow, and the siren faded into the distance. All eyes in the bar turned on Rico.

People were such hypocrites. Being an officer of the law is one of the most despised professions known to man. The thieves, the drug dealers and prostitutes, all criminals would just as soon kill a cop as look at them. The thing that hurt the worst, though, was that law-abiding, 'good' citizens weren't much better when push came to shove. How many times did he pull over a motorist and was told, 'Why aren't you off chasing criminals?' Ironically, they had broken the law, and he, in fact, was doing his job. Somehow, those driving BMW and Lexus luxury cars felt they were above the law. 'I'm paying your salary.' *'Yeah, no shit. I pay taxes too, so I guess I'm paying my own salary.'* He usually just thanked the motorist and handed them the ticket. Nothing was worse than getting into a fray with an old woman. Not even a gunfight. He had been attacked by a purse wielding, graying avenger at least five times. What was he to do? Fight back? There's no way he'd live that down at the station. It never failed that at some point the woman would hurt her hand and stop, and then threaten to sue. Thank goodness for video cameras catching it all.

These people in the bar all looked to him to tell them what to do. Rico was the unanimous leader by default. He was the one wearing the blue uniform.

"Everyone remain calm." He turned to muscle man, who was trying to sit back up. "How bad is your hand?"

The man pulled at the rag around the bite, and it showed no evidence it was bleeding. "Not terrible. Hurt's like hell, but I would expect a bite to do that."

"Pop, can you put some alcohol on it, or something to kill the germs until EMS arrives?"

"Sure. I got nicked up a little too, when I was slinging that bat. I'll get some towels for the guy on the floor and get him fixed up."

A man pulled a girl away from the bar by the hand. "All the other things that were by the window are gone. I'm ready to get out of here." A series of gunshots from outside froze him in his tracks.

Rico raised both hands. "I don't want anyone to leave just yet. We don't know what's going on out there, and we should stay together until we know it's safe."

"How long will that be?" the man said, pulling the girl tightly in his arms.

Rico rolled his eyes and shook his head. "How the fuck would I know that? I was here having a good time just like you when all this shit started. I don't know where these dead looking things came from, if any are still out there, or what else is going down around us. Common sense tells us our decision making will be better when it gets daylight. We just need to stay calm until we learn more."

"Pop, I need a drink," someone by the bar said. A few others chimed in agreement.

"No." Rico's voice boomed. "No more drinking. Only water. We need to keep our wits about us." He turned to a guy standing under a television set. "You, see if you can find us some news. Anybody else with a cell phone start searching for answers."

Blank stares from the crowd answered back.

"For Christ's sake, people, snap out of your funk and do something," Rico commanded.

"But what about them?" a woman asked.

Rico jammed both sets of knuckles on his hips and surveyed the dead bodies on the floor. "Nothing to worry about. They're not ever going to get up again."

"But they scare me. They stink, too. I want them out of here," the woman's voice cracked.

"Ma'am, since people are dead, we can't disturb the bodies until police arrive and photograph the evidence."

"You're a cop. Make a report. Take a picture with your cell phone and draw a chalk line on the floor. Just get them out," her voice sounded even more desperate.

Rico rubbed his hand over his face. "Ma'am, this is a possible crime scene. It doesn't work that way. Please go find some place to sit down—as far away from them as you can. Have some water. Play Angry Birds on your phone. Do whatever you need to take your mind off those things."

"But—"

"Now!" Typical, she forced him to go there. It was difficult to reason with people—especially those who were distraught.

The woman scowled and defiantly dismissed him with her nose in the air before heading to the farthest barstool.

Now he was a dick, an asshole, whatever undeserved label fit. Didn't people realize it is they who made him act that way? Nope, ultimately, they would test him until he put his foot down. Human nature, he guessed. That meant human nature hadn't evolved much from the animal world. The strong ruled. If animals ever learned how to fire automatic weapons, humans would find themselves in trouble.

He turned back to the crowd. "Anybody here a doctor? Nurse? Some type of care giver?" Most had broken from their trance and were either speaking hush-hush among themselves, or fingering cell phones.

"I've had some first aid training," one man said, tending to the computer nerd as Pop handed him some towels. He had already covered the bite wounds with cocktail napkins and quickly covered the shivering victim with the towels.

"How's he doing?" Rico asked.

"Didn't lose that much blood. He's just in shock. I wish that ambulance would hurry."

Far away sirens and gunfire crept in to chill the scene further. Pop stepped over by Rico.

He spoke in a whisper. "What you said earlier about this being a crime scene, am I in some kind of trouble for—beating up on that thing?" The event had really taken a toll on this poor old man.

"Hey, Pop, look, don't worry. I was here, and I ultimately am responsible. It's my bullets that took them all down. You were trying to save lives. Everyone here saw what you did—what you had to do—to those things. You're a hero, Pop. But events have to play out by the book."

"Should I get a lawyer? Whoever it was that I banged up might have relatives who could sue for desecrating the body. And what about the people here that got hurt?"

"Well, having a lawyer in any legal matter is never a bad idea. And I hope your insurance is paid up. I'll think you'll be fine as I don't see any criminal charges coming your way. But certainly if someone drops a civil suit on you, you'll have to lawyer up."

"Ah, well. I guess I'll just take it one day at a time." Pop tried to act as if he wasn't going to let him worry him.

"You want to help me look those things over? See if we can find any identification?"

"Sure."

Rico reached in a pocket and pulled out a pair of thin plastic gloves. He always kept a pair handy in case he handled a bloody victim, or he was sent on a drug bust where needles would be involved.

He and Pop walked over to the first zombie Rico had dropped. The smell roiled Rico's stomach but he managed to escape the feeling with only a dry burp.

"This man died recently. Recent meaning within the last six months. Embalming doesn't preserve the body as long as most people think. After a year, the body generally is nothing more than skeletons and teeth, with slight patches of tissue here and there."

"How do you know that?" Pop asked.

"Eh? Oh, I had the chance to see an exhumed body once. Insurance company believed the guy was poisoned and didn't want to pay the widow. I never found out what happened after that."

Rico carefully searched the clothing for identification and was surprised when he found an envelope stuffed in an inside pocket.

"What'cha got there?" Pop asked.

"Dunno. Let's see." The envelope wasn't sealed. He opened the envelope and removed the letter inside. A rectangular piece of paper fell out. The letter read, 'I told you I would pay you back,' and signed, 'Billy.' The rectangular piece of paper was a hand written check for ten thousand dollars, addressed to Mr. Albert M. Davison.

"People never cease to amaze me," Rico said as he showed Pop the letter.

Pop looked over the letter and then again at the check. He giggled—slightly—then a little harder. The laughter took control as tears pooled in his eyes and rolled down his cheeks in big drops.

"Hey, Pop. It's okay." Rico reached out and gently squeezed Pop on his shoulder. "It's going to be okay."

A police car screeched to a halt outside the door and an ambulance drove slightly past it before stopping. Help had finally arrived.

"Really, Pop, everything is going to be okay." Rico helped the old man to his feet and watched EMS spill out the ambulance. He was tired, but a whole new chapter of the day had to begin and end before he'd be getting any sleep.

At least he freed his mind from pining over Mary Etta. That is, until now, and he started to hate himself for it.

Chapter 4

Two days later

"There you go—a dog with false teeth," Private Andy Wells said, after giving much thought to the situation.

"What in the name of God are you rambling about now?" Private Steve Rogan asked.

Three fallen war heroes shambled down an empty street in Cosper Ridge Estates. The bodies had been mysteriously reanimated to life.

Two wore the dress blues of a Class A Noncommissioned Officer. An overseas service bar adorned each jacket, along with a combat service identification badge and service stripes. The other was naked and in an advanced state of decay—resembling a walking skeleton. There was no doubt they were on the hunt for human flesh.

"The one on the right. That's something I haven't seen before. Look at it. How in the hell can it even walk?" Wells said, hiding behind the cover of an SUV haphazardly abandoned on the street.

Rogan leaned around the vehicle for a better view. "Who knows? How can the dead come back to life anyway? Some force had to rebuild the remaining organic material and regenerate it enough to get the muscles working again. After that, the body expends energy so it has to find a way to replenish it. For some God awful reason these walking corpses need human flesh to keep going."

"That's some high dollar stinkin' thinkin' right there. You a college boy, Rogan?"

"No, just high school. Shut your trap and take out the one on the left. I'll take the one on the right. First kill gets to shoot the one in the middle."

"Wait a minute. There's another thing I ain't figured out yet. How is it that these zombies can break out of coffins and claw their way up from six feet of packed dirt? That's a lot like pussy to me," Wells said.

"Pussy? How is that like pussy?"

"I don't get *it*," Wells said with a grin.

Rogan rolled his eyes. "I remember going to church and hearing the preacher say in the end times the dead would rise. Maybe this is prophecy come true."

"Not buying it. I might have been born at night, but not last night. If this was prophecy, then J.C. would have been riding in the sky on a white horse slingin' a flamin' carrot."

"You mean sword, don't you? Jesus had a flaming sword."

"Well, the painting I saw, it looked like he was holding a flamin' carrot."

Rogan shook his head. "I don't really know how the zombies got out of the ground. What if they burrowed out like a mole?"

"Sounds like bullshit to me. You can't bullshit a bullshitter, and I'm one of the best," Wells said with a nod.

"How about this: Little men from Mars swooped down in UFOs and shot the graves with a super ray-cannon, disintegrating the dirt, and bringing the dead back to life."

"Now *that* could happen. That their theory at least is based in science," Wells said, pointing a finger at Rogan.

"Andy, they were in the ground, and now they're out. That's really all that matters. That, and the fact that," Rogan's mouth twisted, and he lowered the tone in his voice, "they're coming to *get* you, Andy."

"Stop that! Yer scaring me. I was just saying . . . ."

"Shut up and shoot," Rogan said.

Wells slapped a new magazine into his M16 and chambered a round. He leaped to the side of the SUV and peppered the chest of his undead target in full auto.

Rogan steadied his rifle on the roof of the vehicle, took careful aim, and fired. The top of his target's skull peeled back like a pull-top can. The zombie fell backward onto the asphalt, his mouth no longer chewing empty air.

Repositioning slightly, Rogan shot the one in the middle dead center of its left eye. The head exploded, sending fragments of bone and black, putrid goo in all directions. *Dead meat fireworks*, he thought.

Wells continued to shoot his target in the chest. The bullets went straight through, ripping out chunks of meat from the zombie's backside. The dead walker advanced despite the direct hits. It violently shook as each bullet tore through.

"Wells, what are you doing? You wasted a whole clip of ammo and it's still standing. You know to aim for the head, not shoot it to pieces." Rogan took aim and brought down the zombie with a headshot.

Wells grinned. "I know. I was only having a little fun. Just think, if it was wearing a grass skirt, it would've looked like it was doing the hula dance. That gives me an idea. Let's put a grass skirt on a zombie woman. You can get a video camera and film while I shoot her up, making her *dance*. Then, we can upload the video on the internet. We can put a music track on and everything."

Rogan raised a hand. "Wells, you can come up with the craziest shit."

"Are we's going to do it or ain't we?"

"*We's* need to concentrate on our mission. Search and rescue, remember? Some people are probably holed up in their houses, scared out of their minds," Rogan said.

"I doubt that they's had much chance of surviving. Central Texas State Veterans Cemetery is so close that this neighborhood would have been the first course on the menu."

An old woman with a nasty limp ran screaming for help from around the corner, a half block away.

"Good Lord," Rogan said, turning toward the cries. A host of undead chased in hot pursuit. "There must be forty of them after that woman. Call for back-up, now!"

Wells radioed their position and briefly described the situation. He ejected the empty magazine in his rifle and stabbed in a full one.

"Run, lady, run!" Rogan sped off first, shooting as he ran. Bullets flew wide of her position and hit to either side, doing little to slow the advance of the aggressors.

The injured leg proved to be too great a hindrance. The nearest carnivore closed in and pulled her to the ground.

As the two crashed to the street, withered hands from all sides jutted forth, digging filth-encrusted fingers into her soft flesh, ripping her apart. Blood splattered into the air—flying in all directions.

Rogan stopped, took aim, and shot the zombies where it counted as they feasted on the kill. As soon as one fell to his bullet, another fought its way in to share the prize.

Wells arrived at his side with the dash of heels pounding the ground from the other members of his platoon following.

Wells gloated, "Got one . . . and another. Got that one . . . Missed . . . Wait . . . got it. That last one's head exploded like a frog sucking on a cherry bomb. I'm up to about eight points. How many d'you get?"

"This isn't a video game. This is serious stuff, man," Rogan said, squeezing off a carefully aimed shot.

The additional six members of the platoon took down the mass of undead like corn chopped in the field. Apparently, the temptation of the fresh kill was too alluring for the group of zombies to notice the soldiers in the distance.

After a few minutes of combined gunfire, the last of the zombies fell to the street. It took a bullet to the head as it climbed over a pile of its companions, reaching out for a half-eaten piece of thigh. It didn't get the satisfaction of a final bite before returning to the grave.

"I'm glad that's over," Rogan said.

"If this had been the carnival, I would have won one of them stuffed gorillas. You know, big and puffy—with that bright blue fur and a goofy look on its face." Wells bugged out his eyes and poked his tongue to the corner of his mouth.

Rogan turned away, his lips tightening.

Wells rubbed his chin and scratched his head. "At least we found the best way to kill a whole bunch at once."

"Overwhelming fire power wins every time it's tried. Nothing really special about the way we killed them," Rogan said.

"That ain't it. You and I could've took out these goobers by ourselves."

"How on Earth do you figure that?"

"Well, *Mr. I'm so smart*, it's as plain as the nose on yer face. You saw how they acted. They had only one thing on their mind. Dinner. They's didn't even know we was here as long as they had something close by to eat. The way to take out a pile of zombies is to keep their attention away from you." Wells grinned from ear to ear. "All you gotta do is use the right bait."

***

Reports of the dead returning to life were the same the whole world over. Fortunately, the event had been short lived. It only took a few days for authorities to restore order, although it did take a few weeks to eliminate the stragglers. Some areas had been hit harder than others had, but after the initial shock wore off, life for most returned to normal. Casualties in general were few. More people had died in the panic from heart attacks and accidents than had been killed by the reanimated dead. Many, though, did suffer from scratches and bites, most unhindered from the injuries.

Killeen remained the sleepy little town it had always been, just as life went on after the September 11th attack on the Twin Towers. Church attendance had picked up too. Televangelists across the country wasted no time in taking advantage of the situation and raked in huge piles of money.

The people of the world demanded an explanation. Scientists determined the event was a fluke of nature—with a billion to one odds for it to have happened.

It all started when a group of asteroids traveled through Earth's orbit. The asteroids pulled a massive cloud of dust with them. Whereas the Earth escaped the barrage of space rocks, it wasn't so lucky with the dust.

There was little concern when the Earth ran into the cloud. A slight haze filled the sky, but the world didn't go dark as some religious zealots had predicted. Pandora's box didn't open, unleashing hell on Earth. Planes even continued to fly uninterrupted. Active volcanos had more effect on commerce.

The moon at night did take on a slightly different color through the prism of dust. It had a twinge of yellow never before seen. The dust affected the clouds too, and the rain that fell similarly carried the pale yellow color.

It took scientists some time to isolate a unique microbe found in the rain. A group of French geneticists made the first discovery. The microbes resembled a virus—as it had no means to self-replicate. The saving grace of it all was that the alien microbe's DNA was incompatible with DNA found on Earth. There was no fear of some new hybrid plague spreading across the world and destroying all life.

At least that was the original finding. Now, no one knew what to expect.

Chapter 5

Six months later

It was two o'clock on a warm Wednesday afternoon in October. The sun beamed through the window shades and shined on the tables at the rear of Pop's Lounge. The after-work crowd had started to trickle in. Happy hour always attracted an interesting bunch into the bar. College kids knocking down a few pitchers after class. Businessmen in suits relieving stress from the circus of the day. The lonely guy. The lonely girl. People with nowhere to go. People who had places to go but didn't want to be there.

Rico stepped in but stopped at the entrance. He looked around and remembered the events that happened back in the spring. In a way, it seemed like it never really happened—that it was just a movie in a faded memory. A dream even. The attack of the undead was certainly something he wished he could forget—wished had never happened. However, recent reports in the news wouldn't let him. Scientist had an answer for what brought the dead to life, but it was what some others speculated that had him back at Pop's Lounge this day.

He had left his motorcycle helmet on his Harley-Davidson Sportster but brought his duffle bag with him. It was his personal bike with a 'Property of Killeen P.D.' sticker on it. For the three years he owned the bike, no one had ever bothered it.

Pop had his gaze fixed to a television screen and was mindlessly drying a beer mug when Rico stepped up to the bar.

"Hey, Pop. How you doing?" Rico waited as Pop turned his attention toward him and gave him an up and down.

The curious expression disappeared as his eyes widened.

"Rico… That you?"

"Yep, it's me. A trim buck ninety on the ol' pounds meter. Been hitting the gym more these days." Rico patted his belly.

"You look great, son. So that's what you've been up to since—" Pop hesitated for a moment, "since the last time. Come, sit down."

Rico reached out and shook Pop's hand. He dropped the bag to the floor and sat on the wooden bar stool in front of Pop.

"What to drink?"

"Uh . . . ."

"On the house."

"Thanks Pop, but I've given up drinking."

"Ah, come on. A soft drink then, or just some water." Pop placed a cup full of ice in front of Rico and waited to push one of the plethora of buttons on the elaborate drink nozzle.

"Ginger ale."

"Coming up."

"Thanks." Rico waited for his glass to fill. "You know, I feel bad that I haven't come to see you over these last few months. The last time I was here really changed my life."

"Tell me about it. A lot changed for everybody."

"Well, I'm not talking about those dead things that attacked. I mean the talk you gave me before any of that happened. Everything you said about me and my life was true. It was things I already knew, but it's like when you said them, it... it made it seem possible for me to achieve. Your talk pushed me over the edge and allowed me to take control of my life. I started to eat healthy, backed away from the booze, and spent my off time at the gym and not lying around on my ass in front of the TV sulking over Mary Etta. I just wanted to come by and thank you for that. And to check on you, you know, because of the news."

Pop made a shy smile. "I didn't do nothing. It was all you. And don't you go worrying about me. I'm as healthy as a horse."

Rico wasn't so sure about that. Pop looked a bit more haggard than the officer had expected. Sure, he was an old man that only got older every day—but that wasn't it. No doubt running a bar seven days a week would wear out even a young person. Maybe that's all it was.

"I'm sure you know what's going on in France." Rico didn't really know how to get the conversation started without sounding too nosy. Plus, he wanted Pop to open up and not be on the defensive side.

"Yeah. To think it took the Froggies to figure out what brought the dead back to life. What are we paying all our tax dollars for? Hell, our government told us there was nothing to worry about in that space dust."

"At least they got the part about the asteroids missing the Earth right. That cloud of dust that followed has everyone concerned now."

"Ah, it don't bother me none. Other than that yellow rain it caused and the people who recently died coming back to life, there's nothing else going to happen. People who have died since then haven't come back. Like they said, it was just a fluke. They'll figure it out one day. I even heard one scientist say he thinks that's how life originally started on Earth. Alien microbes mixing in with the soil and producing DNA."

"But the microbes they found in the dust couldn't self-replicate. Its DNA wasn't compatible with ours. It shouldn't have done what it did and raise the dead. They're saying now it mutated. What happens if that alien stuff mutates again? And . . . and what do you think about all those people that got bitten or scratched when the dead came back?" That was the million dollar question. Rico wanted to know if Pop suffered from any of the symptoms others had reported.

Pop's gaze turned to his left forearm. Rico saw what he focused on. A red welt a half inch wide and three inches long streaked across his bicep.

"Is that where you got scratched?" Rico asked.

"Yeah, when I was slinging the bat."

"That the only place?"

"No, I got a couple smaller ones. There's one on my elbow and another on a knuckle."

"You been to the doctor?"

"Sure. Those damn places would never heal so I went to one of them walk-in clinics. They cleaned up the scratches and gave me some ointment and pills. Nothing's changed. They're still there. Big deal. Don't bother me that much. Itches from time to time though."

"How about the symptoms others are reporting? Fever, congestion, runny nose, and runny eyes?"

"I don't know. I got allergies. I don't have fever, but I've lived most of my life with congestion." Pop raised his hands. "I know what you're concerned about, but I think the news is trying to make a mountain out of a mole hill. This is an off year for politics so they're looking to make news."

"I don't know, Pop. It's coincidental that those who were cut or bitten when the undead attacked are all having similar symptoms. Those who have shared bodily fluids with them since then are affected too. I heard a conservative estimate put a number of those affected at fifteen percent of the population. Some say it could be as high as thirty. That means millions of people may have some type of illness that no one will know how to cure."

"So what? Colds have been around for years and we can't get rid of them. They'll come up with some more over-the-counter medicines to ease the symptoms. The pharmaceuticals will make millions."

Rico lifted the plastic cup to his mouth. "I hope you're right. I sure hope you're right." Ginger ale fizzed on the back of his tongue as he took another swallow. The walls of the bar felt like they were slowly closing in. Faded memories of the harrowing night stirred as Rico cast his gaze about the room—half expecting to see a slimy handprint on the window. For the first time in a long time, he thought how a shot or two of vodka would mix with the ginger ale.

"Hey, Pop, you ever think much about that night?" Rico felt the creeping fear of that living nightmare return.

"Me? Sure. Well, not as much lately. Right after it happened, everyone who came in here made me retell the story. Business picked up quite a bit, and I had to take on some extra staff. I think the last time I told the story I had killed ten zombies using a toothpick with an olive on the end. I ate the olive after I put the last one down."

Rico chuckled. "Yeah, you should hear some of the shit the guys told at the station. One man Rambos—all of them."

"Remember that bat? Look behind you."

Rico twisted around and saw the muck covered bat hanging on the wall displayed in a rectangular glass case. It had a brass engraved nametag that read 'Denise.'

"You gave the bat a name?"

"Ah, you know. It helps the story—makes it part of the legend. I named the bat after the nastiest red head I ever met in my life. Denise Wannamaker, I sure had a thing for that gal." Pop's distant gaze reminded Rico that lost loves remained with you forever.

"Pop, it's been great catching up. I'm going out of town for a few weeks—taking all my vacay at once. Just hitting the road, and wherever I end up, that's where I'll be."

"Good for you. I hope whatever you're looking for in life you'll find."

"Me too, Pop, me too." Rico slid off the bar stool and picked up his bag. "So, you sure you're okay? Healthy as a horse, like you said?"

"Don't you worry about me none. I'm fit as a fiddle. And one thing's for certain, I'm not guilty of sharing any of my bodily fluids with anyone else getting them sick, too." The old man was hardheaded but Rico always loved his dry sense of humor.

"What the hell? Why not? Give ol' Denise a call. I bet she still has a head full of that red hair."

"That might be true, but at her age, I bet the carpet don't match the drapes."

***

Meeting with Pop was just what Rico needed to clear his head before heading out on what he hoped would be his greatest adventure. He didn't have much of a plan, and felt stupid when his partners at the station gave him hell for not knowing where he was going. *Fuck 'em*, he thought. Something inside pushed him to get away, as if a great reward—or an awakening of some type—awaited him just around the next turn in the road. The fog of depression hung wherever he went in Killen, especially in the gym while he ran on the treadmill. Most of it was because of Mary Etta, but there were other things, too. Failures he suffered in life, and hidden things he had done that no one knew but him. The future was about to change drastically for him. He could feel it, and he couldn't wait for it to come.

The passion he had once felt serving as an officer of the law had dwindled next to nothing. He couldn't blame all of his state of mind on his divorce. It lied deeper than that. At least he'd become honest with himself. As simple as it sounded, that's what really sparked the change in him. That, and 'The Spook,' the street name for the night the alien virus raised the dead.

Hell, just about everyone left alive had taken on a different perspective in life. Some still hadn't gotten over it. For him though, The Spook gave birth to an itch. An itch that could only be scratched by a throttle and holding onto the handlebars of his motorcycle as it glided down the highway. It was time to fly. His wife wasn't his wife any more. She had made sure of that. After The Spook, she was bound and determined to end the marriage as quickly as possible. Rico had secretly hoped that one day she might change her mind and come running back after she initially left him. But she used scorched Earth tactics to push the divorce through as quickly as possible. Mary Etta could only see him as a fat failure in life and didn't have room for him in the picture. He had despised her at first for that, but now he was happy to see her go. It was what he ultimately needed to grow. A little pruning always hurt, but the growth it produces is always for the better.

He needed to change. He had lost his drive, his motivation to ensure he met every expectation of his duties. That attitude would get him into dangerous situations and he would probably get himself killed in the line of duty. Being a hero is something every officer strived to be. Dying a hero was just plain stupid. Two months after The Spook, he had written his resignation and presented it to his Chief, who eventually talked him out of it. Rico kept his resignation letter on a desk at home and looked at it every day. All he had to do was change the date, slap a stamp on an envelope, and it would be done, once and for all.

His true destination didn't lie on a map. Rico would know he reached it when he got there. He felt the chains of his life in Killeen stretch the farther down the road he drove. The wind whistled through his hair, and the mountains of problems shrank down to hills in his rearview mirror. Soon they would be but pebbles he could kick out of his way forever.

The handlebars guided him into the future, controlled by his two hands. The speedometer kissed 75mph down the highway. He wished he had made the break a long time ago.

A fresh start was what he needed, especially after what happened six months ago. Of all the things, his wife, the job, the dead coming back to life, what haunted him the most at night was the fight at the bar. The shots. They rang in his head any time he stopped long enough to think. No matter how many times he felt like he was over it, the images came back. That was why he was on the move. He needed to get away from that town. He needed to get away from his ex, and he needed to get away from that night.

An aging Ford Ranger traveled up the other lane and passed him. The truck sounded like shit, and Rico wondered how long a vehicle in that bad of shape could go that fast before it fell apart. The truck's engine sputtered and backfired, sounding like both barrels of a shotgun going off. Rico jumped in his seat and remembered the time he pointed his gun at the ghoul and pulled the trigger to end its existence. The loud boom, the bullet hitting the eye, the bits of bone and goop that shot out of the back of its head as the bullet smashed through. His bullets entered flesh. It might have been dead flesh, but it was still flesh just the same.

In his years of service, it was common for officers who shot or killed people to deal with stress issues. Hell, there were some that accidently shot themselves, or a police dog involved in the fight. Therapy was always recommended and sometimes it had been a requirement to return to work. Of course, this was something most cops laughed at. Even Rico remembered harassing a few of his buddies over it, but he wouldn't act like that now. Now he understood the real need to open up and let true feelings out. He realized the only way to keep the demon seeds from growing were by being open and honest with himself and everyone else.

The truck backfired again as it gained its distance.

Rico had to focus on his hands to maintain the control of his bike—his mind shifted to the zombie Pop had battled and the bullet fired from his gun taking it down. Rico cut back on the throttle and drifted down to 60 mph.

The truck soon pulled away. It was gone, and so was the memory.

Now there was nothing but the open road and nowhere to be.

Rico liked that feeling. With the road ahead, he hoped to replace those awful memories with the freedom of a better tomorrow.

He may not find his destination in a day or a week, but one thing was certain. He knew that he would eventually find it.

The sun gradually fell to the horizon glowing like a perfectly round piece of hot coal. The heat of the dry air and black asphalt gave way to the first fingers of the cool night air. The change in temperature soothed his sun drenched, wind burned skin.

He felt his cell phone vibrate in his pants pocket. Curiosity got the better of him. He unbuttoned the pocket and fished out the phone. When he glanced down, he saw the number of the last person on Earth he'd ever want to speak to again.

It was Mary Etta's lawyer. He rolled his eyes and set his gaze back on the road. One chain still connected him to Killeen, and it pissed Rico off. He snorted like a bull about to charge, remembering the last time he got into it with that motherfucking prick. His hand tightened around the phone, and if he could have crushed it, he would have. The phone had stopped vibrating, but three seconds later, it started again. "Fuck you!" Rico screamed into the wind. He threw the phone in front of his Harley and tried to run over it with both tires. *If I'm going to leave it all behind, I need to leave it all behind.*

Rico regretted the decision to toss his cell phone after riding a few miles down the highway, but it was too late to worry about that now. A new beginning for him would include a new phone and number, too. He felt even freer, as if the last chain holding him to the past had broken.

He drove on, and the roar of his motorcycle echoed off the wall of mesquite trees lining the highway.

By the time the sun set on the Texas asphalt of Highway 105, Rico was hours away from home.

He wondered if he would ever see the city of Killeen again.

Chapter 6

The stars overhead twinkled like tiny diamonds sprinkled on black velvet by the time Rico decided to pull over and call it a day. He probably would have kept on keeping on, but the gas gauge on his bike dragged him back to reality. Cruising through the cool darkness under the wide Texas sky had an off-world effect. His headlight seemingly opened a wormhole through time and space. Although he knew he hadn't left the planet, he wanted to view the world through new eyes, and not repeat mistakes of the past.

Had his mind not been preoccupied with the thoughts of The Spook, among other things, he might have known where here was. All he remembered of his ride was the fact that he had stayed on the 105 strip for most of it, and turned down an interesting looking highway that looked recently repaved. The ride had been smoother, which only lulled him further into his musings. If he had to guess, he was most likely far south of Huntsville.

It hadn't been an exit ramp with signs to remind him to check his fuel that brought him to a stop. It was a four way intersection where a car to his right had arrived first. He waited for it to speed on and dropped his gaze to the fuel gauge. The needle pointed close to the negative range. Luckily, for him, there was a small gas station-diner combo and a motel just on down the road.

As the car passed, two young boys in the backseat had their faces pressed against the window and waved. Rico raised a thumb up and blew the horn in two quick bursts. He remembered being that young, too, and having a fascination with motorcycles and their riders.

He eased off the clutch and slowly made his way the short distance to the gas station. A sign by the road proclaimed they had the cheapest gas in town. From the looks of the place, that could either mean the fuel at the pump, or the gas a diner would experience after eating a meal there. Rico made sure to park at the pump that didn't offer diesel. Usually, only a select number of fuel pumps would have diesel on the menu. Diesel owners were known to get irate over gas burners hogging the one or two pumps that dispensed the heavy fuel.

At least someone inside was sure to be able to tell him where he was.

He dropped the kickstand, stepped off the bike, and looked around. It was the first time he felt fatigue from his long ride. His hind parts felt a bit numb and the small of his back ached. He arched his back and walked in an irregular circle, trying to shake off the stiffness.

On second thought, might not find out after all, he shrugged. The place looked like it might be closed. Some little towns in Texas were known for rolling up the sidewalks when the sun went down. *Then again, maybe some of the florescent lights inside might just be burned out.*

The only part of the parking lot for the gas station-diner that was paved was the small square of cement that circled the two lone gas pumps out front. The rest of parking area was pretty much just dirt. Any rocks or shells that could have once covered it were now buried underneath the loose ground. Rico imagined a heavy wind could kick up one hell of a dust storm and fuck up this small island of civilization.

He pulled out his credit card from his wallet, but at first glance realized there was nowhere to swipe the plastic on the gas pump. He would have to go inside and pay first.

The gas station was small despite the fact that it stuck out like the monolith from 2001: A Space Odyssey among the desolate asphalt of the highway. The yellow sign above the store read 'Ducky's Diner and Grocery.' A tacky illustration of an alligator with jaws open hung to the right of the building's name. Even in the darkness of night, Rico could tell by moonlight that the sun faded, yellow sign was very old and had probably been a bright masterpiece quite some time ago. Now it was just a crusted dilapidation of ironically negligent marketing.

Rico shook his head, stuffing his card back into his wallet and thumbing a few bills. *A gator on a sign with the word duck for the name? I wonder who had that bright idea?*

Dirt kicked up around Rico's feet as he briskly walked the length of the parking lot toward the store.

He looked toward the seedy motel across the street and considered staying for the night. Amenities were the least of his concern, but cleanliness was a must. No bugs either. He might be a big, strong policeman, but he had no tolerance for spiders and roaches. The thought of a hot shower and a comfortable place to lie down made him feel all the more road weary.

The motel at least showed signs of life. A few cars and trucks lined up in front, parked as if the valet might have been drunk. Rico chuckled at his own joke, the thought of a place like that having a valet! One thing for sure, none of the Texas royalty would stay in a dump like that. Governor George P. Bush would probably sleep in his limo rather than lay his head down here. He wondered if any of the vehicles in the lot had been manufactured in this century. Time and Texas sun had beat up the paint pretty bad. No amount of compounding and waxing would ever breathe life back into these paint jobs. At least there were a few lights on in the motel, and as Rico got closer, he was relieved to see a person standing behind the counter inside the gas station.

He swung the door open and felt something sticky on his fingers. When it closed behind him, a duck quacked, clearly announcing his arrival to the clerk. *It's time to get off the phone, or quit picking your nose. You've got a customer*, Rico thought, and looked for something to wipe his hand with.

"Welcome to Ducky's," the man behind the counter proclaimed with a southern accent thicker than any Rico had ever heard before. "What can I do ya fer?"

Rico nodded, hopeful that his Texas drawl wasn't quite that heavy. "Need to fill up. Do you take credit cards?" He grabbed a napkin by the coffee machine and wiped his hands.

"We sure as shoe shine summer don't, mister." The man smiled, showing a row of missing front teeth. "Shucks, you must not be from around here."

"What gave it away?" Rico said as he reached the counter.

"Hadn't seen ya around these parts before. I never do forget a face."

"Is that so?" Rico said, forcing his rude stare away from the missing teeth and scanning the diner's selection of hot foods. "Not much of a diner is it?"

"Whatta ya mean, mister?" the man's smile melted a bit.

"Nothing," Rico said, eyeing the meager selections beside the counter.

To call this a gas station-diner combo was a bit of an overstatement. The place had all the things any normal gas station would have. Beer, soft drinks, junk food, overpriced engine oil, a microwave with rotating hotdogs, and a cheese dispenser for nachos. You name it, they had it. Nevertheless, as far as diners go, this place earned a major fail rating. Yes, there were a few small tables with a couple of chairs off to one side of the room. But the food selection was confined to a space beside the counter no bigger than a bathtub. A variety of heartburn central dishes baked under heat lamps behind glass. The corn dogs appeared to be the only appealing thing available. Everything else had probably been sizzling under the heat lamps since some time that early morning.

Rico sighed. "Okay, give me four corndogs and . . ." Rico hesitated, distracted by a flashing Shiner Bock sign. "What kind of beer do you have?"

"What kind of beer you want? We got all kinds. You know, Miller, Coors, Bud, and Shiner Bock."

Rico looked over his shoulder toward the coolers and took a deep breath. He had stopped drinking to show he was in control over his life. He met his objective and proved to himself that he could do it. The trip to Pop's had him thinking he could let loose a little, enjoy the simple pleasures again. But, maybe it was too soon—maybe head on down the road a ways before he would start drinking again. "You know what? Let's just make it a soda. And charge me for three gallons of regular. The Harley won't hold much more than that."

"That ain't no problem, mister." The toothless man started smashing his dirty fingers against a battered plastic calculator that had just as many missing buttons has he did teeth. "That'll be twenty-one dollars and thirty one cent."

"Looks like you need to get a new calculator there," Rico looked up and read the clerk's nametag, "Kevin."

"Well, all be. How'd you know my name?"

Rico tapped his forehead with his index finger and closed one eye.

Kevin the cashier looked at Rico like he had just walked on water.

Rico handed him the money and waited for change. "So, you know if that motel is still taking in guests this late? I think I might be ready to call it a night."

"Sure are. Miss Tammy is the night manager. She's over at the office. She can get you all set up and what not."

"Prices reasonable?"

"Hell, I don't know, mister. I don't stay there or nothin'." Kevin broke out into a violent coughing fit.

"No, I suppose you don't." Rico stepped back, waiting for the coughing to subside.

It took a few minutes for the clerk to regain his composure. Kevin made change and handed it off without counting it back. "Don't forget your drink. I set you up on pump 1."

Rico nodded. After retrieving a Sprite and his heartburn hotdogs on a stick, he went outside.

"Leave it to good old Kevin to put me on the wrong pump," he grumbled under his breath. He had to move the bike back to the next pump.

A night bird sang in the distance while he pumped gas into his thirsty machine. A full moon hung down the end of the highway, beckoning him to follow. He wondered where it might lead. Surely somewhere far away. Somewhere with potential beyond the measure of Kevin the toothless, calculator smashing genius.

Somewhere away from that cough.

*

The Western Winds Motel didn't have a flashing neon sign out front inviting tired travelers to rest there for the night. Instead, a dilapidated painted sign relied on colored flood lamps to lure guests in. No pool available for the kids. It just wasn't that kind of establishment. Rico doubted anyone ever stayed here more than one night.

The office door had a vacancy sticker in large yellow letters plastered across the front. Rico opened it to the smell of stale cigarettes and formaldehyde from particleboard. The place was a relic of the 50s. The carpet was well worn and it wouldn't have surprised him if it had been there since original construction. *This would make the Guinness Book of World Records for crappiest motel in Texas*, he thought. If he'd been traveling with a tent, he might rather bunk down in it instead. But, there would be no hot shower, and no soft bed. God, he hoped they had soft, clean beds.

What Kevin at the gas station called an office was nothing more than a 4 X 6 room. It reminded Rico of the bathroom at his house where he grew up, minus the toilet and sink. The woman behind the counter didn't bother to look up as he stepped in. It had to be the infamous Miss Tammy that Coughing Kevin spoke of. She was too engrossed in paperwork to notice he had walked in.

"Uh, excuse me, ma'am." Rico used his soft, polite voice. "Mrs. Tammy?"

"Yeah, you want a room?" She didn't bother looking up from her task.

"Yes, ma'am. I'll just be staying for the night. How much for a room?"

She lifted her head and glanced his way. An angry black mole poked from her left cheek just under her way-too-long salt and pepper hair. "Twenty-five dollars cash. Cost you more if you use a card."

Twenty-five dollars was awfully cheap—even for a shithole. He hoped she hadn't misunderstood him and thought he wanted to rent the room by the hour. This place looked like the perfect place for hooker activity. "How much for your best room? One with a nice clean bed, the bigger bed the better."

"Twenty-five dollars, I done told you. All rooms are the same. You stayin' or not?"

Rico hesitated.

"We got cable. No porn though."

"And the bed . . . ."

"Bed's clean. Heck, mister, soap and water ain't that expensive. This place might be old, but we keep it up."

"In that case," Rico whipped out his wallet and fished for a twenty and a five, "I'm in."

"Glad to hear it." Miss Tammy abandoned the pen in her hand and opened a drawer. She began to rummage through it. "Now, I know I put them keys somewhere. I had 'em just last month when we cleaned them rooms."

"Uh, you haven't cleaned the room since last month?"

"It ain't like that. We clean all the rooms every month. Ain't nobody stayed in the one I'm putting you in since it was cleaned last month."

Rico rolled his eyes, *what have I gotten myself into*, he thought. Miss. Tammy was too busy looking for the room key to notice his conflict. He killed some time by gazing around. The large pictures on the wall made the small space seem even more cramped. One, though, had his interest, a poster of the state of Texas framed in varnished wood. A red thumbtack with, 'You are here' written in black sharpie marked the motel's location.

Well, at least that answers that, he thought while still waiting on Miss Tammy to find the room key she was after. The Western Winds Motel was south of Huntsville, just outside of Brooksville. Mr. Hunts' namesake was a thriving metropolis compared to Mr. Brooks'.

Small metal objects clinked and tinkled from inside the drawer as the old woman continued the diligent search.

He studied the map a little more, wondering where he might end up this time tomorrow. The image of a boat crossed his mind, but before the thought could fully form, Tammy popped it like a bubble with her sharply tinged voice.

"Found it."

"Good." Rico smiled, looking her in the eyes.

Miss Tammy peered back, and for a brief moment, Rico wondered what those tired old eyes had seen in her time. There was a gleam in them that gave him the sense she possessed ancient wisdom. Like she could see his life as a story and she knew how it ended—a Shaman of sorts.

The image he had of her grand stature in the universe came to a crashing end when she smiled.

Rico grimaced, despite his best effort not too. He had to question if this county had ever learned the science behind adding fluoride to the drinking water.

This time, she did notice his disapproval, because her lips quickly dropped back down around her horribly yellowed, crooked teeth and swollen gum line.

The basic pleasantries had run its course. It was back to the business at hand. She needed the money. He needed a room. They both nodded at one another as if understanding they were worlds apart in daily life and the only connection they would make was this transaction. Rico offered a conciliatory smile as she handed him the key. After a few seconds of awkward silence, the simple gesture bought him a reprieve. She smiled back, having the wherewithal to keep her lips together.

"Room 116, right?" Rico held up the key.

"Says so on the key. Room's second to last out front near the end."

"Thank you, miss."

"Have a good night's…," Miss Tammy coughed, "rest."

Rico turned and made a quick exit, hoping to outrun whatever germs spewed into the air. Just as he opened the door of the cramped office space, Miss Tammy called out.

"There's an ice bucket in the room and plastic cups. Just around the corner is the ice machine. Got a soda machine, too. The man just filled it up today."

"Good to know. If you're not here in the morning, it was nice meeting you." He hoped he hadn't offended the old woman too badly. He imagined she was a nice person, despite her physical appearance. It was wrong for him to judge a person's value by their looks. He knew this to be true on some level, but as a cop, his experience had taught him it is possible to tell a book by its cover.

He could still hear that old lady coughing her guts out after the office door closed and he was halfway to his room.

*

It took some jiggling and back and forth motions to get the room key to slide into the slot. The keyway was in dire need of lubrication, and the doorknob felt loose and rattled when he turned it.

The moment of truth, he thought, and flipped on the light switch. *Ta-Da!*

A lamp on a small table by the bed came on, showing one of its three bulbs had gone to be with Jesus. No overhead light at all, not even on the ceiling fan, which wasn't all that unusual as most bottom end motels kept lighting to a minimum to cloak the quality of their care in mystery.

The walls were painted a light tan. Dark brown carpet cushioned his steps, and he imagined it held years of hidden treasures he had no plans of searching for. The twin size bed had been properly made and covered with a deep chocolate colored comforter. The middle of the bed sagged as if a horse had been sleeping in it, or from marathon trick sessions of the local entrepreneurs of the evening. *I would name this room Fifty Shades of Brown*, he thought. Even the pictures on the wall had browns for dominant colors.

The smell was worse than the appearance. It sort of reminded him of his high school gymnasium, only worse. It was apparent that Miss Tammy didn't lie when she said the room had been cleaned. The problem, though, was the musty old sweat sock stench was in a battle with overwhelming bleach odor. It was like trying to mask the stench of jock itch and foot fungus with the entire sanitation department of San Antonio. His nostrils burned as he looked around the room to see if he could find a window to open. No luck, the one covered by thick drapes was just a solid piece of glass.

Rico tossed his bag to the floor and set his helmet on the chest of drawers—the only real furniture in the room— right next to the 20 inch TV.

The room was warm enough for him to run the A/C unit under the window. He turned it on 'Fan' to blow some fresh air in, and found an overhead fan in the small bathroom to get some circulation going. It wasn't much, but it was at least something.

He plopped down on the bed and contemplated where he was on the map and what direction he might be heading. How should he choose? Did he really have a choice anyway? Were consequences in life all from choices by free will, or was everything predestined by God or the universe to begin with? What if he just put a bottle on a map, gave it a spin, and drove toward wherever the open mouth pointed? As intriguing as that sounded, it just seemed too irresponsible. He could head west and find his fate somewhere in New Mexico. Or even just take a simple route and follow the interstate through Louisiana into Mississippi or Alabama. The possibilities were endless. It was just a matter of where. Rico liked it. He liked not having to be somewhere. All those years on the force had him chained to one small area on the planet. His time away from the job had him tied down to a woman whom he strived to always please. Now he only had to please himself. Making a decision tonight on which direction to go was just too much of a burden. He decided on enjoying a little more freedom from responsibility. It could wait until the morning.

However, before morning, he needed to scrub off some of the day's grime and get some sleep. Before he could do any of that, he had to get the dry taste of gym socks and disinfectant out of his mouth.

The air in his room had already begun to clear. Now seemed like a good time to find that ice maker and Coke machine. Too bad he didn't have a decent cigar to light up and enjoy celebrating his new adventure.

Once outside, the cool night air offered immediate relief. There was no traffic along the road in front and no activity in the parking lot. *Looks like everyone's bedded down*, he thought. His footfalls bounced off the sidewalk as he rounded the corner to the hum of machines.

The Coke machine was the most modern piece of equipment he'd seen since stopping off in this neck of the woods. Amongst the variety of cola, diet cola, and un-cola, one brightly lit button offered 12oz of relief in a can of Big Red. He fed the machine a dollar bill and it gobbled it down without choking it back up. The can dropped from the dispenser with a loud clunk. Rico reached down to get his quarter and retrieve the drink.

"Hi there," a woman's voice said.

Rico had been so caught up in his thoughts that the introduction startled him. He froze and jerked his head toward the voice.

The moment he spotted her, Rico just wanted to be back in the musty room, minding his own business. He had seen her kind almost daily on the streets of Killeen. They basically all dressed the same. She wore a skimpy skirt and a tight shirt over an almost meatless frame of a body. Her ratty blonde hair looked like it hadn't been brushed since last week. This one had a set of fake tits—probably a gift from her boyfriend-turned-employer to boost sales. She partially hid behind a dangling purse. Track marks ran the entire length of her right arm. This girl was a junkie whore and didn't try to hide that fact in any way.

Rico had dealt with enough of life's throwaways to deduce she was between the age of twenty-two and twenty-five. Which, to the untrained eye, would seems outrageous, because she didn't look a day younger than forty-five. The daily drudge as a prostitute had worn the glow of youth off her skin and left tanned, wrinkled hide. The obvious drug habit had further depleted precious resources and emaciated her body. Her eyes sunk in and dark circles pooled underneath, exacerbated by her pale complexion. A rash left its mark on her right knee, probably from habitual scratching while on the stuff. The only question was about what the stuff might be—crack, meth, or heroin?

"You a cop?"

Well, it didn't take long for it to come down to business, he thought, and reached out and grabbed his drink. Rico latched his gaze to hers. When it was clear she wasn't scared and wasn't going to run off anytime soon, he played his next hand. "Depends on who's asking." He popped the top on the Big Red and swallowed a mouthful. "You a prostitute?"

"Depends on who's asking," she said coldly, as if she wasn't interested in playing any games. The pain of her condition didn't hide in her expression. It was obvious she was going through withdrawals now. She needed money. How far would she go to get it?

Fuck this shit, Rico felt a haunting memory return. He stiffened his body and tried to push it from his mind. He turned to walk away—hoping to escape both the present and the past.

"You gonna leave that quarter?" she called.

The desperation in her voice jerked at his heartstrings. "You want it?" Rico turned, seeing that he had left the quarter in the change slot of the soda machine.

She bit the bottom of her lip and gazed hungrily into his eyes. A few seconds later, she waved an impassive hand. "No, you take it."

It was just a stupid quarter. This woman needed more than that to get her out of a bind. But even if Rico reached into his pocket and gave her the money she needed, it wouldn't repair what was broken in her. It would only oil the machine for a little while until the rust of addiction would clog the gears once again. Only the machine would have worn a bit further, threatening a final break down. There was simply nothing he could do to save her. In fact, if he gave her the money now, she might overdose and die because of his sympathy. He had to be stronger than that; a bitter lesson he had learned from his past. This time when he turned and left he wouldn't have second thoughts.

"You don't know what you're missing," she called out.

Rico gave a dismissing wave in the air, not bothering to look over his shoulder as he briskly walked away.

Despite his disdain for the woman's profession, he couldn't help but wonder why she was hanging outside this motel. It was basically in the middle of nowhere. Surely, she was smart enough to realize there was more money to be made in bigger cities. He knew that was a bad way to look at it, but it was true just the same.

"Name's June Melon," he faintly heard her say. "In case you change your mind."

I'm sure for the right price I can call you whatever I want, Rico thought as he rounded the corner and headed back to his room.

Chapter 7

Either he had moved enough fresh air into the room, or his olfactory nerves had fried enough that the horrible stench no longer bothered him. The comforter must have weighed thirty pounds and was too warm to cover with. The sheets, at least, were clean, but felt like they were made from a grade of cotton slightly softer than burlap. He layered two of the flat pillows to get his head at a comfortable angle, and after a few minutes of squirming around on the mattress, he finally settled in. Rico wondered if the mattress was stuffed with chicken feathers.

A million thoughts swirled through his mind as his eyes shut. The past and the future posed questions he hoped to have answers for soon. Sleep edged in like a drug, extinguishing the tiny fires of turmoil one by one, easing the officer into its warm embrace.

Bam! Bam! Bam!

The dream began as a nightmare, just as it had done countless times before. He was at Pop's bar that fateful night—aiming the gun at the target. Something was different about it. He lifted his gaze from the barrel sight. The bullets had found their mark, but it wasn't one of the walking dead taking them in the chest and face. It was his mother.

This just couldn't be! His mother wasn't there that night. He rubbed his eyes—praying she would be replaced by the undead—but she remained.

But this wasn't her. Not his real mother. Something inside told him so. He aimed the gun again. She stared back. Her eyes told him she was scared and asked why her own son would raise a hand to take her life. She had always loved him and supported him. Why this?

Bam! Bam! Bam!

The body collapsed to the floor with arms splayed wide. She was dead, and he had killed her. However, when he stepped over and looked down at her unmoving corpse, her face no longer looked back. The dream returned to the familiar scene. A rotting, stinking corpse who had come to life had died a second time.

Rico's eyes opened before the dream finished. The A/C fan hummed in the background, and he tried to focus on the unfamiliar objects in the room to get his bearings.

Feeling miserable, he wondered how long it would be before the nightmares would stop. How many others suffered like him? What else was floating around in the universe, biding its time until finding Mother Earth to infect? It was one thing to fear the horrors of war perpetrated by men. At least both sides had a fighting chance. How would man fare against a much nastier alien invasion? The possible scenarios were endless.

He tried to shake his thoughts away from the unknown. In the dark, his imagination only made the monsters larger. His mother had disrupted his dream. Was she okay?

His mother had been on medication for the past several years to treat her dementia. The pills didn't cure anything but did help make her life manageable. Still, his dad had grown too old to take care of her by himself. She had been in a nursing home for over a year now. Contact with the outside world was near nonexistent. The television in her room stayed on the Animal Channel, so she had been completely isolated from the events of The Spook. The regimented lifestyle of the home suited her well. Wake up, eat breakfast, go to craft class, eat lunch, play bingo, take nap, eat supper, and then down enough drugs to keep her asleep until morning.

Thoughts of his mom shifted to a time when he was a teenager in high school. Back when he was chubby from overeating. Back before he had gotten in shape to join the Coast Guard.

Pete Knoles had been the biggest bully on campus. Rico always wondered what made him tick. Pete picked on everyone— even football players who were bigger than he was. His presence exuded an aura of intimidation.

Rico didn't escape Pete's evil eye. In fact, Pete never missed an opportunity to make fun of his weight if he were in sight. After Rico returned to Killeen from his four years in the Coast Guard, he had never seen Pete again until the day after The Spook. Pete had met with some bullies much tougher than him. The guy who dished it out the most finally met his match.

Rico remembered a time when Pete had him on the ground:

"Leave me alone, Pete. I didn't do it."

"I don't care if you didn't do it, Rico the geek'o!"

Rico was 15 years old. Pimples and braces all over again. He was just outside the gym by the soccer field. His jeans were covered in grass stains. Pete put on a show as his classmates gathered around.

"I swear I didn't do it."

"Somebody took my Little Debbie Zebra Cake from my locker. And the only person it could be was you, you fat fuck!"

Pete kicked Rico in the chest, leaving a shoe print on his striped shirt.

Most of the other kids laughed, something Rico never understood. There was nothing funny about violence. As Rico gazed around for help, there wasn't one sign of sympathy in his classmates' expressions. He wanted to cry but willed himself not to. Not in front of everyone.

Pete started making piggy grunts, which made most of the other kids join in. The event was one of the most humiliating of his life.

"Rico the geek'o ate my Little Debbie cake. You'd eat the whole world if someone let you."

But that had happened years ago. And it proved to be a pivotal point in his life. From then on, Rico made a conscious effort to limit how much food he ate while in high school. The void he had been trying to fill with empty calories for momentary pleasure was overshadowed by his desire for respect. Mostly the desire for self-respect.

And what of Pete? Despite every negative thing Rico could think about the man, he would have relived Pete's abuse over and over again if it meant Pete wouldn't have died the way he did.

Rico had taken a statement from an eyewitness to how he met his death. Pete had come back to Killeen to visit a few of his buddies on April 1st. They were smoking outside a bar when one of the walking dead approached him. Despite the amount of blows he threw into the thing, it never went down. When more zombies showed up, his friends scattered. Pete only got more pissed off, and vowed to 'Fuck them all up.' That had turned out to be the worst—and last— decision Pete made in his life.

The ghouls that overwhelmed him didn't bring a quick death. They went for the arms and legs first. Pete had screamed until he was hoarse. When EMS collected the remains of the body, the only thing identifiable was a tattoo on a chunk of flesh.

Rico watched the ceiling fan slowly spin overhead. The moonlight leaked into his room past the curtains, casting distorted shadows on the wall, just as the past leaked into his mind, distorting the hope he held for the future.

Was he being selfish? Was he guilty of deluding himself that there was actually a new salvation that awaited him somewhere else?

Maybe I should just go back home—spend some time with Mom, he thought, knowing her days were near the end. *I could try to heal the gap between Dad and me too.*

Too many questions and second guessing finally tired him to the point where he fell asleep again.

When he became aware in the nightmare, he was aiming down the barrel of his pistol. This time, the target was Pete, the school bully. Pete was no longer a teenager, and what remained of him could barely be able to be called a man. Pete was torn to ribbons and covered in blood.

Rico's stomach twisted in knots. The killing never got any easier.

Bam! Bam! Bam!

*

A noise startled Rico from his sleep. He felt a bit more rested, but his body ached for more. The ceiling fan blew cool waves of air over his cheeks. The room had no clock, and if he still had his cell phone, he would have used it to check the time. The remote control for the television was on the nightstand. He reached for it and pointed it toward the television.

Before he pushed the 'on' button, something bumped hard against the wall.

That's just great. How much longer am I going to have to hear the headboard in the next room bang? He wished the guy next door would hurry up and shoot his wad to get it over with. *Well, at least she's not screaming, Oh God! Oh God!*

Then he did hear a scream. It was a female's voice, but it didn't come from the other room.

He sat up in bed, pushing the cobwebs from his mind. The screams came from outside his door, sounding distant. *Really?* For a place this backwoods, he would have thought the last thing he had to worry about was getting a good night's sleep.

"What the hell's going on?" he said under his breath.

Rico tossed the sheets aside and stretched his tired muscles when he stood. Hopefully someone had just arrived drunk and was still in a partying mood. He certainly didn't want to deal with any shit going down tonight.

Rico was at the window pushing back the curtains when he heard the screams again. Fortunately, the moonlight was bright enough to fill in the areas between the anemic street and parking lot lights.

Nothing unusual was going on out front. His bike was right where he left it, as were the other vehicles he parked next to when he arrived. However, there were more cars parked by the road than he remembered. He must have slept harder than he thought not to be bothered by the rumble of engines and headlights flashing through his window.

A mini-van was parked behind his bike. Beside that was a nice vintage Corvette. Whoever had decided to stop for the night in such a fine car was probably lost.

He looked over at the gas pumps. An older white Ford pickup set at pump number 2. For some reason the truck's hazard lights were on. There was no one at the pump, and the gas station didn't appear to be open. Maybe that's how this motel made its business.

If a motorist found themselves in the middle of nowhere and the only gas station for miles is closed, they just stayed for the night until the pump opened. Not a bad racket.

The *thump* that had awoken him hit the wall again. Rico didn't know if was from a headboard, but whatever it was chapped his ass.

He almost decided to forget it and lie back down when he saw a manly figure run out from the gas station toward the truck at the pump. In his haste, he fell to the ground about halfway there. Dirt plumed up around him as he slid to a stop. It caught Rico's attention that the runner never looked at where he was running. His head craned over his shoulder as he made the mad dash toward the truck. The man didn't waste any time on the ground, springing back to his feet to close the distance between him and the pumps.

"Looks like the suburbs aren't the only haven for knuckleheads." Rico sighed. *I'm not in the mood for this.*

Then Rico saw what the man had run from. It was hard to see at first because of the uneven lighting and shadows. It was only one person in pursuit, and they didn't look like they were in all that big of a hurry. But they kept going at a steady pace—a bit jerky, like they had an injured leg. Then the person lifted their arms. The realization hit him like an electric shock.

The Spook! It's happening again, he thought.

No way. This had to be a rare case of a straggler just now escaping from where it had been. Maybe from an Army facility where some of the undead had been captured and studied. The dead didn't come back to life anymore. The scientists had assured everyone of that.

If he had stayed back in Killeen, he wouldn't be here and have to come face to face with the undead again. As much as he would have liked to crawl back in bed and cover his head, he knew that was something that he couldn't do. A man outside needed help, and his job was to protect and serve.

He pulled on his pants and socks as quickly as he could and reached for his gun on the nightstand when he stepped into his boots. The extra clip was in his bag, so he reached in and grabbed it. His heart raced as his hand hit the door, and he snatched up his jacket as he stepped outside.

Get a hold of yourself, man. Think it through and don't let the excitement make you do something stupid, he thought.

Rico took a deep breath and slipped his jacket on as he headed toward the pumps.

Screams echoed across the parking lot, but there was no telling from where they came.

A quick scan of the surroundings showed the man frantically trying to unlock his truck at the pump and the ghoul shambling toward him. The parking lot appeared to be devoid of activity.

Rico called out, "I'm a police officer. What's going on?" He hoped to accomplish two things. One: let the man know help was on its way. And two: distract the undead.

"What the fuck does it look like?" the man still trying to get into the truck shouted. "It's The Spook! It's happening all over again. That dead guy bit me!"

As Rico stepped closer—his heart pounded in his chest like a steel drum. It matched the *thump, thump, thump* of his footfalls.

"Fuck! Fuck! Fuck!" Rico mumbled, pissed about the situation. He was able to get a better look at the man at the truck. Each time the hazard lights flashed, he saw that the man's chest was covered in blood. He had almost gone to his aid until the zombie giving chase moaned eagerly in anticipation.

Rico aimed the gun at the ghoul. It was at pump number 1, reaching out as it shuffled over to the truck.

"Shoot it!" the bleeding man cried.

Rico's hands shook. His mind flashed to his nightmare. He saw the first zombie he shot at the bar, and then his mother's face, then Pete's face, before reality returned him to the present. The zombie in front came into clear view as he pulled the trigger.

Bam!

The gun blast in the still of night slapped him awake from the momentary shock the situation had on him. The zombie fell between the pumps before he could reach the man.

Rico hurried over to the undead lying on the ground. He lifted his gun, prepared to fire again if it showed any sign of movement. It didn't though. It was dead, again. The undead who attacked the man was none other than Kevin, the friendly gas station attendant who had waited on him earlier.

The cough, Rico thought. *Kevin suffered from that cough. Did he have a cold, or was he suffering from whatever ailed those affected by The Spook?* His worst fears took root and began to sprout.

The man by his truck let out a sob.

"Are you okay?" Rico asked, turning his attention away from Kevin.

The man jerked his head around and peered over Rico's shoulder. His watery eyes went wide in abject fear.

"Fuck this! I'm outta here!" The man found the fortitude to insert the key in the lock and opened the door. He slid inside, and the engine roared to life as soon as his ass hit the seat.

Rico turned and saw what had the old guy in such a panic. Two women had just rounded the corner of the motel and they were heading straight for him. Close on their heels, at least a dozen zombies gave chase. It wasn't much of a surprise that Miss Tammy, the motel manager, led the way. She had the same cough, and now she was a member of the walking dead like Kevin.

"Shit." Rico gritted his teeth—the worst of his fears coming true right before his eyes.

He turned to jump in the bed of the truck, but it was too late. The white Ford barreled away from the gas pumps with tires spinning in the dirt and kicking up debris. The driver didn't take into account the dirt parking lot after his tires left the cement by the pumps. The rear of the truck fishtailed from side to side, and he overcompensated the steering each time, trying to regain control. The truck arrived at a light pole before the driver succeeded. It hit the pole and skidded against the curb where it rolled off balance upside down. Metal screeched as it folded under itself, quickening Rico's teeth.

When the truck came to a rest, it was half on the grass and half on the road. With Rico's ears ringing, he wasn't sure if the moans he heard came from the driver, or the group of zombies heading his way. It didn't take long for him to find out. The moans carried the desperate pangs of hunger. There was no doubt those very moans came from the cab of the overturned truck. The man had been bitten, and it hadn't taken long for him to turn into a flesh eating zombie.

That meant the alien virus had mutated again. Those who were bitten during The Spook must have incubated a new strain of virus. Now that it had transformed them into undead cannibals, they were able to propagate by wounding a member of the living. Realizing this had Rico wishing he had a full suit of riot gear and body armor. He was about to be an eyewitness to one of the new zombie firstborns.

"Help! They're going to get us," one of the two women headed toward him shouted.

Rico looked for a means of escape and felt his keys in his front pocket. He could see his motorcycle from where he stood, but there was no way he could carry both women with him. He was going to have to steal a car unless the women had one. No time to think about it now. It came down to fight or flee, and he didn't know if he had enough bullets to take down the zombie horde.

"Follow me!" No point in running to them if he was only going to have to lead them away. He stepped past dead-man Kevin and darted for the gas station. "This way, hurry!"

Fortunately, the women easily outpaced their would-be attackers. Rico waved them over and held the door open. The two quickly shot by, and he stepped in behind them. Once safely behind the door, he twisted the knob on the deadbolt.

"My name's Rico," he said. "I'm a police officer."

"I don't give a fuck what your name is, mister. Just help us get out of this mess," the woman closest to him, a brunette, said.

Yep, par for the course. Just do what we pay you for, shut up, and protect my ass, Rico thought. The zombies had crossed the road and were heading straight for them. "Well, looks like that bunch would be the last to reach the finish line at the Boston Marathon. We can at least out run them for a ways. Either one of you have a car we can take?"

The unified moans from outside grew louder. Even though Rico knew a layer of safety glass protected them, it still creeped him out that they were so close. Miss Tammy was the first to step up and mash her face against the glass. The ancient wisdom she may have once harbored gave way to an unquenching lust for raw human flesh.

"I don't," the brunette said.

"And you?" Rico took notice of the other woman for the first time and realized it was his date wanna-be, June Melon, who he had met by the soda machine.

The blonde shook her head. A bewildered expression gripped her face. Rico wondered how fucked up she was on drugs and maybe just thought she was having a bad trip.

Rico turned to the brunette. "Do you know where all these zombified people came from?"

"The trailer park behind the motel," she said, gasping to catch her breath. "We was over there trying to find a little work... I, um... I mean trying to find a friend, when the shit hit the fan."

More of the undead gathered by the door. Hands with crooked fingers pawed against the glass. June snapped to attention and slowly stepped backward. "They want in—they're going to get us! We have to leave before they break in."

At least June was aware enough to be scared for her life. "That's probably a good idea. I'm sure there's a back door. Let's lose these fuckers and get the hell out of here!"

Chapter 8

"Hold on." Rico stopped in his tracks. He closed his eyes and shook his head. "Let's not run off right now without thinking this through a bit." He turned and pointed a finger at the brunette. "There's a pack of zombies out there wanting to eat us. Those people were alive a few hours ago. We're not dealing with a small number like back when The Spook happened. That means once we leave here, we're going to face a hell of a lot more than before. We'll have to steal a car and make a run for it. I don't know where we'll go, but we'll need supplies. We need to grab what food and water we can here before we make our escape." Rico scanned the store, looking for the most practical food and drink to bring along with them. No chips, but maybe some crackers—with peanut butter or cheese filling. Something with protein, like tuna, or even Vienna sausages. Water would be heavy but it was what they would need the most. Maybe some energy drinks, but hell no to any alcohol.

Before he could bark out any orders, a jolt to the door hit so hard it made the electronic entry warning—the duck quack—activate. It startled Rico enough that he raised his arms and lowered his head for cover. *I'm too fucking jumpy over this,* he thought. *I've got to get my shit together.*

He turned to the door and watched the mass of zombies fervently push against it. They pushed so hard, Rico thought he could hear tiny pops from stressing glass. He hurriedly stepped away on a frantic mission.

The brunette spread her hands and shifted her weight from side to side. "What the fuck are you doing? I thought you said we were leaving?"

"We will in a minute. We have to buy a little time to grab some supplies. I'm looking for something to barricade the door with."

"Wait, where's Kevin?" The brunette turned her attention away from Rico and ran to the counter. She looked behind it and craned her neck to one side.

"Don't worry about that goofball clerk. Come and help me move some stuff in front of the door." Rico grabbed a display shelf featuring various flavors of beef jerky and started dragging it toward the entrance. June was too distraught to be of any use. This was no time for the other woman to lose her focus on the dire emergency at hand.

"But Kevin can help us. We can't leave him here." The brunette turned her attention away from Rico. "Kevin?" She yelled.

The moans increased outside, reacting to the woman's cry.

"Shut the fuck up!" Rico briefly stopped pulling the display and watched the zombies increase their efforts to break in. "Kevin's dead. I'm sorry if he was your friend, or one of your customers. He turned into one of those things and attacked a man by the gas pumps. I had to put him down."

"You did what?" The brunette brought the back of her hand to her mouth. "Kevin's dead? You're lying." Her face instantly turned red. Tears welled in her eyes and began to roll down her cheeks.

Rico grimaced at the sudden burst of anguish. Now was not the time for her to pull this shit. Damn women, wearing emotions on their sleeve.

Before he could chastise her, the teeth quickening sound of glass cracking froze Rico in his steps.

"They're going to break in and get us!" June cried.

"What gave you that idea?" Rico glared at both women. He pushed the display against the door the best he could. It was heavy and a little awkward. The chips in the floor tile didn't make his job any easier. "Now help me with that ice cream box by the counter."

Rico ran to the cooler and pulled one end away from the wall. It was heavy, which was good to use for a barricade, but not too heavy for him to move alone if he had to, which was even better. He reached down and unplugged the electrical cord.

He pulled the other end away from the wall and pointed it toward the door. As he went to the back to begin pushing, another set of hands appeared and latched on too. June had finally broken out of her funk enough to make herself useful. She gave him a reassuring smile, but it was obvious to Rico she was just putty inside. At least she was trying, and he admired her for that.

As for the brunette, she had gone from the self-centered, more level headed of the women to some hysterical mess that needed to be shot with a tranquilizer gun. Good grief, was Kevin her boyfriend?

Rico braved a look at the faces of the hungry ghouls outside as the cooler inched its way toward the door. Miss Tammy's eyes were milky white and vacant of life. She was horrible to look at. It reminded Rico of a shark's eyes as it searched for prey in the waters of the deep. Cold, uncaring, hell bent on one thing alone— to feed. As Rico and June moved closer to the door, the savage lust of the undead increased. The storefront door rattled like a disjointed tune played on a hollow drum.

"Think it will hold?" The quiver in June's voice had Rico thinking she was about to lose it again.

"I have no idea," Rico said, watching the creatures desperate to get inside. "All we need to do is buy some time, and then get the hell out of here."

The glass cracked again, noticeably louder this time.

The dead moans seeped through the crack and wrapped icy fingers around Rico's spine.

June must have felt that way, too. Her mouth fell open, and her eyes grew as wide as saucers. The brunette was still lost in her own little world, ignoring the threatening death.

Rico snapped out of it and tried to command June to action. "That shelf over there. Help me move it." He dashed over to a shelf lined with canned goods and junk food. He leaned against the display and put his back into it. "Shit." The damn thing was bolted to the floor.

Glass creaked again until pieces broke and fell to the floor.

"What are we going to do?" June cried.

"Find the back door and get out of here." Rico quickly looked for a gallon jug of water to grab. They could do without food for a while, but water was something they simply had to have.

June didn't wait for him, and when more glass hit the floor and the barricade shifted, Rico forgot all about the water. He caught up with June just as she reached the brunette.

"Get her back to her senses. What's the story with her and Kevin anyway?" Rico asked.

June made sad eyes and raised her lower lip. "Kevin was her baby brother."

Fuck. Kevin was her brother, and I killed him. I wish I had kept my big mouth shut. Rico cleared his throat. "I'm so sorry to hear that. I . . . didn't have any choice in the matter." Rico walked over to a door in the back and opened it. It was a closet housing brooms, mops, and other cleaning materials.

June shook her head. If the brunette had heard him, she must have not cared for the apology, because she didn't respond in any way.

When the regret had rolled off Rico's lips, he realized he didn't really care she had lost her brother. He didn't know them well, and what time he spent with Kevin certainly didn't cement any emotional ties. What was sad about the situation was his drastic change in attitude. He would have sympathized with the brunette if he had just met her yesterday and learned of her brother's death. He would have genuinely felt something inside for anyone who had a lost a loved one. Something had died inside—a part of his humanity. It didn't matter to him now that Kevin had been a human like him hours before. Kevin was no different from a wild animal in his undead state. Now it was kill or be killed. There would be no remorse for eliminating the living dead.

Rico didn't like what he had become. "Damn, where's the door leading out of this place?"

"There's an emergency exit behind the counter," June said.

"Grab your friend and get ready to make a run for it. We're wasting time." Rico ran behind the counter and found the emergency exit down a short hall leading to the office. He waited as June dragged the brunette by the hand with her.

"Okay, get ready. I'm going to lead, and you both stay as close to me as possible. Got that?"

June nodded her head.

"Good, here we go." When Rico said, 'go,' he opened the door and stepped up with gun poised in the lead.

Someone waiting outside immediately crashed into him and knocked him backward to the floor. *Damn! I should have known better—looked outside first. I got in too big of a hurry and now I'm fucked.*

When he hit the floor, the pistol jarred loose and skittered from his hand. The metallic clang spiked amongst the desperate moans of the undead and gnashing of teeth. The zombie had apparently been waiting at the back door, and Rico made the mistake of inviting it in.

Six months ago, Rico had been in the fight for his life with a zombie on top of him at Pop's. The scene repeated itself. A scene he had never thought would happen again. He fought to keep the zombie's fingers from digging into his skin. The zombie clawed with abandon to gain dominance.

This zombie didn't smell of death and rot. It had the familiar rank of a homeless person. Lots of body odor simmering under a layer of grime. There were notes of rotted fruit mixed with spoiled milk. The smell was still bad enough to make Rico gag.

After turning his head for a gasp of fresh air, he called, "My gun! Get my gun!"

The zombie's head struck like a snake toward his face. Rico barely managed to keep his nose from getting chomped off. Its teeth clacked against empty air.

Fortunately, Rico was in better physical shape for this dance with the undead, because the zombie's muscles weren't reconstructed by alien DNA as with the first. Its muscles were fresh and invigorated by the off world life force.

He gripped the attacker's throat with both hands and spread his forearms wide to wedge against the flailing arms. Footfalls to his left had him wondering if the two women didn't have the stomach to come to his aid and had decided to leave him behind.

The brunette sobbed. Maybe June was leaving her behind, too.

The heavy breathing he heard was his own. Despite his efforts to overcome the assailant, he was barely holding on. His arms were tired and muscles burned as if he was trying to raise a heavy barbell for that one last rep.

Fatigue was just about to become his master when a gun fired right near his head. His ears rang, and the concussion from the blast felt like an open palm slap to the face by Hulk Hogan.

The creature's body immediately went slack. Rico tossed it aside and took a moment to refocus on reality. He hoped there weren't any more zombies waiting to storm in the back, and if they didn't hurry out, the things in front would soon be on them.

"I just shot old man Glen," June said, gun still aimed at the unmoving body.

"Good grief. You knew this guy? Why'd he smell so bad?" Rico rose to his feet and rubbed the soreness from his arms.

June didn't answer. She acted as if she didn't even hear him.

"June? You okay?"

She turned to him, and said, "His . . . his wife kicked him out of the house for drinking too much. He's been living by the dumpster in the back of the diner for the last couple of months."

It was difficult for Rico to hear her soft words. He was able to read her lips and the shocked expression on her face helped him realize how she felt.

"We don't have time for this shit." He grabbed the gun from her hand, and she made no resistance to keep it.

Moonlight spilled onto the floor through the door opening.

Rico raised the gun and headed for the exit, determined not to be taken by surprise this time. "June, grab you friend and get your ass in gear. Let's move!" His voice resonated in his head as if his ears had been stuffed with cotton. He poked his head out the door, careful to keep his gun close to his body.

Had June not pulled the trigger right next to his head, Rico might have heard the brunette's cries of sorrow turn into screams of terror. Might have heard the glass on the front door give and shatter. Might have heard the rack of beef jerky topple over and crash to the floor.

To his left, one lone sodium security lamp illuminated the dumpster about a hundred feet away. To the right, the escape route was cloaked in darkness. He waited for his eyes to adjust to the dim light.

So far, so good. Rico extended an arm behind to wave the women to follow. His hand hit something, and when he jutted his head around to look, June crashed into him and tried to push him out the door. Then he saw why.

The barricade had totally given way to the onslaught of the undead. Zombies shambled over one another to get inside. Some had tripped over the displays but were already getting back on their feet.

June had left the brunette behind. The brunette looked up at the ceiling with a blank stare and open mouth. She raised her arms as if asking someone above to lift her up.

The first zombie to arrive descended on her shoulder, taking a large bite out of the soft flesh. The violence pulled her from the imaginary safe place, and she screamed out at the top of her lungs.

Blood gushed from the opened wound. Rico thought for a moment that he saw the white of bone. He went to rush to her aid but put himself in check. It was time to think and not react.

Two zombies arriving next joined in on the feeding. She fell to the floor, and more undead dropped down and ate like hungry hogs to the slop.

The last image he caught of her was an arm shooting up from the mass of ghouls like a drowning victim going down for the last time.

Rico stopped resisting June's attempt to push him outside, and both passed out the door. The area was quiet with no other dangers in sight. The hidden dangers, though, were always the worst.

*

Rico ran with June out front leading the way, keeping a watchful eye out for zombies from all sides. June was holding up better in the escape than he had imagined.

His hearing had started to come back to normal. As his feet hit the ground a couple of minutes into the run, it was as if someone turned up the volume on the TV. The dull thump of boots hitting ground and the wisp of the tall grass shoved out of the way made noises he hoped wouldn't attract any unwanted attention.

"I think we can cross the street and head back over to the trailer park behind the motel," June said.

They were far enough from the gas station-diner for its lights not to be an issue. "Sounds good to me. Try to stay low and keep the noise down." Damn, this girl was doing good for a junkie. She was leading him to safety, and if she hadn't killed old man Glen, he might not even be alive right now.

June nodded and crouched over as she began her trek. Rico pulled on her dress when they reached the street to slow her down in fear his boots would hit the pavement too hard. Once around the back of the motel, June came to a stop between a row of trees that separated the business from the trailer park.

Rico whispered in her ear, "Where're we going?"

"Kevin lived in the trailer park. He's got a clunker for a car. If it starts, it'll at least get us out of here."

Before he could say, 'Let's move,' it dawned on him. There were only two now. They didn't need a car. "Hell, I've got my motorcycle. It's parked up front, and it'll take us anywhere we want to go."

"What about the keys?"

He produced them from his pocket and jingled them before her.

She nodded. "Then lead the way."

The two wasted no time, running down the side of the motel past the Coke machine where they had first met. Rico was so focused on reaching the motorcycle that he didn't even think about his duffle bag and other belongings in his room. He just kept one foot in front of the other. By the sound of it, so did his new friend.

"It's over there." He had kept his voice low enough, but in his haste to reach his bike, he kicked up a pile of loose gravel and sent it clanging against the side of a car. *Shit, the last thing I needed to do was draw attention.*

A few zombies had wandered their way out of the gas station and were out front. The noised had them shambling back toward the motel.

"Just keep running," Rico called. If June saw the zombies, he didn't want her to halt in her tracks and second guess the situation. "We're almost there!"

Rico jumped on the bike, kicked up the stand and put in the key. He hoped like hell he could find somewhere safe to hide out. The motorcycle roared to life. He felt June jump on and grab hold of his hips. The thought of his ex-wife appeared in his mind, but was gone just as fast. The moans of the dead filtered through the rumble of the Harley and brought him back to the here and now. "Hang on, June!"

"My name's not June," she hollered in his ear.

Well, that wasn't a real surprise. Rico gave the throttle a twist and lifted his boots from the ground. Dirt kicked up as they sped away.

They hit the highway and passed by the old, turned over, white Ford truck. The zombie inside had managed to find its way out. It had reached out in hopes of satisfying its hunger. It didn't have the slightest chance of reaching Rico and the woman, but it reached out just the same. A mindless robot programmed for survival.

***

"Holy shit. She and that guy just jumped on his bike and tore out of here," Gus said, looking out a window in the room next to Rico's.

"What the fuck?" Marcus rolled off the bed and darted over to see, a cigarette dangled from his chapped lips. "Fucking bitch."

Gus scratched the gnarly growth under his chin. "What do we do? Go after her?"

Marcus sucked the last bit of life out of the smoke and exhaled like a pissed off bull. Then a smile curled on his lips. "She won't go far."

"She won't?"

"Nope, not far at all."

"What makes you think that?" Gus asked, mashing his cigar in the ashtray next to the bed.

"Because she's got an appointment with the tooth fairy."

"You really think she'll head back that way?"

"One hundred percent." Marcus reached in his pocket and tried the fit of his new brass knuckles. "And we need to get there before she does."

"But what about that spic that was with her? I think he was a cop."

"Think I give a flying ass bat about one little cop? Look around, Gus. The Spook is going down again, and this time, it's happening to people who are alive. I have a feeling it ain't going away like last time."

"You really think so?"

"I do. I been thinking about it. You saw the same thing I did. That old woman manager was coughing one minute and trying to bite us the next. We barely got back to our room."

"You sure are smart. You know that, Marcus?"

"Yes, I do, and that's why I'm where I'm at. You're the muscle, and I'm the brains."

"That's right," Gus said, holding the shotgun across his chest. "What you want to do now?"

"Pack our shit. We're going on a trip, and we need to get there before she does. That skank owes me a bundle. I aim to work it out of her until I'm paid in full."

Gus laughed. "While we're out, we need to score some supplies. I'm running low on blow."

"Then we'll get that, too."

Marcus pulled a pack of Lucky Strikes from his shirt pocket and lit one. The match cast his face in an eerie orange glow. The dancing light accented the scar on his left cheek. He sucked on the smoke and the end smoldered and fired up. He turned to the mirror and adjusted the gold chain around his neck connected to large gold letters that spelled his name.

Only one girl had tried to quit the game on him before. Marcus taught her a lesson she would never forget.

Angie would be the next to learn his simple code of justice.

Chapter 9

June hollered something over the Harley's roar.

"What?" The wind whistled around Rico's ears as he tore down the highway. This was no time for his new companion to play twenty questions. God, he hoped she didn't need to pee.

The road took a sharp bend up ahead. By the time he saw the turn, he realized they might be in a heap of trouble. He was going fast. Too fast in fact. The adrenaline rush had him so focused on escape that he hadn't bothered to look down at the speedometer. Had he done so, he would have known he was outrunning his headlights, jeopardizing his ability to react to an obstacle in the road.

The desolate highway careened left and right like a black snake. The headlights lit up the center stripes of the road. Because he dared maintain his speed, the white stripes took on the appearance of a continuous line. He maneuvered across both sides of the highway—*straightening* it out the best way he could.

June yelled again and squeezed him tightly around the waist.

Even if he couldn't hear her, he got the message. Now that he was returning to his senses, he was at least going to slow down before wrecking the bike. The road rose up a small hill, and he had no idea what was on the other side. Rico gazed down at the speedometer for the first time after letting out on the throttle. They were going almost 90 miles an hour, and for how long, he had no way of telling. All he knew was that he wanted to get as far away from everything as fast as he could.

The motorcycle slowed as it traveled up the incline.

"Where're we going?"

Well, at least she didn't ask, 'Are we there yet,' he thought. Rico had started to feel more like his old sarcastic self again. It would have been useless to answer her over the Harley's growl.

He waited until they made it over the top of the hill and found flat road before bringing the motorcycle to a halt. The engine stopped at the twist of a key, and he planted his feet on the asphalt to keep the bike upright.

The blonde uttered a few indecipherable curse words when she un-assed herself from the seat. Rico waited for the thirty minute lecture of how, 'You drove so fast you could have got us killed.' Just like his ex-wife. Never grateful for all the good he did for her. All she could concentrate on was what he didn't do right. Maybe he did drive too fast. He was genuinely scared. Still, he managed to get them both out alive and now they were safe somewhere. Shouldn't that be all that mattered? This girl probably wasn't even going to acknowledge the fact that he had played a part in saving her life.

She came around to the front of the bike. The harsh illumination of the headlight underscored the years of drug abuse cratering her face. Her hair was a tangled mess.

"Thank you." She leaned forward and gave Rico a hug.

For a moment, Rico had been so taken off guard he almost lost his balance holding up the bike. He dropped the stand and turned off the headlight.

"You're welcome... I think. I thought I was about to get an ass chewing."

She let go her embrace and stepped back.

It was so dark now he could barely see her. In the darkness, only their souls would shine.

"We came pretty damn close back there, didn't we?" she said, ignoring his sophomoric comment.

"Yeah, I guess we did." Rico rubbed his tongue around his dry mouth. "To be honest with you, I thought I was a goner until you picked up my gun and shot that old man. I . . . I thought you and that other girl were going to leave me behind."

"I was scared, and I'd be lying if I said the thought of leaving you didn't cross my mind, but I couldn't do that. For whatever reason, my self-preservation didn't have me running out that door. And . . ." her voice cracked.

Rico thought she was going to cry.

"And it was hard for me to shoot old man Glen. He wasn't a bad guy. He just liked to drink." She began to sob.

It would have been insensitive to tell her to suck it up and put it behind her. She deserved a few minutes to release pent-up emotions. Rico waited until she seemed to regain control.

"It's okay—what you did. The old man had turned into a monster. He wasn't the old man you remembered. And I might not be here now to thank you if you hadn't shot him. Not many other people I know would risk their life for me. I thank you." Maybe a compliment might help her pull it together.

She sniffed a few times and said, "I wouldn't go pinning any medals on me right now. I can't promise you that if the situation happens again that I'll react the same way."

The confession took Rico by surprise. He thought about it a minute and said, "Don't lose confidence in yourself. If you did it once, you can do it again."

"It has nothing to do with confidence."

"What do you mean, then?"

"I may not care next time if you live or die."

Rico wasn't quite sure how to take such an honest remark. Was she saying that self-preservation might rule the next time? What if she meant she might be so strung out on drugs she wouldn't know which end was up? The conversation had gotten too deep for two lost individuals on the run during the zombie apocalypse. It was time to take things in a different direction.

There had been no traffic on the road for most of the trip. Even more importantly, not one of the undead had presented itself either.

Clouds hid a good part of the moonlight now. As far as Rico could see, which in this case wasn't very far at all, there was nothing in the immediate area but trees. There was no artificial glow in the distance to pinpoint closest civilization. Darkness appeared to have swallowed all.

"Sorry for going so fast. I should have had things more in control. I have a problem with that. I have to constantly remind myself to think before I react."

"It's okay," she said. "We made it here without getting hurt. That's what's important."

An owl's hoot carried across the night breeze and something rustled in the trees nearby. Rico placed a hand on the pistol grip just in case there were any surprises. As peaceful as things seemed, he didn't want to be lulled into a sense of false security.

"So, why did you want me to stop now?"

"I had something on my mind that I felt we needed to talk about sooner rather than later." She cleared her throat and followed that with a cough. "I wasn't sure if you had a destination in mind, or if you were just driving for the hell of it. And from the speed we were going, I tend to think it was the latter of the two."

Rico shrugged. "Yeah, I guess I didn't really have a destination in mind. At least not a place I was intentionally heading to tonight. I have been considering a few cities to visit while I'm on vacation. I seriously doubt I'll be going to any of them now."

"Before we go any further I want to tell you my real name. It's Angie. Angie Kinnum." She awkwardly reached out her hand. "Tell me the truth, you a cop?"

Rico climbed off the bike and grasped her hand dangling in the darkness. "I am—or was. My life's story is kinda long. After tonight, I have a feeling that nothing about the past is going to matter much anymore. It doesn't make any difference if I'm a cop or not." Rico wanted this girl to trust him. If she trusted him, she would take orders. If she hesitated at his commands, they both might end up dead. It was time to inject a little humor. "But what the hell, woman? I thought your name was June Grape, or something like that?"

Angie laughed. "You mean, June Melon?"

"I guess. I don't really pay that much attention to last names when I meet someone."

"It's just my handle. You're a cop. Surely, you know what I do for a living?" She ran her hands down the skimpy blouse.

"Yes, I know what you do for a living. And I probably know why you do it, too."

"I change my name a lot. Usually it's a combination of a month and a fruit. I like to keep it simple, you know? June Melon. September Peach. May Berry."

"January Cobbler?" Rico laughed.

"No, silly." Angie chuckled. "You get the point though."

"I got it. Your name is Angie Kinnum. Now Angie, why did you want me to stop?"

"I just told you my name. Now, aren't you going to tell me yours?"

"I introduced myself at the gas station. The brunette said she didn't give a fuck what my name was. I guess you were too distraught to remember. My name is Rico."

"Rico. That's a nice name. I like it. No last name?"

"Does it really matter?"

"No, I guess not, but I don't see what's the big deal about you telling me your last name. It's not like I'm going to hunt you down later on and claim you the baby daddy."

From the way she said the words, he wasn't sure if she was pissed, or just making a sarcastic joke back at him.

"Hey, don't get your panties in a bunch. My last name is Cruz. Rico J. Cruz. Don't ask me what the J. stands for." Rico was teasing, of course, and waited to tell her the J. stood for Joseph.

Angie took a deep breath and hesitated before speaking again. "This time *is* different, isn't it?"

"What do you mean?" Rico asked, wondering where Angie wanted to steer the conversation.

"The dead coming back. This time it's different. I don't think it's going away this time."

"There's no real sure way of knowing, but I think you're right. This might be it."

"What do you think will happen?"

"I have no idea, honestly." Rico ran his fingers through his hair and looked up and down the road. "I guess there's a good chance if the military reacts fast enough they might be able to put this uprising down. There are probably a lot of people who've been affected. No doubt, some of those are in the military. Hell, cops too. Damn, just thinking about how bad things could get worldwide makes me have some doubts now."

"How so?"

"You saw what happened back there just as well as I did. Earlier, everyone was basically fine, dealing with their little coughing fits, and not long after, they're all stark raving mad. No one could have planned for something like that, at least not that drastic of a change happening as fast as it did. What we saw tonight is nothing. We were the lucky ones. We managed to be out in the middle of nowhere when it happened."

Angie remained silent through his long pause.

"The chaos we just witnessed was just a taste of what's probably happening everywhere right now. Think of New York City and places like Austin that are thriving with people. Sick people. Sick people that are no longer sick, but undead flesh eaters."

Angie gasped. Rico had painted an effective picture.

"About nine million people live in New York City. That means maybe two to three million are zombies on the hunt right as we speak. There's no way the police force could handle an emergency like that. And no time for the military to have a plan they can put into action."

"Oh, Rico, what are we going to do?"

Great, now he went too far thinking aloud and had her upset again. "We're not in a big city. As long as we keep to less populated areas, I think we'll be okay... really. We'll just have to keep our eyes open and take things one day at a time. Maybe the military will set up a safe zone. If they do, we can go there."

"Megan is dead!" Angie covered her face with her hands and started to cry.

He had made her so upset he wondered if she had heard the last words he just said. In truth, Rico wanted to slap her across the face and say that a lot of people are dead. A lot of people are probably dying. Hell, Pop from the pub back in Killeen was dead. No doubt about it. Worse, Pop was one of the walking dead, but nothing was going to change that now. Nothing was going to take back the alien microbes that fell to Earth, or the dead rising from their graves. The six months of internal terror the world had endured could not be erased. The sudden rebirth of chaos that now had them in the middle of a deserted highway was here to stay. It was a changed world, and it stood a great chance of never being the same again.

Rico took a deep breath and tried to undo the mess he made.

"It's going to be okay. We're going to make it. Don't worry, we'll make it," he said, leaning in to embrace Angie.

She grabbed ahold of him and sobbed, digging her fingers into his jacket.

It was actually strange to hold another woman in such an intimate embrace other than his ex-wife. Rico wasn't a touchy-feely kind of guy to begin with. At first, all he could think about was what kind of disease might pole vault off her and get on him. The darkness hid her Earthly façade of flesh. Right now, she could be any woman, and there was no doubt how much she hurt inside. Rico felt small for being so judgmental. Sure, she was a drug addict and a prostitute, but she was a person like him just the same. He wondered what Angie's life was like as a little girl and what awful tragedies occurred to turn it into such a disaster.

*

It was quite some time before Angie stopped crying.

By then, it had grown cooler. The wind had picked up, adding to the chill. The clouds had thinned and Rico saw his surroundings better. The increased visibility loosened the built up tension, but not by much.

Wiping away the tears and running mascara from her eyes, Angie looked up at Rico and half smiled.

"I'm sorry."

"No need to be sorry," he said. "I know what you're going through. We've all been through a lot in the last six months. Life as we knew it has been turned upside down."

"You can say that again." She took a deep breath and huffed it out.

"The world's been turned upside down." He smiled.

Angie half-giggled.

"Come on," he said. "It's getting colder and it's late. We need to move on."

"Yeah." She nodded and pulled strands of hair from her face. "I uhmm . . . I wouldn't mind stopping by my place, if that's okay." Before Rico replied, Angie shot back, "It's my mom. She… she uhmm… lives alone."

Rico thought of his own mother. He wondered how she was doing, too, or if she were *doing* at all. That was something he didn't really want to think about right now—not about his father either. They were too far away for him to do anything about their welfare. It would be up to others in the community to save them. Angie was here, and he could help her. Deep inside, he knew why. She reminded him of his older sister, Jennifer. Jennifer had been dead for years now, though her memory haunted Rico nearly every day of his life.

"I understand the concern for your mom, but—well," Rico dropped his head and chewed on his bottom lip. "Uh, how far away are we from her house? Hell, I don't even know where we are right now."

"That's the good thing. I do know about where we are. Out here, there aren't many highways, so you always basically either head north, south, east, or west. We've been heading west. I think we can make it to her house in less than an hour."

"I don't know if it's safe to go. She doesn't live in a big town, does she?"

"No, she lives off in the sticks, down a road that's so old the asphalt has practically worn away."

"I have to ask you this, and you must tell me the truth. Had your mom been sick since The Spook? You know, do you think she's infected?"

"I'm a hundred percent sure she's not. Don't worry. She won't be waiting to eat us."

"All right then, I'll take you there. Being with your mom in a time like this will ease your mind, but..." If Rico was going to bring her home, it might be time to part ways. He was comfortable with the idea of only having to look out for one person. Being responsible for someone else was something he wasn't ready to take on if he didn't have to. "I, uh, I won't be staying with you though. I hope there are some other members of your family you can huddle up with for safety."

"Oh? You won't stay?"

"I don't want to be the odd man out with your family. I'll catch a few hours sleep there, but I'll at least be gone by noon."

"But you shouldn't go out by yourself, not after tonight. Not after what has been going on for the last six months. You said so yourself. This thing is going to get worse before it gets better."

"You know, I say a lot of things. Maybe that's a problem I have, too—saying things I've been thinking. Yes, there's safety in numbers. If you have family to protect you then I don't have to stick to my earlier plans. I might rather find the nearest town and see if I can hook up with the local police. If we can round up enough good old boys in the area, we might be able to get control of the situation before it gets out of hand. My mind's been racing in a bunch of different directions."

"What, can't make up your fucking mind? You have ADD or something?" Angie placed her hands on her hips.

"Yeah, so what? I took medication for it when I was younger. I got better control of it so I don't need to take it now." *Bitch*.

"Whatever." Angie threw her hands to the side. "Can we go now?"

"Sure." Fuck, did this woman expect him to have all the answers right now? Hell, he was making plans as he went along. There was so much to consider, because truth was, no one had any idea how bad things were. He might change his mind ten more times before he actually made a final move, and that had nothing to do with him having a mild case of Attention Deficit Disorder.

He climbed on his bike and helped Angie find her footing as she shimmied her way onto the seat. The motorcycle roared to life. The loping thump, thump, thump of the engine cut through the silence. Rico feel like a giant spotlight now shone on them. Still, the purr of his Harley was a welcome relief. He loved having all that power between his legs.

"So, we just keep heading in the direction we were going?" he called back to her.

"Yes," Angie yelled into his ear.

"You don't have to yell so loud."

"Sorry," she pointed. "Just keep heading west for another twenty minutes, or so, until we come to the next intersection. Take a right, and we'll go down an old road that will eventually bring us to Mom's. Don't speed once we get on that road. It's winding and not in good condition. Watch out for deer and armadillos."

Rico kicked up the stand and let off the clutch. "Remind me when we get there. Hold on."

The bike eased forward and picked up speed.

Chapter 10

Angie had spoken the truth about the road's conditions leading to her mom's house. Fortunately, no one drove in the opposite direction down the narrow road throughout the arduous trip. Rico had dodged potholes along the way and almost hit a possum avoiding one. Some of the potholes were so bad they had potholes in them. The street jutting off the highway leading to the house was in even worse condition. The saving grace of that was the two didn't have to travel far to reach it.

"Slow down, we're coming up on it," Angie said.

If Rico went any slower, the bike would have fallen over. He thought he could make out a gravel driveway cutting through some tall weeds to his left. After a slight turn to the right, he swung his path into a hard left and drove down the driveway. A single bulb on the porch cast enough light for him to see where he was going.

This was Angie's mother's house? It looked more like the city dump. This might be a place to call home, but it wasn't a house. The dwelling was a singlewide trailer on cement blocks. A metal overhang serving as a second roof covered the length of the trailer.

As bad as it looked, this certainly wasn't the first time Rico had seen a living quarters in this bad of condition. There was junk strewn about all over the yard and a burn pile off to one side. Hell, the whole placed looked like it would benefit from a carefully placed match. The only thing missing from the stereotypical sight was a car set up on blocks with the tires off—oh, and a washing machine. He guessed the family was too poor to afford those luxuries. Jeff Foxworthy had a series of jokes that would go well right now.

All too often, the inhabitants of such deplorable conditions shared a similar M. O.: Poor, ignorant, drug users, alcoholics— usually a combination of some or all. The kids had no choice but to suffer under such unfortunate parenting. Many abusive parents didn't even enroll their kids in school.

Despite Angie's obvious problems, she at least seemed to have an education. How far into high school she had gone, he hadn't a clue.

The trailer leaned slightly to one side. The cement blocks propping it up had visible cracks and one or two were partially crushed. Rico wondered if it was safe to go inside.

He parked the bike near a swing set, and the two dismounted. The swing set was so old that it had metal seats instead of plastic. Two of the seats had completely rusted in half but one was still partially intact. No way would that seat support the weight of a new rider.

Over from the swing, a few garbage cans overflowed onto the lawn, sending out a rich stink of rotted fruit and meat. It was obvious this trailer wasn't on any garbage truck route, and Rico wondered why bags of trash were left to pile up here rather than just thrown into the burn pile and gotten rid of once and for all.

Something shifted in the garbage. Rico looked and saw a slinky black and white cat scrounging through the mess. He took a few steps toward it and heard a chorus of nearby baby kittens calling for their mother. *That's just fucking great*, he thought. *A starving animal making more starving animals.* Rico never understood why pet owners didn't have their animals fixed.

Momma cat came toward him. She must have been more hungry than scared. She laid on her back and squirmed around playfully. The cat's many nipples were swollen and stretched. One of them looked like it might be infected.

That poor cat, he thought. *That thing has probably been through half a dozen litters.*

The animal's hair was matted in places and in dire need of brushing. She turned her head slightly and the porch light illuminated her eyes an eerie green. He reached down to pet her, but as his hand approached, she rolled back on all fours and trotted off. *I guess she just wanted to make friends but didn't trust me enough to let me touch her.*

"What are you doing?" Angie asked.

"Checking on the cat. Why doesn't your mom feed her?"

"The cat's fine. Come on." Angie turned and headed for the trailer, not waiting for Rico.

The porch area in front of the trailer basically looked like a tornado had touched down on garage sale grade gym equipment. A bench press set with chain and bar laid out beside the house. There were weights scattered across the grass. The steel weights had a harsh layer of rust covering them. No one had worked out with these in quite a while, especially those in the yard with grass growing around them.

Angie waited by the door and said, "Watch your step," and pointed downward.

Rico saw her place her foot on the third step of the short stairway leading to the door. The wood looked rotted and probably had been infested with termites.

Angie grabbed the screen door and yanked it open. The door groaned against the hinges. If the roar of the motorcycle hadn't told her mother they were here, the door had. Rico looked over his shoulder to see if any uninvited guest stirred about from all the noise, they had been making.

Satisfied things were cool for now he pulled the door shut behind him. He heard Angie stomp her way through the living room. When he turned around, she was gone. Rico was left to face the horrors of the trailer alone.

And a house of horrors it was.

The dim light cast weird shadows on the wall. An old CRT television was on, showing nothing but fuzzy gray static. Rico had read once that some of the static on TV and the radio is actually caused by radiation left over from the Big Bang. Thinking of that discovery made him wonder, if the zombie apocalypse destroyed civilization as we knew it, how long it would take mankind to learn of that little gem of information again?

The TV's volume was low but still filled the room with agitating white noise. He turned it off without affecting the light in the room much. Not that there was anything worth seeing to begin with. There was so much crap stacked everywhere that there was nowhere to sit. The couch was a cluster of dirty laundry. The La-Z-Boy had stacks of pornographic magazines on it. A dinner plate balanced on the left arm of the chair. The remnants of pizza crust and crumbs lined the edges of the plate. Pizza and porn. Angie's mom sure did have strange tastes.

Framed photos lined the walls. Rico tried to make out faces in a few of them, but couldn't see well in the dim light.

Where was Angie's mom? He heard a faint rustling noise coming from another room. Hell, what was Angie doing? A barely discernable path on the floor led him into an equally trashed kitchen.

On second thought, the kitchen was by far the more disgusting of the two rooms. Plates and glasses piled in the sink and discarded junk food packages lined the counter.

"How can people live like this?" Rico didn't care if anyone heard him. Animals took care of their habitats better than this.

He eased his way past the trash down a narrow hall. As he walked, he came to opened door and looked in. It was a bathroom. Opposite the bathroom, a back door led to outside.

"Good God," he said, taking in another masterpiece of mess. There was so much junk on the floor, there was no way of not stepping on something to go in. The counter was a cluster of things covered in hair and dried toothpaste. Then he noticed the icing on the cake. The window in the bathroom was cracked open. At first, it looked like an eight foot snake had found its way in. It wasn't a snake though. It was a regular garden hose. The end of the hose led into the bathtub, which was full of soapy water. Curiosity got the best of him, and he reached over to the sink and turned on the faucet. Nothing. Something must have gone wrong with the plumbing, or God forbid, maybe the trailer never had running water to begin with. The thought of cooking and cleaning with water from a hose brought a grimace to his face.

"Son-of-a-bitch!" Angie shouted in obvious frustration.

"What is it?" Rico called out.

He passed up another room to his right and walked through the open door into a bedroom. Angie had her arms up to her elbows digging through an open dresser drawer. No sign of Angie's mom anywhere.

"What's the ruckus about? What in the hell are you looking for?"

"I can't find it," Angie said through clenched teeth, continuing her frantic search through another drawer.

"Can't find what?" Rico asked. "Where's your mother?"

Angie ignored his question and continued her search. "Damn it!" she said, and started tossing the contents of the drawer over her shoulder. Socks started to fly his way, and then underwear followed. Rico doubted this was Angie's mom's room, as he didn't know of any women who wore tighty whities.

"I know he had it hidden somewhere. Where is it?"

"Had what hidden? Who's he?"

Again, Angie either didn't hear him, or didn't feel the need to acknowledge his presence.

Rico stood there for a moment, watching her frantic behavior. When she was done with the dresser drawers, she turned to the closet. A jacket flew out the door onto the bed.

"Will you please explain to me what the hell is going on?"

A shoebox came next and landed on the jacket. When the box hit, the top came off and a load of Polaroid photos spilled out.

"Angie!" Rico stepped closer to the closet. "What are you doing? Where's your mother?"

"Yes," Angie said victoriously as she pulled a small wooden box from a shelf near the floor of the closet. She turned, dropping to the floor with her legs crossed.

Whatever was in that box certainly had her excited. She started to open it, but then looked up at Rico as he moved directly in front of her.

Angie's excited expression melted into one of bewilderment. It was as if she hadn't even known Rico was in the room until just now. "I... uhmm..."

"Angie, your mother?"

She made a face like she was afraid Rico was about to hit her. "My mom doesn't live here."

"What the fuck, woman?"

Angie didn't reply. She was too focused on the box, holding it tightly as if to keep what was inside a secret.

"If your mother doesn't live here, then whose house is this?"

"Marcus."

"Who's Marcus?"

"My boss."

"Oh, you mean your pimp? That's great. Just great." Rico thrust his hand toward the box. "Give me that!"

"No, it's mine! I've got to have this."

Rico tried to take if from her, but Angie held firm.

"Let go," she demanded.

"Not until you stop playing games and are honest with me." Rico continued the tug of war.

"Please... no. Just leave me—" Angie cut her words short as the box came loose in her hand—sailing into the air. The top fell off, and the contents of the box scattered across the floor.

Rico gazed upon syringes, glass vials, packets of white powder, and shook his head.

"Look at what you did!" Angie cried, and crawled toward the drugs.

"At what I did? I didn't bring us to a pimp's house to steal his drugs. Are you crazy?"

"Just leave me alone," she shouted. She reached out to gather up the spilled contents of the box.

"You're pathetic. I've been a cop long enough that I should have seen this coming. I let my emotions cloud my reasoning. Your type is all the same. You're just like Jennifer. Nothing's really important in life except the next fix, even if it means selling your body. Even if it means you one day shoot up too much and die." Rico stomped his foot on a syringe near his foot. The glass shattered under his boot heel. "I don't have time for this shit. I'm out of here."

"Look at what you did," Angie shouted. "Wait, don't go. I need this. Let me just shoot up this once. You know—to get us down the road. I'll stop. You can help me. I'll stop. I just need it one more time. I can't just go cold turkey. Not tonight. Not tonight!" Angie broke down crying, reaching out for Rico as he stepped away.

Rico didn't care. He had heard this all before. There was nothing he could do to help Angie. No matter what he'd try, he could never trust her. He turned around and headed his way back through the narrow hall of the trailer.

Angie shouted something else, but Rico didn't hear the words.

"I don't care," Rico shouted back. "If you haven't noticed . . . everyone's in danger. The dead are coming back to life. It's the end of the world, and all you can care about is your next fix!"

Rico stepped past the kitchen, and just as he entered the dim light of the living room, he turned back, about to give one more 'fuck you' to the woman who had used him.

That's when everything went black.

The last thing Rico saw before the darkness engulfed his vision was Angie's right hand holding an iron skillet coming down on his head.

Rico fell unconscious.

***

An old El Camino slowly drove down the bumpy road with its headlights off and turned into the trailer's narrow driveway. Gravel cracked and popped under the tires, and the engine died when Rico's motorcycle came into view.

Marcus pulled the key ring from the ignition switch and rubbed his thumb over the attached rabbit's foot key fob.

"How long you think they been here, Boss?" Gus asked. He straightened himself in his seat and leaned forward, looking above and below the cracks in the windshield.

"Shhh..." Marcus said. "I'm trying to think." There were a few ways he could handle the situation. The rise of the undead complicated the basic plan a bit. He wanted to have a little fun before bringing the matter to a conclusion. Maybe tonight he might just get it over with real quick like. Maybe he would flip a quarter when the time came to make the choice.

Too bad the cop didn't have a car. Marcus loved his El Camino—had it since high school. However, the car suffered a few casualties in a recent turf war with another drug dealer. A giant web of cracks marred most of the windshield on the passenger side. The side mirror was also missing. It had been knocked off by the same baseball bat that had cracked the windshield and made some sheet metal modifications on the hood. Marcus had won that battle, but never got around to fixing the damage. He thought there would be time for that later. If the cop had a car, he could take it and leave his beloved El Camino at the trailer where it would be safe. Well, at least his car still ran well, dented hood and all.

"Sorry, Boss," Gus whispered.

"Damn straight," Marcus said.

"What's that supposed to mean?" Gus flicked a cigarette out the window.

"It means I agree with you, Gus. You *are* sorry." Marcus laughed.

Gus scratched the back of his head and closed one eye. "What's so funny? I don't like it when you laugh when I don't get what's so funny."

"Forget it," Marcus said, lighting up a cigarette of his own. "It's time for us to focus on the task at hand now."

"What's the task, Boss? What do ya want to do with them?"

"I'll tell you what we're gonna do with them. We're gonna teach that cop a few lessons. No one takes out one of my Betties and doesn't pay. So, the first lesson's gonna involve a fist and a pair of brass knuckles. And then we're gonna make him pay."

"I don't much think money is going to do any good now, Boss—what with the zombies and all." Gus poked a little finger in his ear and twirled it around.

"I know that, stupid."

"Then how do ya plan to make him pay?"

"I aim to take that motorcycle of his, for one thing."

"What about Angie? I like her."

"You say that about all the Betties. And besides, it ain't like she hasn't pulled some shit like this before. We handle her the same as always. With care and respect."

"So... rough her up too, but..."

"That's right," Marcus said, a plume of smoke bursting from his nostrils. "Just not too hard in the face. We're going to use this end of the world shit to our advantage."

"How's that, Boss?"

"With money out of the picture, like you said, commerce will go back to a bartering system. And do you know what goes for a high price in the bartering system, Gus?" Marcus grinned.

"Motorcycles?"

"No, you fuckin' dip-shit!" Marcus tossed his half smoked cigarette out the window and blew out a plume of gray. "Betties!"

"Betties?"

"Yes, Betties." Marcus patted Gus's broad shoulder. "We're going to be rolling in the dough."

"You know I'm allergic to gluten." Gus frowned.

"I'm talking hypothetical, man. Jesus, get a clue." Marcus shook his head.

"Oh... So that's a good thing, then?"

"Hell's yeah, it is! Even if paper money isn't worth anything, we can always trade for other stuff. Food, guns, ammo. Hell, gold and silver might even make a comeback. Somebody will give us something we want if we have something they want."

Gus smiled. "You sure are smart. That's why you're the boss."

"Damn straight." Marcus tapped a little drumroll on the steering wheel. "Damn straight."

Chapter 11

Andy Wells turned over in his bed for what must have been the tenth time since hitting the sack. The barracks at Fort Hood were modern enough by today's standards. His room accommodated two, akin to a college dorm. Nothing like the sleeping quarters back in the day, where men slept in bunk beds in what resembled a large warehouse.

The problem was his roommate, Alex Edwards, kept wheezing and coughing. Just as Andy would be about to drift off, Alex would hack up a lung, or sneeze with the force that whale did when it blew Jonah out its nose.

As bad as Alex had been, Andy was surprised that he hadn't caught the *croup* his buddy suffered from. Andy put his pillow over his head and tried to muffle the annoying sound. If this shit didn't stop soon, he was going to go outside and find a comfortable Humvee to bunk down in.

It took a few minutes of mully-grubbing for him to realize that Alex had finally quieted down. Was his platoon mate really asleep, or just gearing up for another round?

Andy removed the pillow and listened to the sweet sound of Alex's shallow breaths. *Finally*, he thought. He turned over in the fetal position and placed a hand between his thighs.

Then it hit him. He had to pee. Of all the danged luck! Just when the opportunity presented itself, nature called to ruin it. He tried to ignore the pain in his bladder, but the more he tried not to think about it, the more it bothered him.

I give up. With the stealth of a ninja, Andy moved the sheets aside and crept to the bathroom. The room was dark, but he knew his away around well enough that he could maneuver even with his eyes closed.

He eased the bathroom door open and carefully lifted the lid—keeping his fingers between the lid and the tank so as to not make a *clunk* that would wake Alex. Andy was secure enough in his manhood that it didn't bother him to sit down when he peed. Still, he had to keep the stream pointed to the side of the bowl to keep things silent.

A minute or so later, after the blessed relief, he lifted his ass off the toilet and headed back to his bed. No need to wash his hands, he hadn't peed on them.

Alex was quiet, still fast asleep.

A few steps later would have him snug under the covers and the Sandman closing his eyelids.

The little toe on Andy's right foot struck his desk in mid-step.

"Sumbitch!" Andy yelled, and then clenched his teeth shut. He grabbed his foot as his ass plopped on the bed. His toe throbbed like a blacksmith pounding on an anvil. *Great, I'm going to wake up Sleeping Beauty.*

The cold flush of pain that cascaded over his body slowly passed. Miraculously, Alex remained silent. *Thank you, little blonde haired, blue eyed baby Jesus.* Andy leaned over and felt the fluffy pillow under his head. *At last, I'm going to get me some shut eye.*

The darkness wrapped its tenderness around Andy's mind and slowly dimmed all conscious thought.

"Uhgg."

Andy snapped from pool of dreams back to reality.

"Ahgg."

Dammit! Alex was awake again. *Maybe if I stay quiet he'll go back to sleep.*

The mattress squeaked, feet hit the floor and dragged against it. Alex ran into the foot of Andy's bed.

Andy sat up. "Hey, you big gorilla, the head's the other way." He turned on a lamp just in time to see his platoon mate reach out to grab him.

"She-it!" Andy cried when he saw Alex's face. His square jawed buddy who favored George Clooney had turned into a flesh eating zombie.

Somehow, Andy managed to roll off the bed and avoid the deadly embrace of the man turned monster. Alex probably had forty pounds on him—all of it muscle. There was no way he could take on the big man hand to hand and expect to win.

A Bowie knife Andy had since high school set on his desk next to his computer. As Alex pulled himself off the bed, Andy grabbed the 9 inch blade from its sheath. Before he could defend himself, Alex tackled him to the ground.

The wind *oofed* out of Andy's mouth as Alex growled like a wild animal. If the zombie took a chomp, his life would be over.

A gunshot rang from outside—then another. Some kind of commotion sounded from the hallway linking all the rooms on the floor of the barracks.

The carbon steel blade came up in Andy's hand and landed smack dap in the top of Alex's head. The big man shuddered a few times and went limp.

Andy pushed the dead man off and felt around his chest for a wound. He found nothing, and breathed a sigh of relief as chaos ensued in the hall.

A gun fired in a nearby room. Andy opened his door to see Steve Rogan come out of his room two doors down rubbing the sleep out of his eyes.

"What the fuck's going on?" Rogan asked.

Andy ran up to his friend and grabbed him by the arms. "The zombies have come back! And they is us!"

Chapter 12

Rico opened his eyes and saw a torn Coors Light carton not far from his face. He was lying amongst the trash on the floor. Something in the trash poked against his cheek. His head felt like it was in a vice and someone was pounding it with a sledgehammer.

He put his hand out and pushed himself up into a sitting position. A wave of nausea had threatened to take him back down, but he overcame it. Things were still hazy in his mind, but then, just as he reached up to his head and felt the lump, he remembered.

That stupid bitch, he thought. *No good deed goes unpunished.*

When he touched the lump, it felt like he had just stuck himself with a thousand needles. He brought his hand away expecting to find blood. There was none. At least he was lucky on that account.

He eased himself up, holding onto the arm of the couch. The flickering television caught his eye. *I thought I turned that damn thing off?* When he looked directly at screen, the bright dancing static made his head throb even more. Next to the TV was a small pyramid shaped plastic box he hadn't noticed before. It had three LED lights and 'The Clapper' etched into the plastic. The clang of the frying pan hitting his head must have activated the switch and turned the TV back on. *Motherfucker.*

He reached down and was happy to find that Angie hadn't taken his gun. He pulled it off his hip and popped out the clip. Satisfied all the bullets were in place, he shoved it back under his belt

The room was quiet. Too quiet, in fact. He half expected to hear Angie throwing things around in the other room like before, but he knew better than that. She had already found what she came to get. She had lied to him.

Rico gritted his teeth at the thought. How stupid could he have been to trust the word of a drug addict? Did he allow himself to be so gullible because she was a woman? Was he trying to right the wrong he had done to Jennifer?

Rico snapped out of his pity party and felt lucky he wasn't injured more than he had been. Sure, his head hurt. The blow with the frying pan must have just grazed him though. Had she made full contact he might be saying hello to St. Peter at the Pearly Gates about right now. He saw his motorcycle parked by the swing set through the window. He seriously doubted Angie would have tried to make an escape on foot.

He made his way back through the kitchen toward the master bedroom. In a way, he knew what to expect to find when he got there. And he had been right. Angie was sprawled across the bed next to a belt and an empty syringe. She lay there breathing, but unconscious. Other drug paraphernalia lay scattered across the end table beside the bed. The same scene he had seen time and time again over the years while in the force.

He sighed.

Part of him wanted to leave her there on her own. She would be fine as long as the door to the trailer stayed shut and she had a supply of drugs. Beyond that, who knows what would happen to her? There was nothing he could do to fix her problem. She would just slow him down anyway, and then he'd have to deal with her drug addiction all over again.

Another part of him said that as a cop he was to protect and serve. The caring side of his humanity told him it was simply the right thing to do to help a fellow man in need.

Guilt washed over him as he turned around and stepped back in the hall. Then he thought how he'd be putting his life in danger by bringing her with him. She had attacked him, after all.

He reached up, and the lump on his head throbbed anew when he touched it. Angie proved herself to be unpredictable. Most junkies were. That was the last thing he needed to deal with right now with the dead returning to life. There was no telling what was going on out in the real world. He thought of his cell phone and wished he hadn't tossed it. Then again, even if he had the phone, he thought the towers were probably so jammed with users that he couldn't have made a connection anyway.

Rico looked back into the master bedroom at Angie's pathetic excuse for existence. Then he turned his gaze to the hall. It was time to leave before she woke up and did something else reckless. He didn't need her, and she sure as hell didn't need him, because he wasn't going to help her feed her drug dependency.

He looked at Angie and gritted his teeth—then down the hall again. *Time to leave. Just cut and run, and try not to think about it. Tough love is about all I can give that woman.*

Just as he approached the bathroom, he heard a vehicle creep up the gravel driveway. The low hum of the engine stopped.

"Shit," he said under his breath. "I've got company."

Rico ducked down and eased his way to the bathroom window. This was no easy task, considering the horde of crap piled in the room. Once in position, he maneuvered his gaze through the small gap under the window and saw the front end of an old car not far from his motorcycle. After a few minutes, two men got out of the vehicle.

The passenger by far was the larger of the two. His basic build reminded Rico of The Rock back when he watched him in WWE's heyday. The driver didn't look much over five feet in height. He was thin and had a scraggly looking beard. It was hard to tell the age of either one.

The big guy had a shotgun slung over his shoulder, and the little guy had something gripped in his right hand that reflected light as he moved it.

Both stepped over to his motorcycle with obvious interest. They spoke in a low tone so Rico couldn't hear what they said, but he was able to see their lips when they moved to one side of the bike.

The thin man reached out and touched the bike, mouthing words that looked like, *'let's wait and see,'* or *'all we need is the key.'* Rico had no doubt their interest lay in obtaining the key.

The big guy nodded. The two left the Harley and started toward the trailer.

Rico's heart pounded in his chest. He reminded himself to keep calm and stay focused—a discussion he had been having a lot with himself lately. *What the hell have you gotten us into, Angie?*

The back door. It was his only chance to escape before they came in. Rico kept low as he stepped through the bathroom. His elbow whacked a shampoo bottle on the sink. Luckily, it made little noise as it collided with the array of junk scattered about the floor. It was momentary relief for the tension that gripped his chest. His headache was all but forgotten.

As his hand touched the knob on the back door, he stole one last regretful glance at Angie before making his escape. This was her world. She lived in it at her choosing. He wanted no part of it.

The back door's hinges were as rusty as the door in front, squealing like an alarm when he opened it. Rico cursed under his breath and hoped no one heard.

The wooden steps leading to the ground were in bad condition too. The top board felt spongy and bent under his weight. He hurriedly made it to the ground and noticed a greenhouse about half a football field away.

Overhead, the clouds had blown out and the moon shone brightly above. The night would eventually give way to day. Rico had honestly never wanted to see daylight again as badly as he did now. Tonight seemed like the longest night of his life—even longer than the first night of The Spook. Checking in at the motel and the events at the gas station felt like they happened weeks ago.

Rico pressed his back against the trailer and listened carefully. The front door squalled and two pairs of feet tromped on the trailer floor. These guys knew he was here and acted as if they didn't give a damn. He pulled the pistol from his belt and held it at the ready by his shoulder.

"Come on out, June Bug!" one of the men shouted. "We know you and that cop fellow are here! No sense in hiding. If he's a customer, that's fine, but I want my money!"

This douchebag must not know the world has gone to shit. All he cares about is his fucking money, Rico thought. *Or maybe he does know and he's too much of a money grubber to care.*

Now that he knew their location, it was time to make his move. He bent over and kept his gaze to the ground, careful to avoid tripping over anything and making noise. He rounded the side of the trailer and stopped once the car and his bike came into view.

Rico reached in the front pocket of his pants, and his heart instantly sank to his stomach. The keys weren't there. Had Angie taken them while he was unconscious? He frantically patted the other pocket and felt nothing. His hand stabbed into his jacket and crashed into what he was looking for. He must have mindlessly put his keys in his pocket when he dismounted the Harley. Fortunately, they didn't fall out while he was laid out on the floor.

He removed the keys and found the one to his bike. On second thought, he would wait and start the motorcycle after he pushed it down the driveway and got to the road—to buy a little escape time. The keys went back in his pocket, and he eased his way past the trailer's side.

The trailer was small, and surely by now the two men realized he wasn't in there. Rico half expected to see the front door pop open, and was ready to shoot first if he had to. Time to go.

Just as he trotted toward his bike, something clattered loudly in the trash pile. Momma cat emerged from a mound of beer cans with a field rat trapped in her jaws. *Why the fuck did this have to happen now?* It was time to double down on his plan. If he were going to leave, he didn't need to give them any more time to come outside.

His feet bounced across the ground as he raced for his ride. The throb in his head returned and matched the rhythm of each step. Should he go ahead and fire up the bike now, or stick to his original plan and push it to the road?

By the time he reached his bike, he had the key ring out and quickly inserted the Harley's key. No one had come out of the trailer yet. Maybe they were still in the back trying to rouse Angie. Rico resisted starting the engine and pushed it off the stand.

The Harley was heavy and pushing it across the gravel driveway took more effort than he wanted to give, but he was almost there, mere moments away from freedom. All he had to do now was start the bike and get the hell out of Dodge. However, when he turned the key in the ignition he couldn't bring himself hit the start button.

Pop's voice forced its way into his mind. "You took the job to protect and serve. You're one of the few men who truly care about the job. About the people. You can't leave Angie back there. What would your mother think if you did a thing like that?"

That bitch could have killed me back there, Rico internally argued. *And she was the one who got me into this mess in the first place.*

"You act like that matters, son," he could hear Pop say. "That woman needs help, but not just any help. She needs *your* help."

Rico grunted, weighing out the possibilities.

"Just think," Pop continued. "Think of what those two men are going to do to that poor girl. What have they've already done to her? You don't really believe she wants to turn tricks to make a living, do you? Do you think she wants to be messed up the rest of her life? She has a mother, too."

Yeah, one that apparently doesn't live here, Rico groaned.

Rico waited for Pop's rebuttal, but nothing came. He had been indecisive all of his life, but this was the first time he had an internal conflict with another person in his head. Was sanity slowly slipping away?

He shook off the question and blamed it on stress. Pop had been an inspiration to him, and it made sense for Rico to think of Pop when it came to making the right choice. Pop was dead now, but the old man could continue to live just as he remembered him in his memory.

Leaving that poor girl here would be leaving her to die. She was just one girl amongst millions—hell, he had just met her tonight! He had no obligation to protect her, but fate, God, or whatever, had brought them together.

Before he could talk himself out of his latest decision, Rico dropped the stand on the bike and headed for the trailer. The gun came up from his side, ready to end this situation as quickly as possible.

***

"She's doped up, Boss." Gus ran his hand through his oily hair and wiped his palm on his pants.

"Tell me something I don't already know." Marcus pushed past Gus and shook Angie's shoulder. "Angie, wake up. Where's the cop? Wake up. I know he's with you, now where is he?"

Angie grumbled and rolled over into a fetal position.

"Angie!" Gus had leaned over close to her ear.

"Wh…what?" her left eye slowly opened

"Wake up, I said." Marcus slapped Angie hard against the cheek. "The cop. Where is he?"

Angie blinked a few times and finally opened her eyes. She was awake—drugged up, but awake. "Hi there, Marcus," she said softly, wearing a faint smile. "What are you doing here?"

Marcus continued to shake her—more violently now. "The cop. He came with you. Where is he?"

"I… uhh…" Angie started to fade again, the drugs still her master.

"Like I said, Boss." Gus rested the butt of the shotgun on the floor. "She's all doped up."

"I can see that, dipshit. Help me find that cop before he causes us trouble." Marcus put his hand on Gus's arm and gave it a shove. The big guy didn't budge, and Marcus's hand slipped off. "Go… take care of it."

"Okay, Boss." Gus turned and walked down the hall.

"And don't kill him," Marcus called out. "I want to have a little talk with him first."

***

Rico waited against the trailer next to the front door. He was wide ass out in the open, but hoped to use the element of surprise when the two stepped out the door. From the sound of things, the opportunity was about to present itself. Footsteps pounded through the living room and neared the entrance.

The sad truth of the situation was that Rico didn't have much of a plan. Either he was going to get these guys to surrender, or he would play O.K. Corral and put them six feet under. Adrenalin pumping through his body helped clear the pain in his head

The front door groaned open. Rico saw the barrel of the shotgun lead the way pointed toward the ground. The big guy turned immediately and looked down at him.

Rico raised the gun. "Police! Drop your weapon and show me your hands." Rico stepped into view and steadied his pistol.

He had regretted his outburst right after he made it. Years of police training had him reacting automatically. He didn't have any backup coming to help, and the other guy was nowhere to be seen. Rico should have shoved the pistol in the guy's side, threatened to kill him if he made a sound— and shot him if he did!

"Throw the gun to the ground," Rico said, waiting to shoot if the barrel lifted his way.

The man smirked, turned his head, and spat. It was clear he had no intentions of giving up his gun. He began to laugh.

"You sure are one crazy cop. Put that little peashooter away before you put an eye out."

"I'm serious," Rico said in an even tone. "Put it down."

"You must be confused," a voice called from behind. "This is my house, and I didn't call no law."

Rico turned his head and saw a fist brandishing brass knuckles zipping toward his face. Things went black at the sound of a sickening crunch. Hearty laughter came from the trailer's direction. It seemed so far away.

Chapter 13

Rico had only thought his head hurt before when Angie banged him on the head with the frying pan. In comparison to how his head felt now, her blow would be considered a love tap. His entire face throbbed from the back of his head down to the tip of his chin.

The pain dominating his thoughts gave way to emerging consciousness. He was sitting down with his arms behind him and unable to move. Even though his eyes were closed, he knew exactly where he was. The trailer pimp-shack had a unique stench, and he was still there.

Voices grew in the background. Scumbags, party of two, were in the room with him. Rico took a deep breath, and it hurt so bad that he groaned.

"I think he's finally comin' around, Boss."

Feet shuffled to his right side.

"About time," the other voice said.

Before he had a chance to lift his head, an open palm stung his cheek. Had he not already been in so much pain, he might have felt it more. He struggled to open his eyes in the bright room. Sunlight shone on him directly through a window. He had to take it slowly, blinking a few times so his eyes would adjust to the light.

"Looks like Sleepy finally decided to wake up, Gus." The smaller of the two men stood in front of Rico, slightly bent toward him, with his hands on his thighs. "Good to see you coming around, brother. Wasn't sure I had it in me to wait much longer." The man grabbed the back of Rico's hair and peered down on him from above.

"I don't think he knows where he is, Boss."

"Just give it a few more minutes, Gus. This sort of thing takes time, unless he has brain damage. You got brain damage, boy?"

"You know what's best. That's why you're the boss," the large man said.

Gus... Gus must be the big guy's name, Rico thought, trying to focus on his interrogator as he forced his eyes to peer up. The boss wore an evil grin that displayed yellow-brown stained teeth. There was a wildness in his eyes that told Rico he was in deep, deep shit.

The boss let go of Rico's hair and stepped away.

Rico let his jaw drop to his chest and rolled his head around a couple of times to loosen up. His hands were bound behind the back of the chair, with what he didn't know. Similarly, something held his ankles to the chair's legs. All eyes were on him, so now was no time to test the restraint's strength. He was weak, and in his condition, even if he could take the boss down, the big guy still had to be dealt with.

How long had he been unconscious? Daylight flooded the living room, and from the intensity, it certainly wasn't morning. As he took in the surroundings, looking for something to use as a weapon, he saw all the crap in the room the dim light had hid. Was there something hidden underneath that mess he might be able to use?

His gaze came to an abrupt stop when he saw Angie sitting on the end of the couch. Well, she actually sat on a pile of clothing strewn about on the couch. From her expression, Rico figured he had assessed the situation correctly. She thought they, too, were in the deepest of shit. From the looks of things, Gus and the boss had spent a little special time with her.

Angie's upper lip was swollen, and her right eye was black and blue around the edges. Both hands pressed unnaturally against her left side, and she grimaced in obvious pain. *I guess the cost of dipping into the boss's drugs is a good ass whipping,* he thought. Angie looked about as battered as he felt.

Rico turned his head around and looked at the two men. Dust specks danced in the sunlight beaming between them. Gus had moved over into the kitchen and leaned on the counter. He picked up a can and gulped a mouthful from it. His shotgun was propped against the refrigerator not far from him.

Boss man rocked on his heels with his arms crossed over his chest a few steps away. He didn't wear the brass knuckles at the moment, and Rico didn't see a gun of any sort on him. That was, until the boss turned to address his large counterpart.

"You see that, Gus? Look at his eyes. He's all busted up and tied down and he's still sizing us up? He thinks he can take us on."

Rico spotted a pistol tucked in the back of the short man's jeans at the small of his back. He only got a glimpse of it and couldn't tell if it was his Glock or not.

"You really think so, Boss?" Gus shook the can a few times and crushed it.

"I know so," the boss said. He stepped up and grabbed the top of Rico's hair this time.

"Leave him alone, Marcus," Angie pleaded. Her voice quivered and sounded weak. "He saved my life back there. He did a good thing for you. I'm still yours. I can get your money back."

Marcus gripped his fingers into Rico's hair and shook his head back and forth a few times before abruptly letting it go. Rico's head jerked to the side. He grunted in relief.

Marcus mumbled something and walked away, turning in a small circle.

Rico went to wet his lips with his tongue to say something and tasted blood. His lips were swollen, but he hadn't realized until now his teeth were no match for the brass knuckles. He opened his mouth and searched for missing teeth with his tongue.

"Yeah, sorry about that," Marcus said, and giggled. "Kinda knocked a few teeth loose there, didn't I?" He pointed his finger at Rico and narrowed his gaze. "You had it coming to you, motherfucker."

Rico spit crimson filled saliva on the floor. Marcus reared his hand back as if he was going to slap him again when something banged against the front door.

"Uh, sounds like we got company," Gus said, craning his neck to look in the living room.

"Yeah, no shit." Marcus rubbed a finger under his nose and sniffed.

"You think it's them zombies?"

"What would make you think that? It's probably the neighbors coming over for tea and cookies." Marcus grumbled under his breath and shook his head as he marched to the window and looked outside.

"How many, Boss?"

"Got a few of 'em out there," Marcus said, one eye closed and roaming his gaze. "Got Bill, that auto mechanic from up the street, and about a half dozen others. I think one of them might even be his son."

"That's too bad," Gus said. "Ol' Bill treated us right when we needed a repair."

"Yeah, that's only because we treated him right when he needed a favor." Marcus turned and jutted a finger toward Angie, then brought the finger to his lips and said, "Shhh...."

Angie cowered, sinking deeper into the couch.

Fists continued hitting the door, and then more fists joined in, pounding on the side of the trailer as well.

The shit had already hit the fan when Rico ate the brass knuckle sandwich. He had hoped he had a chance, no matter how small it might have been, to outsmart his captors and escape. Now, the undead had arrived to make a bad situation worse. Rico looked frantically about and pulled at his restraints.

"Aw, don't worry there, little man," Marcus said, turning back to Rico. "We're safe from them out there. We got ourselves an honest to God cop to protect and serve. Oh wait, he looks a little tied up right now. Sucks to be you, eh?"

"What do you want?" Rico's dry throat barely eked out the words through swollen lips.

"Oh, I think you know what I want," Marcus said. "I want to know if you have been protecting Angie, here? Or, have you just been serving her?"

"What?" Was this guy insane? Zombies were outside trying to get in and all this douche could worry about was his petty vendetta?

"You see." Marcus reached around his back. His hand came back with the pistol. He stepped over and placed the barrel against Rico's head. "I have good reason to believe you owe me some money for the date you went on with my Bettie over there. And seeing as to how it's the end of the world, I don't think money is going to buy me much anymore. I might prefer that Harley of yours. And as a matter of fact…" Marcus reached into his pocket and pulled out Rico's keys. He dangled them in the cop's face. "I have already taken the liberty of ridding you of that ride anyway."

"Look, you've got all the cards. The only wrong thing I did to you was save Angie from certain death. I haven't harmed her— haven't touched her. You can have the bike and any money, or anything else I have. The world has gone to shit. Let me take Angie, and let's go our separate ways. You don't need her anymore. She'll just slow you down," Rico said. This time he was more subtle while testing the restraints. They were tight, but not that tight. If he had enough time, he could work his way free from them.

Marcus laughed. Gus wandered over to his side wearing a confused expression, then forced out a laugh himself.

"You don't get it, do you, copper? Angie and me is like family. There ain't no you and her. If I let you go, you'll go alone. Angie needs me. She needs her medicine. If she runs off with you then that means no meds. We wouldn't want our little Bettie getting sick, would we?"

Marcus said the words with such odd concern, Rico wondered if the man truly had a soft spot for Angie. Perhaps he felt like his manhood was challenged because Rico took her.

If that were the case, it didn't help matters that Angie had pleaded with Marcus to leave him alone. A jealous pimp was far more dangerous and unpredictable than an angry pimp.

The pounding on the trailer from reanimated hands grew louder. A window in the kitchen cracked, and a few blows later, glass rained down to the garbage covered floor.

Gus hurried over to the refrigerator and snatched up his shotgun. He pumped once and pointed the barrel at the window. A squeeze of the trigger brought a horrific blast muffled only by the walls of the trailer.

Rico felt like his head was inside a brass gong and someone had struck it with a mallet. The loud noise even made his teeth hurt. The shit was about to get real, and Rico was tied up for lunch.

"Please," Rico said. "Let me loose. I can help you. We need to get rid of the undead outside before they get in. This trailer won't hold them off forever. Call a truce. I give you my word, you can trust me."

"Please, let me loose," Marcus mocked. "If I were your prisoner, would you give me a gun?"

Rico turned his gaze to the floor.

"Give me a break. I wasn't born last night. We got a bunch of dead people walking around outside who want to eat us. Big deal. I'm used to dealing with deadbeats. They ain't no different than a lot of my regular customers. They want to sink their teeth in my Betties. Well, they have another think coming. It's going to cost them, same as everyone else."

Now he knew Marcus was completely off his rocker. Was it genetic, or just a burnout from all the years of drug abuse? "What are you talking about?" Rico protested. "That doesn't even make sense. Untie me and let's get them before they get us. I'll leave right after, and you'll never see me again."

"And where exactly would you go? Just cause you're a cop doesn't mean you got it all figured out. You think we don't already have a plan? Well, we do. It started with teaching you a lesson. That lesson ain't over with yet." Marcus grabbed Rico by the shirt.

Gus stepped in the living room and waited to watch.

Another window from somewhere in the back shattered. Something large thumped on the floor a minute later. A ghastly snarl followed.

"I think one them found a way in. Gus, head on back there and take care of it. Don't go get yourself bit neither," Marcus said

Gus nodded, gripped the shotgun in both hands, stepped past Marcus and Rico, and then headed toward the back rooms.

Marcus hurried over to the window and looked out front, seemingly distracted from dishing out any of his special justice.

Rico gave a quick glance back at Angie, hoping Marcus wouldn't notice. She looked distraught, and mouthed the words, *'I'm so sorry.'* Rico shot her a furtive wink.

"You blowing kisses to my girl?"

Fuck! Busted, Rico thought.

Marcus grinned. "I knew it. I knew it. All cops got a thing for Betties. You're no different, boy. You might as well own up to it and take your ass kicking like a man."

"Untie me and fight me like a man!" Rico yelled.

"Just leave him alone," Angie cried out. She looked as if she were about to say something else when Marcus glared at her. Angie's mouth froze open, and then her bottom jaw started to quiver. She folded within herself and sank back down on the couch.

"Can you tell I got her trained good? She's like a huntin' dog. Takes orders from her master. You ain't her master. I am." Marcus made an animated wink, mocking Rico's stealth communication to Angie.

Rico boiled with anger. How could anyone treat another living human being like they were just a piece of meat? How much has Angie had to suffer serving under this man's thumb? If he managed to make it out of this alive, he was going to give Marcus and his muscle a taste of their own medicine.

"Hey, don't look at me that way, or I'll—" Marcus's words were cut short by the loud report of the shotgun in the other room. After a few moments of pause, he called out, "You okay back there?"

"Yeah, Boss!" Gus called back. "One of 'em climbed in through the window. Looks like more of 'em gathering out there, too."

"Please listen to me," Rico said. "This trailer's not much stronger than a wet cracker box. We need to find some place with solid walls to hole up. I don't know if that TV will do any good, but if you have a radio, there might be some news on it that will tell us where it's safe to go."

Gus stepped back into the room with the shotgun over his shoulder. Blood splattered his shirt in various places it hadn't before. "I heard him say we might need to find a better place to stay. I think he might be right, Boss. This here ain't no place to make a stand. Won't be long before—"

"Won't be long before I crack your skull open!" Marcus shouted. "Who the hell gave you permission to think?"

Damn, this Marcus character must be one bad dude to treat the big guy like that, Rico thought.

Gus dropped his gaze to the floor and back shuffled into the kitchen.

"That's right," Marcus said. "Get on back there and keep an eye on things. Take care of it if it becomes a problem. I'm in charge here. No one else." He pulled up the gold chain around his neck from under his shirt and pointed to the letters spelling his name. "See this? It says Marcus. Do you know where my name came from? Well, it's ancient, is what it is. Came from the Roman god of war—Mars. I am the god of war. You got that?"

"I didn't mean nothing by it, Boss. But it couldn't hurt to get an idea what's going on out there. It would give us some options. You always say it's a good thing to have options."

"I tell you what, Gus." Marcus ran his fingers through his hair, clearly agitated. "It is a good thing to have options, but after we do that, it's back to business. And seeing as to how you think this cop is so bright, you get to clean up the living room when we finish with him. Got it?"

"But, Boss—"

"But, nothing." Marcus cut the big guy's words short and walked toward Angie. She lowered her head and raised her arms after scooting over out of his way. He leaned over an end table by the couch and grabbed hold of an electrical cord plugged into the wall. His fingers followed the cord down to the floor under the trash and fished out a radio.

"Here it is, but you don't realize what's going on. All the copper's doing is stalling. And you don't have the brains to see that, but I do. Nothing good is going to come of it. There's nothing airing on the TV, so I doubt anything would be on the radio. Even if there was some information, why would we follow the rest of the sheeple? We need to be outside of the main group—away from the authorities where we can be our own bosses. We'll set up fort and get customers to come to us. Do you know what they call that, Gus? When you get to make your own rules?"

"Uh, being boss?"

"Well, yeah, but that's not what I'm driving at. When you don't take orders from no one, then you're what's called autonomous."

"Anonymous?"

"No, dill weed. *A-ton-o-mus.*"

"I'm sorry, Boss."

"Damn straight, you're sorry." Marcus set the radio on the table and eyed Angie. He leaned over, pooching out his lips as if he was going to kiss her. She braced herself but didn't pull away. His lips came closer until they touched her swollen cheek. Angie held her breath until he made a big smacking noise and stood straight.

"You think you can manage to work that thing, June Melon?" Marcus nodded at the radio.

Angie fidgeted on the couch until Marcus moved away. She slid over by the radio and flipped the 'on' switch. Static blared through the small speakers. She turned down the volume and gazed up at Marcus.

"That's the strongest station in these parts. See, I told you it was a waste of time. Nothing. Now let's quit stalling." Marcus laced his fingers together and stretched them outward until they cracked. "All good things must come to an end." An evil smile curled on his lips as he dipped into his pocket and pulled out the brass knuckles.

"Try another station," Rico pleaded.

Angie didn't wait for permission and began turning the knob. The radio popped and crackled through white noise. The background beat of the undead against the trailer intensified Rico's feeling of hopelessness.

Marcus slid his fingers through the holes of the polished metal. He flexed his grip a few times—making a fist. "It ain't dark outside yet, but you're about to be seeing stars."

Before Marcus made another move, the radio spit out a half word amongst the static as Angie turned the knob.

"Wait, go back. I heard something—go back," Rico cried.

Marcus rolled his eyes.

"I heard it, too," Gus said.

Angie slowly twisted the knob, trying to find the station. She tuned and found a low monotone voice.

"Turn it up," Gus said from the kitchen.

As the volume increased, so did the static, but the voice beneath became clearer.

Gus hurried into the living room and turned an ear toward the radio while keeping an eye on the kitchen.

"Martial law has been instated by the President of the United States. Any person, or persons, showing signs of aggression to police or military will be shot on sight. Please remain indoors if at all possible. Avoid traveling to large towns or cities as traffic is set for contra flow leading away."

The news took some wind out of Marcus's sails. His shoulders slumped, and he dropped his hands to his side. He now listened as attentively as the others did.

"Military bases are being set up for safe zones. Evacuees are advised to report to the nearest military base. Evacuation points for the state of Texas include: Camp Bowie—Brownwood. Camp Bullis—San Antonio. Camp Mabry—Austin. Fort Bliss—El Paso. Fort Hood—Killeen. Fort Bliss—Bastrop County. Martial law has been instated under the Presid—"

"It's just a recording," Rico said. "It will keep repeating itself."

Angie turned the radio off. "What does that all mean?"

"Yeah, what should we do, Boss?"

"It means nothing, and we should do nothing." Marcus grumbled, stepped forward, and yanked the radio from the wall. "None of those bases are close to us. Besides, you heard them. They said to stay put. I bet people are leaving the cities like ants hightailing it out of a kicked over pile."

No sooner had the words left his lips than the hinges on the door rattled as the ghouls outside pressed against it. A screw head popped off the upper hinge and fell to the floor. All gazes in the room turned to the small piece of metal.

Rico pulled at his restraints to free himself and grunted in frustration. Before Marcus could turn toward him to do anything about it, the top door hinge pulled free from the frame.

Chapter 14

Marcus bounded over to the door and threw his weight against it. His efforts were too little, too late, as the bottom hinge pulled free next. He cursed and tried to hold the intruders back with his shoulder pressed against the door. As he reached for the pistol, the weight of the zombies forced him to his back on the floor. The gun slipped free of his grasp and bounced only a few feet away from Rico.

Angie screamed through ghastly sounds emanating from the zombie horde. She clambered to her feet atop the pile of junk on the couch.

Gus lifted the shotgun and fired into the lead ghoul from the kitchen. The blast only added to the mass chaos engulfing the room.

The zombie caught the buckshot across the face and chest. The steel balls ripped out chunks of flesh and sent jet black blood pouring out the wounds. One of the projectiles found its mark in the brain. The zombie fell forward and landed on the door, unmoving.

Marcus groaned against the added weight and struggled to push the door off him.

As badly as Rico wanted to see Marcus disposed of, now was not the time. He needed that scumbag and his muscle to keep the zombies at bay until he could break free.

Rico rocked in the chair as he fought against the restraints. The struggle tipped him off balance and onto the floor. The chair was constructed out of cheap wood with a wicker back and seat. He felt it flex some and the bonds loosen a bit. It wasn't enough, and he pushed through the pain as he redoubled his efforts to escape.

Where was Angie? Why wasn't she helping him? He wasn't sure if she were even still in the room. Gus fired the shotgun two more times. Rico saw chunks of flesh explode and the zombies at the door fall back. Marcus yelled for help. Rico writhed and thrashed about as a wild animal caught in a trap. With every move, he felt the bonds give a little. Moans of hunger grew from outside. He craned his neck around and saw three more zombies shuffle into the doorway.

Gus must have been too excited not to have realized he had one foot on the door Marcus was trapped underneath. The massive man's eyes bugged nearly out their sockets, and a faraway expression of uncertainty gripped his face.

"Get this door off me," Marcus shouted. Gus fired the gun again until it clicked empty. He pulled a shell from his belt and began reloading.

Angie jumped off the couch and leaped over Rico. She slid on some magazines as she tore down the hall.

Rico couldn't believe she had been in the room the whole time and didn't give him a hand. Now was not the time for this girl to lose it. "Angie, come back and help me!"

However, it didn't look as if she were coming back. He jerked and tugged. No matter what, he couldn't break free.

Two zombies lumbered inside and sent Gus back on his heels, heading toward the kitchen. A third entered and must have noticed Marcus squirming from underneath the door. It knelt down and crawled toward him.

The doorway was empty of new guests for now. Marcus was about to get the surprise of his life, and Rico couldn't figure why Gus hadn't blasted the ones after him.

Gus cursed, "Dammit! It's jammed!"

Okay, that answered that question. Gus picked the wrong day to have trouble with his shotgun. Outside, Rico saw more undead heading up the gravel driveway toward the trailer. It wouldn't be long before the place was totally overrun.

The groans of the walking dead approaching intertwined to form an ethereal hymn of sadness—a beckoning call for more to join in the pursuit to satiate the unquenching hunger.

"Gus, help me!" Marcus shouted. He had managed to work his head and left arm from under the door, and was having one hell of a time keeping the hungry monster from getting him. The thing's teeth gnashed at the air, only because Marcus had a tight grip around its throat. "Gus, what the fuck are you doing? Help me!"

Rico strained with all he had against his bonds. His eyes darted from the open doorway and the creatures making their way toward the trailer, at Marcus's gun—and to his shock, his keys—just a few feet away on the floor, and then back at the open doorway.

If he didn't break free soon, he was a dead man.

Gus held the shotgun in both hands and used it to shove the two undead back toward the front door opening. One of them crashed against the wall and slid to the floor. The other righted itself and continued to advance on the large man. He fumbled with the ejector and a spent shell flew out. "Got it!" His fingers felt for more ammo on his belt but came up empty. He darted to the kitchen counter and dug into a box of shells. In a blind panic, he attempted to reload.

Gus should have paid more attention, because the zombie lunged for him before he could get the first shell in. It grabbed him on the arm, but he managed to push it off. It stumbled to the ground, and before it rose, he slammed the shotgun's butt against its skull with a mighty heave.

Rico heard the zombie's head crack above the pandemonium stirring up the room. A stream of brain goo shot out and landed near his feet as the zombie collapsed motionless to the floor. Gus still didn't have time to reload before the second zombie was up and attacking.

A rotting corpse stepped up into the front door and made a gurgling hiss. Rico turned his attention from Gus and couldn't believe his eyes. The zombie was mangled beyond recognition. Its lower jaw was torn away, revealing a gaping grin of blood stained teeth. Its right arm reached out, ready to grab anything in front of it. Its other arm was dislocated at the left shoulder. Nearly all of the skin and muscle was pulled away from the shoulder down to the elbow. The wind blew in the warm, rank smell of decaying meat. As it entered the room, Rico saw a swarm of flies busy laying eggs in the festering skin.

Rico's arms went slack. This was it. This was the end. In all the ways he had thought he might die, this wasn't one of them. He used to have a fear of catching a bullet, or being stabbed by a knife in the line of duty. Now either of the two ways to go out would be a blessing compared to what was just about to happen.

He closed his eyes and begged God to let it end quickly. A lifetime of regrets flashed through his mind as his body turned cold and numb.

Someone grabbed his arms and pulled. He looked and saw Angie with a steak knife in her hand sawing away on his bonds.

"Angie, thank goodness. Hurry!" Rico blurted it out and instantly regretted it. The last thing he needed to do was attract Gus's attention.

The zombie with the severed arm and grinning maw looked toward him. It stumbled over the fray between Marcus and the other zombie, creeping forward.

"Hurry," Rico said, wiggling to get free.

"Hold still, or I'm going to cut you!" Angie shouted, slicing through the thick rope.

Rico felt the knife come to rest but couldn't free his hands. "Don't stop!"

Fear must have gotten the best of Angie because Rico's command jarred her back into action.

A few more passes of the blade and Rico's hands came free. "Give me the knife!" She handed it to him blade first. He managed to flip the knife around without cutting himself and quickly severed the bonds on his ankles. The knife was dull, but fortunately, the rope binding his legs to the chair was smaller than that around his hands.

The zombie was back on its feet, so was Rico. It lunged toward him with the good arm in the lead.

Rico brought his forearm up and blocked the creature's blood covered fingers away—within inches of scratching his face. With his other hand, he slammed his open paw against the side of the zombie's head while keeping a distance from the thing's teeth. He managed to slip around the creature's backside and ran him headlong into the television. The thick glass shattered as the zombie's head went inside. Blood oozed out of the ghoul's already blood soaked face and skull.

The zombie fell limp with its head still inside the television.

Rico spun around. Angie had backed up against the wall and gritted her teeth. There were several unmoving zombies on the floor in the kitchen. Gus was covered in blood, lifting the door and two dead zombies off Marcus.

There was no time to lose. It was now or nothing.

"Let's go." Angie tugged at him.

Rico dropped to the floor and snatched up Marcus's gun and the keys. He grabbed Angie by the hand as he ran past her and pulled her down the narrow hall.

"Don't let them get away!" Marcus shouted from the living room.

The master bedroom window was busted. A lone zombie lay sprawled across the bedroom floor with its brains scattered across the carpet among the shards of glass from the shattered window.

Loud thumps shook the house, signaling that Gus was on the move.

Rico picked up the lamp from the nightstand and busted the rest of the loose glass from the blood-covered window. He held onto Angie as she stepped out toward freedom.

"Were the hell do ya think you're goin', piggie-wiggy?"

Rico looked back. The large bulk of a man splattered in blood from head to toe stood before him. Gus had the shotgun up and ready, but the barrel wasn't pointed in Rico's direction.

Rules of engagement didn't allow a police officer to fire his weapon at an assailant unless his life was directly threatened. Gus wasn't aiming at him, but there was no time to play by the rule book. Rico lifted his gun and fired. There was no second guessing or regret this time. He felt a hard coldness inside which calmed the earlier fears that threatened to incapacitate him.

Gus fell back out of the doorway into the hall. Rico had found his target. Where the bullet hit and how bad the big guy was hurt, he wasn't sure. He wanted to care, but he didn't. Gus had shown him some mercy by not blasting his way into the room. Mercy or stupidity? It didn't really matter. Rico made a hard, fast decision and felt confident he had made the right choice.

With no time to waste, Rico stuck his feet out the window and maneuvered his body around to let himself down. He expected to land on soft grass outside. Instead, he stepped down on an A/C unit. The zombie that had broken in must have used the window unit to step up. His foot slipped off the sheet metal, and he tumbled down next to it. His ankle twisted as he stumbled to maintain his balance.

He quickly brought the gun up and scanned the surroundings. A few zombies shuffled his way, several yards behind. He ran to the front of the trailer and saw several more zombies making their way inside.

Angie crouched down near the rear tire of Marcus's truck. She had the steak knife in her hand and waved him on. Rico kept low and tried not to make any noise as he hurried over. His ankle stabbed with sharp pain and limited his speed. He dropped to one knee by her side.

"We can't stay here long. There are more coming from the back and they'll see us for sure."

"Do we run for it?" she asked.

"Yeah—wait. Give me the knife."

Angie laid the knife on the ground next to Rico. Most of the zombies in front had made it near the front of the trailer.

"Head for the bike. I'm right behind you." Rico gave Angie a push and picked up the knife. He jabbed it into the sidewall of a rear tire. The blade bounced off a few times, but then a hiss of air announced his success. If the tire hadn't been in such bad shape he would have been wasting his time trying.

When he looked up, Angie was already half the distance between him and the ticket out of that hell-hole. He brought the keys out of his pocket and held them tightly in one hand. The gun was at the ready with white knuckled fingers on alert to pull the trigger.

Through the trees to one side of the yard, he saw a number of walking dead heading over. Some of the zombies that had made it to the front of the trailer must have noticed Angie. They turned and shambled toward the bike.

How many zombies in the area? More than twenty, for sure. More than Rico wanted to deal with.

At least they're spread out, Rico thought, as he fast stepped his way down the driveway.

The toll from the past 24 hours weighed heavily on his body. Whatever adrenalin rush that had gotten him this far had petered out. He felt like his body was running out of gas. Waves of pain cascaded in his head each time his foot hit the ground. The blood in his mouth tasted awful. He coughed and felt his stomach roil. A crown from a tooth came loose. He spit it into his hand and put it in his pocket. His ankle began to swell inside his boot.

Angie made it to the bike, looked down both sides of the road, and waved him on.

Gunshots erupted from the trailer. Rico hoped like hell the bullets were aimed at the undead. No time to look now. Another round of shots went off, and then someone shouted from the trailer. It sounded like Marcus.

His last few steps brought him to his bike. Angie waited with a panicked expression. He rammed the gun between his belt and the small of his back and stabbed the key into the ignition. Before he could get on the bike, a zombie neared the exit to the road.

Rico ran with the knife raised high in the air and plunged it down on its skull with all his might. He had no idea how a steak knife would fare against cranium bone. The blade sunk in with a sickening *thunk*. The zombie dropped to its knees. Steak knife: 1, zombies: 0.

He went to reach down and pull the knife out but Angie beckoned him to get his ass back over there.

He made it to the bike and jumped on. His finger hit the on switch and the Harley purred to life—no sweeter sound had ever been made.

Angie left the side of the bike and ran a few steps toward the trailer.

"What the hell are you doing?" Rico eyed the growing numbers of undead getting closer, looked back at the trailer, and then at the undead once more. "We don't have time for this."

Angie shot him a victorious smirked and lifted both hands sporting the American 'fuck you' bird toward the trailer.

"What are you doing?"

"What does it look like I'm doing?"

"Stop this silly shit now, and let's get out of here!"

Angie shook her hands back and forth a few times before heading to the bike.

She smiled on her return. One side of her lip was so swollen it looked like half her face was paralyzed. She hopped on the seat and reached her arms around his chest.

Ugh, pain shot up Rico's ribs into his left arm. She didn't squeeze him tight enough to hurt him. Maybe he had a fractured rib, too. There was no telling what Marcus did to him after he passed out.

As the motorcycle sped away, kicking up dirt and gravel, Rico stole once last glance back at the trailer. He saw Marcus stepping out onto the steps. Blood covered his shirt. He had one hand tightly clutched against his shoulder. Either he had been bitten, or Gus accidently shot him. If the man was bitten, he was as good as dead. If that were the case, then Rico was happy. Gus poked his head from the trailer doorway. Rico didn't stay around long enough to notice his condition.

When they hit the road, two zombies reached out to grab them and came up with empty air. A few more walking single file on the road formed an obstacle course Rico weaved in and out of. It was tough going on the nasty highway, and every hurt on Rico's body felt the brunt of each rough spot.

Nevertheless, the important thing was they were back on the road and away from the trailer. A strange giddiness ran through him. He felt like he had cheated certain death. As crappy as life had become, he now felt uncanny euphoria. All his senses seemed to sharpen—even through the tiredness. He was alive and life never seemed so precious. Rico had read of near death experiences changing the lives of people, but he never imagined it would be like this. Being alive was a blessing. Each moment needed to be savored. Even pain, as it was part of what living had to offer.

A smile crept across Rico's lips he felt might never wear off.

Chapter 15

Marcus groaned as he stood outside the trailer and clutched his shoulder. Watching that damn cop escape and Angie flipping him off only added fuel to fire his anger. If he had any bullets left in his pistol, he would have taken that bitch out. No, he'd shoot her in the leg or something—incapacitate her so she couldn't run away. Then, he'd wait for the zombies to get her ass and eat her alive.

Rocks flew up from the Harley's rear tire and peppered a few zombies reaching out in vain to claim a prize. The loud roar of the motorcycle diminished as it disappeared down the road, only to become a distant hum that faded in the air.

As bad as he felt, now was not the time for regrets. Even though he and Gus had taken care of the immediate zombie attack, others shuffled up the driveway for another wave.

He turned to head back in the trailer and a sharp pain in his shoulder almost dropped him to his knees. "Son-of-a-bitch!" he whispered.

Gus backed away from the doorway and held out his hand to help Marcus up the steps. Marcus's lips withered as if he had just sucked on a lemon, and he scowled. Gus backed away farther, almost tripping on the trailer door.

Zombies littered the floor of the living room and kitchen. Blood had been slung in every direction. The walls looked like the abstract impressionist Jackson Pollock had taken buckets of black cherry blood and created a masterpiece. Marcus walked around the door and stepped over the dead bodies strewn on the floor. There was no way this mess would ever get cleaned up. Gus followed him into the master bedroom.

Marcus closed the door behind them and pushed in the lock. Gus let the shotgun drop to the floor and plopped his ass down on the bed. He breathed heavily through his nose and coughed.

"You let them get away," Marcus said, barely moving his lips over gritting teeth.

"I'm sorry, Boss." Gus looked up with tired eyes from the bed. He scooted over near the headboard and leaned his back against it. His hand pressed against the bullet wound on his side. Gus ran his tongue over his lips, and said, "He shot me."

Marcus opened his mouth to tear his muscle a new one but stopped himself before wasting the energy. What's done was done, and they were both fucked. "Yeah, I see that. How bad does it hurt?"

"Uh, a lot. If a can rest just a few minutes, I might be okay." He turned his head and looked at the drugs on the nightstand. "Might be something here to help fix me up."

Marcus stepped over the zombie on the floor and looked through the window. So far, no others ghouls had gathered around back.

Gus looked over at him. "I ain't no doc or nothin', but I think the bullet went all the way through. That's a good thing, right?"

"Yeah, Gus. That's a good thing." Marcus bit his lip as blood oozed between the fingers pressed against his shoulder.

"You look a mess, Boss."

"I feel it." Marcus coughed. Even he noticed his cough sounded a little different than the one Gus had made. His raspy hack foreshadowed further complication from the zombie bite—something far worse than the loss of blood and permanent scars. "We, uh, we should leave."

Gus nodded and gingerly eased himself off the bed. He took the sheet and wrapped it around his chest to cover the wound. "What's the plan, Boss?"

"We waylay those fucks outside, and then load the car with gear."

"Where're we going?" Gus slowly reached down and picked up the shotgun.

Marcus pulled off a pillowcase and blotted it against his shoulder. It didn't hurt quite as badly as before. In fact, it felt kind of numb. "We're going to a place where I can finish what I started. No one fucks over Marcus Jones and gets away with it. We're going to find that bitch and her new boyfriend and eviscerate the dog shit out of the both of 'em!"

"How do you know where they went, Boss?"

"You just leave the thinking to me, Gus."

Chapter 16

Time had become meaningless as Rico cruised down the highways. The exuberance of cheating death he felt earlier had faded long ago. The wind stung his face, and Angie felt like a new appendage growing on his back. Pain and fatigue joined forces and were slowly but surely winning the war. He didn't know how much longer he could take it. How much longer he could go on. He didn't want to think of how much farther he had to go, either. How many more miles? How many more hours?

He had to stop.

College Station, near Bryan, Texas, was only a few miles up ahead. Rico could have made better time if he had taken a main highway, but it wasn't worth the gamble. He did get turned around a few times on the back roads and drove in the wrong direction. His mind and sense of judgment suffered as much as his body.

The college town wasn't a bad place to stop and get some supplies and rest, as long as they stayed on the outskirts and avoided the main population. He would have preferred driving all the way to Killeen, having finally settled on a destination.

They had come upon an abandoned truck with lawn equipment on a trailer. He helped himself to a gas can on it and filled his tank. Killeen was only about a hundred miles away, so fuel wasn't an issue.

Ever since Rico heard the emergency instructions on the radio, he knew that if they had managed to get out of the trailer alive, to head back to Killeen. Killeen, an Army designated safe zone, was the best possible move for survival.

This early in the game though, he had no way of knowing how successful that plan was going. As they neared College Station, he had noticed the skies above the city were darker. A little bad weather didn't concern him, but the closer they came, he realized the darkness wasn't from clouds of inclement weather. Black smoke rose in large columns from various locations, forming a dark blanket above the city.

This certainly was bad news. Fire is an unforgiving assailant. Even if the local fire department was operating on some level, there was no way they could handle that many fires at once. It made Rico wonder if things near Dallas or Houston were even worse.

College Station, and Bryan, Texas, were both relatively active, populated areas, but he had to take that risk. The populated areas would have more supplies, and supplies at this point were a must. Preferably something to kill the pain and fill the gullet. He was starving. He knew that Angie was, too. He felt her stomach rumble several times against his back as they drove toward what he hoped to be some semblance of civilization. Sadly, the closer they came, the more he realized that hope was nothing more than a pipe dream.

Thinking the whole world might catch on fire over this mess was something he hadn't considered before now.

He slowed the bike as they passed a sign that read *'Welcome to College Station, Texas. Population 97,801. The Lone Star State'*.

"Are we stopping?" Angie yelled into his ear.

"Yeah, I can't go on. I need to rest. I think I need a doctor."

"Well, I don't think you're going to have any luck finding one of those."

"Then I will settle for something to eat and some Advil."

"I can get behind that," Angie said, squeezing him tighter.

Rico groaned, trying to fight the pain. She relaxed her grip and he wondered if Angie had just shown him some affection and given him a hug.

After a few miles, the rural view of trees and clear pastureland gave way to the outskirts of city life. Signs posted along the road advertised fuel, lodging, and the fast food places available at the next exit. Rico imagined himself hitting the next Taco Bell and scarfing down a whole twelve back of Supreme Tacos by himself.

"What's the plan—"

Rico raised his hand, instructing her to wait. As he made the turn to the exit, civilization and its state of dismay presented itself. He killed the engine and coasted slowly toward the intersection until he braked to a stop.

In a low voice, he said, "Look for a CVS, or a Walgreens, or something like that. And please, don't do anything that will attract any attention."

"Oh, my God," Angie whispered. Her fingers dug into Rico's side.

The area looked like an army had rolled through with a scorched earth agenda. Crackles and thumps of burning buildings collapsing interrupted the eerie silence. *If things are this bad here, I can only imagine what the rest of the country looks like,* Rico thought. Fumes from the burning debris stung against the back of his throat.

The road in both directions was deserted. Abandoned cars littered the streets. A building to one side, a Chase Bank, was engulfed in flames. A gust of wind picked up and blew toward them. Heat reached out like gripping hands, beckoning them into the pits of Hell along with everyone else.

In the distance, several other buildings smoldered and burned. Other structures had windows busted out. A car not far away was parked haphazardly on the sidewalk, a half mangled body hung from the driver's side door. Streaks of blood covered the entire side of the car and pooled on the pavement below. Farther down, a lone fire hydrant gushed its water onto the street like a horizontal version of Old Faithful. The flood of water steadily worked its way toward them. It reminded Rico of the dead, building in number by the minute to flood the world. That thought brought up a whole new question. Where was everyone—the living? Where were the undead?

The place was like a ghost town. It took less than 24 hours to turn an average city filled with every day activity upside down.

Rico shifted his gaze up and down the road. There had to be people somewhere. Maybe they had taken refuge in churches or schools—large buildings where masses could huddle together. Safety in numbers sounded reasonable. Then, more people gathered together would require more resources. He remembered reading stories about New Orleans after Hurricane Katrina hit. Some humans quickly degenerated into animals. There was no way he was ever going to subject himself to a situation like that.

No life. And no *unlife,* as it were.

For the latter, he was thankful.

"Which way should we go?" Angie whispered.

"I don't know," Rico said. "That's what I was trying to decide. We need to stay away from fire though, if at all possible. You know how that stuff can spread."

Just then, as if to make the decision for them, a cluster of undead ghouls shuffled into sight between some vehicles less than a block away.

"Look there," she said, and pointed.

"I see them." Rico turned his head, looking for the best way to avoid the crowd. "Uh oh, there are some coming from over that way, too."

The second pack of zombies was fewer in number but closer.

"How do they know we're here?"

"Probably heard the bike before I killed the engine," Rico said. He looked over his shoulder back the way they had come and then straight ahead. "Straight it is."

"Sounds good to me." Angie sighed and wrapped her arms around Rico's sore ribs as he brought the engine to life.

***

Going straight down the highway bypass kept them out of harm's way but didn't put them any closer to a pharmacy. Rico turned right after a few blocks and then headed back toward the main road. He weaved in and out of abandoned vehicles and found his reward at the next major intersection.

Angie tapped him on the shoulder, and he raised a thumb to let her know he got the message. The entrance to the CVS was just up ahead. Nothing was on fire for a few blocks. Rico killed the engine once again and coasted the bike as quietly as possible toward the store. The bike rolled to a stop near the door.

It appeared so far no one dead or alive had taken notice of their arrival. Angie hopped off the bike, and Rico set it on its stand. He brought his pistol out from the small of his back and prepared for the worst.

"It's so strange to see a town deserted like this. Where are all the people? You don't think they're all dead, do you?" Angie whispered.

"I hope not. Maybe they're all hunkered down at home right now. Most people probably have enough supplies to last a few days."

"Did you see those two guys loading up a TV by that electronics store?"

Rico crunched glass under his boot as he eased toward the entrance. "Yeah. One man's zombie apocalypse of doom is another man's winning lottery ticket. People never cease to amaze me."

Angie looked about as if she were afraid a wild animal was about to attack from her blindside. "Are we going in? I'm scared."

"Yeah, but I'm just as concerned as to what might be inside as I am out here. Just keep an eye out while I check things."

Angie stepped up behind him and grabbed onto an elbow. Rico pulled his arm away and shook his head. He moved inside the pharmacy.

The doors in front had been taken out by someone who must have known what they were doing. Rico didn't imagine a brick or a tire iron couldn't have broken through without taking all day—if at all. He guessed it was possible someone used a vehicle like a battering ram to lay waste of the door. It certainly made entering easy, but it also left the pharmacy wide open for any stray zombies to wander in.

The front counter was to the left and clear of any dangers. He had a good view of the right side of the building and it looked clear, too. A few steps later had him down the center aisle. He didn't waste any time heading to the back, scanning each aisle as he passed.

"I can't believe this place is empty," Angie said in a low voice.

"It's too good to be true. Almost feels like a horror movie, where just when you think it's safe, something jumps out and grabs you."

"What are we going to do? Grab some stuff and leave? It's getting dark."

"No, I'm thinking we barricade the front and stay for the night. There's just no way I can keep going."

"I'm exhausted, too, but I feel like I might be too scared to sleep."

"We're just going to have to try." Rico stretched his elbows toward his back and yawned. "Tell you what, I'm going to find a back door and push the Harley around. We can store it inside. I don't want to leave it out in the open."

"Okay."

Rico headed to a doorway with an 'Employee's Only' sign above it. Angie followed closely behind.

*

Once the bike was safely stored away, the two walked to the back of the store where the pharmacy was located.

Angie stepped behind the counter, turned, and faced Rico. "What kind of drugs are we looking for? Are there any drugs you're allergic to?"

"I don't think I'm allergic to anything. Don't really go to the doctor much since I got off my ADD medicine. If I get sick, I just take whatever the doctor gives me. Don't pay much attention to what's in the bottle," Rico said, thinking for the first time that maybe bringing a junkie to a drug store probably wasn't the brightest of ideas. "Something for pain. If I don't get some relief soon, I think I'm going to pass out."

"How about something with opioids or NSAIDs? That should do the trick." Angie turned and perused drug bottles lining the wall. She came to a stop, picked up a white container and shook it. "How much do you weigh?" She removed the top and poured a few into her hand.

An insulated display that looked like a barrel had sodas floating in mostly melted ice. Rico reached in and grabbed a Big Red from the bottom—delighted it was still cold.

"Honestly," Rico said, popping open the can. "How do you even know what you're looking at?"

"My boyfriend... I mean, my ex-boyfriend, was a cook, remember?"

Rico drank from the can and handed it to Angie. "I thought he was a pimp. He didn't look like he had the brains to be a *cook*."

"Marcus had a cousin who was a pharmacist. His cousin taught him how to make meth—even helped with supplies when he could. Of course, Marcus had to give him a cut of the profits. Marcus isn't as stupid as you think. He's pretty smart. He just kinda loses his shit when he gets mad. He gets mad over money— and his women. You still didn't answer the question."

"What was the question again? I keep trying to picture Marcus in a white lab coat mixing up drugs. All I get is Wile E. Coyote with a burnt face from exploding chemicals."

"How much do you fucking weigh? You want me to give you the correct dosage, don't you?"

Angie's tone told him she wasn't amused. It amazed Rico how people who suffered from abuse had some protective bond with their abuser. He had seen it firsthand way too many times when answering domestic disputes.

"I'm glad you found something back there. I worried they might keep the pain meds locked under key. I'd take Advil or something if that's all we had. I do feel like I need something stronger, just not too strong. I want to keep my wits about me." Rico hobbled over to her with his drink in one hand and his other hand against his side. "I weigh a buck ninety."

"Then this should do the trick." She handed him four small white pills.

"You sure? This many?"

"Uh, yeah. They're for children and an adult dosage is four. I think I might take a few myself."

Rico popped the pills in his mouth and chased it down with a swallow of Big Red. He leaned against the counter, and said, "You need to be real careful about what you take. You don't need to be treating this place like a candy store."

"What kind of person do you think I am?"

"Really?"

"I've got a problem. I admit it, okay? You don't have to be so insensitive. Don't worry, I'm not going to eat up all the meds when you're not looking." Angie stormed from behind the counter past him as she headed toward the restroom.

He let her go by without protest. It would only make matters worse. Plus, he didn't have the energy. He was starving, but at the moment felt too tired to eat. There was still a problem with the wide-ass open door in front. That was something that needed immediate attention.

Rico turned around and leaned his back against the counter, taking in the lay of the store. There were sections in various aisles where items on the shelves were missing or upset. The cash registers in front were turned on their side and the drawers open. Funny, the cash registers at the pharmacy were untouched. Whoever broke in must have gotten all they could carry, or were spooked the hell out. The shelves in the liquor section were noticeably empty. Some items lay on the floor as if someone just walked by with their arm sticking out and knocked them off. A surprising numbers of shelves looked untouched.

Rico walked toward the front, contemplating what to use to block the doorway. He came to the cold medicine aisle and looked across more empty shelves. Yep, the thieves were chefs who need ingredients for their next batch of goodies.

At least there were basic medical supplies available. Rico thought, after he barricaded the door, he might try to wrap a bandage around his aching ribs. The crown to his back tooth was still in his pocket. He needed to find some superglue and cement it back on.

One thing for sure, none of the undead had made it inside the building yet. No signs of struggle or blood anywhere. No spent bullet casings. Something did have the thieves' hightailing it out before they were finished, though.

There was a shit load of candy and gum for them to eat. There at least had to be something with better nutritional value—like nuts or something. The frozen food section should have something with meat, even if it was just pepperoni on a pizza. If the electricity held out long enough, they could use the microwave in the break room. All they needed was to lay low for a couple of days and heal a little before heading to Fort Hood.

Rico sure as hell hoped their luck would hold out that long. He brought the can of Big Red up to his lips and threw his head back as he chugged the last bit down. That's when his brain turned a double somersault and landed in a bowl of strawberry pudding.

Angie walked from the back of the store toward him. The atoms making up her body moved around like busy bees on a honeycomb. "It's getting dark. I take it the plan is to stay here tonight?"

Rico nodded, rubbing his hand against his cheek. His head felt numb. It was his hand on his face, but it felt like someone else was touching him. Strange.

"You okay?" Angie asked, stepping toward him, her words slurred and slowed in Rico's mind. As if playing a record on its slowest setting, Angie said, "You feeling okay? You don't look so…"

Rico felt his knees buckle.

The last thing that went through his mind before closing his eyes was that this crazy bitch drugged him. And for what—saving her life? Rico's heart began to harden just a little bit more.

Was there not anyone good left in the world?

Chapter 17

Rico awoke in a dark room with only a small glow of light on the wall near the ceiling providing illumination. What a surprise. His last thoughts placed him in the main area of the store and going weak in the knees. Angie had drugged him for some unknown reason.

The back of his throat felt like it had been abraded by a sandstorm. Other than that and the aches and pains he had been living with, he was in decent shape. Angie had even been thoughtful enough to make his sleep more comfortable. A spongy pillow was under his head and a bed sheet of some type covered him.

He sat up as his eyes adjusted to the light. A few bottles of water lay to one side next to his folded socks, boots, and belt. This had to be some back room in the store. Why would she bring him in here? Maybe he was now her prisoner.

One thing at a time. He reached over and grabbed one of the water bottles. The top came off with a twist, and Rico gulped the entire thing down.

The water was warm but not hot—at least it took care of the dry mouth. He popped open another bottle and took a few sips. Taking in the rest of the room, he surmised that he was in a storage room of some kind. A small slit of a window over his head on the far wall leaked in light. Shelves filled with cleaning supplies lined the walls on either side.

Rico took in a deep breath and stretched out some of the soreness. His ribs didn't feel much better, but at least his teeth didn't hurt quite as badly as before. The water in his stomach churned and reminded him his belly was still empty.

Patting at his midsection, he said aloud, "I could eat a horse and the rider."

"Angie?" he called out, without really expecting her to call back unless she was right there by the door.

He called again.

After a second attempt with no response, Rico put on his socks, boots, and belt and then he rose. Half expecting the storage room door to be locked from the other side, Rico reached out and hesitantly twisted the knob.

It turned freely, and the door swung open.

A few steps down the hall into the store had him right next to the weird machine that took pulse and blood pressure. That thing was about as useful as tits on a bull right now. It was daylight outside, but he had no real way of knowing what time or even day it was. He must have been out for a while, because Angie had apparently been busy. Some of the crap on the floor had been picked up, or shoved out of the way enough to clear the aisles. A good amount of supplies that would come in handy for the stay were stacked neatly over by the pharmacy counter. He guessed Angie wanted to stay close to the drugs. Bitch.

That was the dilemma. Why in the hell did she drug him and then attempt to set up house? The girl didn't sit on her ass popping pills while he was out. Most of the glass was swept out of the way by the front door. Displays and other items had been piled up to block the entrance.

A warm breeze blew in from around the blockage with notes of ash and rotted meat that irritated his nostrils. For a moment, he thought he was going to dry heave.

How that thin little woman had managed to move some of the things was beyond Rico's imagination. Upon closer inspection, the array of junk merchandise, drink coolers, lawn chairs, small grills, and displays looked more substantial at stopping anyone from forcing their way in than perhaps they actually would be. Hopefully the makeshift wall would intimidate anyone or anything from trying.

Rico called out again, stepping over toward the checkout counter, "Angie, you back there?"

His peripheral caught movement from outside through an opening in the barricade right as the words left his mouth. "Oh, shit," Rico whispered. A little voice inside told him he should have kept his voice lower. When he turned and peered through the opening, he regretted he had been right.

A zombie loomed not far from the opening. Fortunately, its back was toward the entrance. Rico held his breath, anticipating the thing to turn around and follow his voice, but it didn't. It just stood there, swaying back and forth, occasionally shifting its weight from one foot to the other. What the hell was wrong with it?

He kept low and scanned the rest of what parts of the street he could see. So far, there only that one zombie in sight. Although the sun was out, the sky looked cloudy. Some of the clouds were dark and gray enough to foreshadow rain.

Minding his step so as to not make too much noise, Rico walked back toward the center of the store, quickly scanning each aisle. Angie was nowhere to be found.

"Angie!" Rico called out, his voice raspy and low. "Angie." Now he started to get a little worried. He hadn't checked the back where the Harley was hidden. There was no way that woman could have driven that thing by herself. What if—what if she found someone else to ride off with?

He was to the back of the store again and seeing a can of deluxe mixed nuts with pistachios reminded him, he needed to eat. But not only did he need to eat, he needed to piss like a race horse. That was when the thought occurred to him. He hadn't checked the bathrooms.

Rico stepped over to the door and slowly pushed it open. There she was, lying on the cold, hard floor. Not set up comfortably like he was.

"Oh my God, Angie!" Rico stepped into the bathroom and dropped down to her side. She was lying in a fetal position, but her arms and legs were tensed up. Was she having a seizure? He pulled the hair away from her face. Her mouth foamed with drool and vomit. The room smelled like puke and piss. That was because she had actually pissed herself. He called her name, watching her eyes for movement. "Angie, can you hear me?"

Angie blinked a few times and struggled to look his way. Her lips quivered, and her brow creased like waves in rippling water. She was in deep, deep distress.

"Talk to me. What happened? Did you take too many pills? You didn't go outside, did you? You're not bit, are—"

She reached over and grabbed his wrist. "I... I need," Angie gritted her vomit-covered teeth and dug her fingers into his skin. "I need a... fix."

"A fix?" Rico said. "Withdrawals? You're having fucking withdrawals already?"

Angie nodded her head, and then kicked out her legs and screamed in pain. Spittle and puke sprang from her mouth, splashing across the floor as she cried out.

Once the horrendous fit died down, Rico said, "I want to help you, but I don't know what to do."

Angie tried to reach for a bottle of water that had rolled over by the wall. Her frail, thin arm seemed much more skeletal now.

Rico leaned over and snatched up the bottle. He twisted off the top and gently turned it up for her to drink. Most of the contents of the bottle just spilled across her lips, cascading to the floor and pooling around Angie's already vomit drenched hair. At least, through it all she managed to down a gulp or two.

Angie closed her eyes for a brief moment and began to smile. At least that's what Rico thought. The smile instantly turned into a grimace, and Angie's legs kicked out straight again. Her fists clenched white as she held them in close to her chest.

Angie cried out in pain, spitting up more saliva and chunks of whatever she had eaten last. Rico reached up, trying to wipe her mouth with his hand, but Angie kicked hard again and he jumped. She cried out more. Her wails of anguish reverberated off the bathroom tiles.

Rico didn't know what to do. He rose and went to the sink and washed his hands. The automatic paper towel dispenser spit out a few sheets, on which he dried his hands and leaned over to wipe Angie's face. Fresh urine ran down Angie's boney leg onto the floor. Gas rumbled from her backside. The stench assaulted Rico's nose. My God, he hoped she hadn't shat on herself. Using the wet towels as a filter over his mouth didn't help much.

Something thumped outside the door. It sounded like it came from within the store. That was when Rico thought of that lone zombie lingering in the street. Angie's cries certainly were loud enough to bring unwanted attention.

"Be quiet. They'll hear us," Rico said.

Angie moaned and drew her legs toward her chin.

She was calm for the moment, so he eased the bathroom door open. Something fell and crashed to the floor. There was no doubt someone or something was inside the store.

*

The last thing he needed was to be trapped inside a bathroom with a junkie going ape shit and a bunch of flesh eating zombies banging to get in. Rico eased the door open and lightly stepped to the outside, careful to release the doorknob without making it click. His stealth efforts mattered for nothing as Angie let out another barrage of cries.

Fuck me! Rico clenched his teeth momentarily until the pain forced him to stop. Even with the bathroom door closed and her voice slightly muffled, he could still hear her wails. And so could anyone out in the street not too far from the open doorway. The barricade did little for noise reduction and it sure as shit did little for protection, as evident by the arrival of the new guest or guests.

He reached around to the small of his back out of habit. His gun wasn't there and wasn't in the storage room when he awoke. It wasn't in the bathroom. Angie had to have taken it—probably had it with her while she was out battening down the hatches. Where the fuck was the gun?

Rico eased over to the end of the aisle and looked down to the front of the store. The barricade had been breached. A portion of it had been shoved aside, large enough to accommodate a man. In this case, the interloper was the zombie that had been idling out front earlier. It was on the floor—apparently tripping on some shampoo bottles knocked off a display. It reached out and used a shelf to pull itself up.

It was halfway to its feet when it saw Rico. Milky white eyes glared back at him. The creature opened its mouth in a wide snarl, so wide that Rico thought the monster was going to tear its cheeks apart. Just when he thought the thing couldn't open its mouth any wider, it hissed a guttural moan. The zombie's face was pale. Dried blood flaked around the corners of its mouth and chin. In its former life, it might have been a salesman, or had some other white-collar job. Its suit and tie were disheveled; the tie flung over one shoulder. The other shoulder and a portion of the neck bore the mark of its undead transformation. Blood covered skin and clothing, with mangled, reddish pink meat dangling from the wounds.

It's party time. Where's my damn gun? Rico ran his gaze over to the supplies Angie had stacked by the pharmacy counter. If it wasn't there, he was going to be in a world of shit.

With no need to hide now, he darted over to the pile of supplies and found it on the backside. He guessed she placed it there just to keep it out of sight. Barricading the door, gathering supplies, hiding Rico in a closet to protect him—despite all Angie's problems, she really had tried to do the right things to keep them alive.

The gun was up in his hands against his shoulder with the barrel pointed to the ceiling. He stepped over to the aisle leading to the front.

There was Mr. Well Dressed Zombie of the Day shambling toward him. Its neck bent unnaturally to the wounded side. Both arms rose toward him as it lifted each foot forward in a wide, mechanical gait. Feet scraped across carpet with each persistent step. The thing's black eyes transfixed on Rico.

He lowered the pistol and aimed for the zombie's head. Angie started up another series of wails. His eyes shifted toward the doorway and the barricade, toward the zombie closing the distance, then back toward the doorway again and the street beyond. He had to eradicate this creature. The pistol felt heavy. He couldn't do it like this. The report of the firearm might draw more unwanted attention. There was no telling if there were any more of the undead nearby. And if so, how many? The gun's blast would only alert them. He couldn't take that chance.

The creature shuffled closer. The distance between them was half the length of store now. If he were going to make a move, he had to do it soon. The thing would be on him in only a matter of moments.

He aimed the gun, but the weight in his hands reminded him once again of the potential threat of making such noise.

Sighing, he lowered the gun.

"Come and get me, you rotten pus bag!" Rico shoved the gun in his belt, knowing he had to take it down or die. The only question now was how he aimed to accomplish that goal. Playing chase with the thing would certainly buy him some time.

He waited for the zombie to come within ten feet before making a quick exit right, down an aisle with medical supplies on either side. Rico's eyes frantically scanned the shelves for anything he could use as a weapon. "You want me? Come and get me!"

Nothing presented itself as much use for a weapon. The only item that seemed promising enough was a rectal thermometer. An image flashed into Rico's mind of him jamming the metal end of the device into the zombie's ear. He had seen that work one time in a movie. In real life, he doubted he had much of a chance to kill the zombie that way. Plus, there was no way he was going to get that close to the thing if he didn't have to.

He had spent more time in thought than he should have. The zombie turned down his aisle and he was still empty handed.

A quick jog had Rico to the end of the aisle right next to a display rack of reading glasses. He caught a reflection of himself in a small mirror on the display. He looked like hell warmed over—even worse than he felt, but now wasn't the time to worry about that. He snatched up a walking cane out of the bucket next to the display and turned to face the zombie.

The zombie's pace quickened as it realized Rico was soon to be in its grasp. Its fingers scratched through empty air, waiting for that sweet second when it could tear flesh.

Rico saw jagged red veins like lightning bolts in a milky white sky around its black pupils. Its jaw dropped open, and it let out a moan so eerie his colon quivered. The moan sounded similar to a bear in the wild, only more ominous and nasally. He tried to shake off the net of fear threatening to immobilize him.

Raising the cane over his head, Rico waited for the zombie to be in the right spot. Close, but not too close.

It shuffled forward.

Rico gripped the cane tightly.

The zombie grew closer.

Then, when the undead son-of-a-bitch was within swinging distance, Rico came down as hard as he could on the ghoul's skull. The zombie went down on both knees, but that wasn't all that happened. The wood cracked over the thing's head, splitting in half like the piece of cheap junk from China that it was. The part Rico held in his hand wasn't even a foot long now. Bits of hair and pale chunks that looked like skin embedded the jagged end of the cane.

The zombie may have gone down, but it wasn't out. It grabbed Rico by the leg.

He tried to jump away, but stumbled back and fell to his ass. His empty hand slapped against the floor as he pushed to free himself out of its grip.

It pulled itself toward him, teeth snapping in anticipation. Rico's heart pounded in his chest. His palms grew damp with sweat, but he held fast to the splintered piece of broken cane.

Just as the zombie was about to take a bite from his leg, Rico sat up and jammed the jagged end of the cane into the creature's ear; just like he had imagined he could with the thermometer. Only, it didn't play out quite like he had anticipated. There was a hell of a lot more blood. And a lot of convulsing. Through it all, he maintained a firm hold on the slender stock of the makeshift weapon and pressed harder. Blood oozed from the wound like too much jelly on a sandwich when taking a bite. The red substance oozed out in high volume and soaked the carpet and Rico's pants leg.

The zombie shuddered as if it was freezing to death.

Rico worried it might break free and survive somehow. He struggled to keep the piece of wood securely in place.

Then it fell to its side and lay still.

Rico put his hand against his chest, released the protruding object that jutted from the side of the zombie's head, and fell to his back on the carpet. He took a deep breath and sighed with relief.

It only took a few moments lying there like that for Rico to calm enough to focus again. Angie's groans helped pull him back to the urgency of the situation. A zombie had broken through the barrier and now the entrance of the store was wide open.

A noise rose in the building that sounded like wind rising. Was there a storm brewing outside? Or worse, a tornado? Rico listened intently for a continuous rumble, a sound similar to a freight train on a track.

Rico hurried to his feet and headed for the front of the store. Outside looked less like rain now. In fact, the sun brightened the area as he gazed onward. It was silly for him to think bad weather was the source of the noise.

He knew better.

The dead were out there, and Angie's incessant cries were leading them right to him.

Chapter 18

A faded green Dodge Caravan sputtered to a stop in the middle of the highway. Gus put the transmission in 'Park' and tried to start the engine without any luck.

"I think we're out of," he coughed, holding his blood soaked side, "gas, Boss."

Gus' skin was as pale as his knuckles on the other hand that gripped the steering wheel. He coughed again. This time, the taste of blood filled his mouth as crimson colored spittle ran down the corner of his lips.

It took a great bit of effort to acquire the minivan; too bad that it was low on fuel. The back of the trailer was free of the undead, but leaving in the El Camino was no longer an option. The two managed to huff it through the woods to a trailer park despite their injuries. Once there, picking a vehicle to escape was a no brainer. The owner of the van was one of the zombies taken down by Gus's shotgun. Marcus pilfered the keys to the minivan from the corpse before moving out. Once they had the van and were on the street, it was time to find that bitch and the cop.

Not long after the chase began, they reached a fork in the road where Gus needed Marcus to give him directions. Marcus had passed out and was snoring. So Gus just played a quick game of eeny meeny miney mo and drove. He hoped Marcus wouldn't be mad at him if he took the wrong direction. Hell, he could always lie and say Marcus told him where to go before he passed out. Whatever, he just couldn't idle in one place unto his boss woke, so he kept the pedal to the metal.

Marcus opened his eyes a time or two and looked around as if he had no idea where he was. When Gus spoke to him, he was mostly unresponsive. Marcus just groaned and held his bleeding shoulder.

The farther they drove, the worse Gus began to feel. His bullet wound needed medical attention. That was when he got the idea of going to a hospital—if he could find one. He had no idea where he was, or where he was headed. Everything all looked the same: a narrow winding highway and an expanse of trees on either side for miles.

Now it didn't matter where they were going.

They were stranded.

No hospital.

No civilization in sight.

No Angie.

No cop.

Just Gus coughing blood and Marcus passed out against the passenger door. His eyes were closed. The man had lost all natural skin complexion. The area around the bite on his shoulder was enflamed. Gus wasn't as smart as Marcus, but he knew a bad situation when he saw one. They were in trouble.

He checked himself out in the rearview mirror. There were dark rings around his eyes and he was sweating heavily. Blood lined one corner of his mouth. Fighting back a fit of coughs, the large man lost. A fresh lining of blood filled his mouth again.

Once the bout of coughing was over, Gus wiped his mouth with his arm and stared at Marcus.

Marcus didn't move and was cold to the touch. He studied the man further and noticed that he wasn't even breathing.

"Marcus," Gus gently shoved his friend's arm. "Marcus… you okay?"

Of course, he wasn't okay. Neither of them were.

Marcus shifted in his seat, his head sliding down toward his lap.

Gus sighed, looking out the window. "I can try to go for help, Boss."

He knew better than to think he would make it very far. Nevertheless, at this point, what options did he have?

Marcus sat upright in his seat.

Gus turned to him. "Boss?"

Marcus craned his neck. The color in his eyes was gone, matching the chalky tone of his pale skin.

"Boss?" Gus reached out, touching Marcus on the elbow. "You... you don't look so good."

Marcus's maw dropped open, revealing nicotine stained teeth.

"Boss?"

Marcus lunged. Had Gus been attacked in an open space, he might have had a fighting chance. Even with his wound and current condition, he would have easily been able to push away, but not now. Not in the confined space of the front seat of a minivan. He had nowhere to go.

The van rocked.

As Marcus sank his teeth into Gus, the large man cried out. His shouts echoed across the open highway with no one there to hear.

Gus's blood splashed across the windshield as Marcus tore away a chunk from his face. Bone and cartilage crunched in the dead man's mouth as he swallowed down the meaty bits.

"Boss, no!" Gus gurgled, bloody bubbles billowing out where his nose had just been.

With the flesh consumed, Marcus struck again. And again. And again.

The expanse of trees on either side didn't protest.

Eventually, the van stopped rocking.

Chapter 19

Two days had passed since Rico slept for more than five minutes at a time—sometimes sleeping while standing up. His eyelids felt like they weighed a ton, and even the skin on his face drooped so badly it forced a perpetual scowl. Zombies taking notice of the fortress had been steady. Thus far, the numbers of undead had been manageable. How much longer would his luck hold out?

Angie still had fits of withdrawal pains which had her screaming in agony. If she were getting any better, it was impossible for him to tell. At this point, Rico wondered if Angie might die.

While Angie's cries led zombies to the store, the battles to keep them at bay drew more. Once a fray kicked up, any zombie in the immediate area seemed to instantly know and hurried over.

For the first day, he had gathered enough makeshift weapons to dispose of the undead without making too much noise. The wooden canes were total shit. He had gone through the supply in no time. He had found some adjustable height metal canes which really came in handy, along with some long screwdrivers in the hardware aisle. When he wasn't fighting for his life, a lot of time was spent fortifying the storefront barricade.

The electricity had been out for more than twenty-four hours. There were enough flashlights and batteries to make getting around in the dark easy enough. The challenge was not to attract any unwanted visitors.

Food in the freezer had defrosted, and the ice cream had turned to goo. At least Rico enjoyed picking the pepperoni off the once frozen pizza and having it for a snack. Eating room-temperature soup and getting past the gelatinous wad of oil was something he just had to get used to. That was, if he were able to survive the next onslaught.

It was the second day when a situation arose where he had to use his pistol. It was either shoot or die as the numbers of undead attempted to overwhelm him. He survived but had spent a good portion of ammunition. There were six bullets left in the clip. Six shots before he would lose his advantage. Now was the time to pack things up and head elsewhere, but Angie was in no condition to move. He had to bide his time while he could.

The CVS smelled of rotting corpses. Bodies littered the storefront, and a few were scattered up and down various aisles. Rico had become quite proficient at killing zombies. He considered keeping count but abandoned the thought when the novelty wore off.

The sun lowered on the horizon, casting its warm orange rays across the ravaged buildings across from the CVS. He maneuvered himself over dead bodies and various items of the barricade that had been pushed aside to sneak a peek of what the future might bring. Sharp pains shot through the hand holding the gun. Rico had been so tense he didn't realize he was squeezing it so tightly. But tension didn't reside in just his hand. His whole body was a tight bundle of nerves, and he was breathing like he was out of breath. If he didn't get some relief soon, his body was going to give out.

At least Angie had been quiet for a good while now. Maybe she was getting better. Maybe she was dead. That would be some shit. Holed up, trying to save a junkie's life, only to have her die—and him so worn out, he might be too weak to fight his way out of the store to freedom. It was past time he should have checked in on Angie, but that had to wait.

The undead gathered from either end of the street out front heading toward the store. A first, he thought there were just five heading his way. Then he saw a few more, followed by a few more. A dozen gave way to two dozen. Another ten or so joined the deadly ranks before it was over. It would only be a few minutes before his resolve would face its greatest challenge. His body tensed so much he thought he felt his eyes bulge. Running low on ammunition, Rico wasn't sure he was going to survive the next wave of zombies. His arms were tired. His legs were tired. He was tired. The gun felt ten times heavier than normal.

The ghouls lumbered forward under a sky that drew Rico's gaze. It was ironic how the heavens, so breathtaking and peaceful, framed something so destructive and chaotic below. Yellows, light purples, baby blues, oranges, whites, and even a tinge of pink cascaded through the billowing clouds. The breeze felt cool, sliding into the store from the gaps in the barricade. Rico wished the air smelled as fresh as the momentary relief it brought, but it didn't.

The zombies in the street sang a chorus of moans worthy to praise Satan himself.

More walking corpses came into view from around the corners of buildings and from behind trees. Rico's pistol discharge and Angie's cries had nothing to do with what was drawing the undead. The zombies were drawing themselves at this point.

Rico's mouth felt instantly dry.

Aiming the pistol through a gap in the barricade, he targeted the nearest zombie. It was a woman wearing mom jeans dragging the left leg as she lumbered toward him, only 30 or so feet away. Her arms were at her sides, but he knew that would change once she had him in her sight. Arms would rise up. Eyes would go wide. Mouth would drop open in a snarl. Pace would quicken, albeit slightly. Then that moan. It would just go on and on and on and on.

Rico waited until another zombie stepped in line directly behind her before he pulled the trigger.

The female zombie's head kicked back violently. She went down—a splash of black cherry red jutted from the back of her skull onto the zombie's face behind her. The bullet leaving her skull hit it in the forehead. Both dropped to the ground, never to get up again.

Only five more bullets. Five more shots and things were going to get up close and personal.

He and Angie weren't going to make it.

Rico bit his lip and looked back toward the bathroom. His best chance for survival was to lock himself in there with Angie. If worse came to worst, there were enough bullets left for the both of them.

***

Angie lay on the bathroom floor, trying to muster enough will to get up. Her muscles ached from the constant spasms of withdrawal. She felt as bad as she smelled. Vomit, sweat, and shit combined to form one rank-ass stench. Getting off the smack had left her with a giant sized void in her life that perhaps nothing else would ever fill. It wasn't until now she realized what heroin had truly become. As long she could score a fix, she had a friend, a lover, a constant companion to help her get through whatever degrading horrors life presented. Heroin was her savior, her God, her most intimate lover who she shared her body with.

Now that intimacy was gone in a way that she had never felt before. Now she was alone. Death waited as her only companion with its arms around her, and if she just gave it a simple nod, it would take her away. She'd been through withdrawal before, but Marcus had always come through at the last minute with the goods. She had never gone the distance to break the habit. Heroin was one hell of an addiction.

She was at least thankful for Rico, although he hadn't been to her aid in the last few hours. There was no way she could have gone this far without him.

Angie had heard stories of people going through withdrawals and not finding the courage to fight it. They would either give in and find a fix, or in worst case, die. There had to be a desire to live. There had to be a reason to fight through the pain. It was mind over matter as the body threatened to shut down.

However, what did she have valuable enough in life to fight for? Hell, the world was turning to shit. The undead were taking over. That was no world to come home sober to. Yet, here she was, fighting the fight. Why had she lived?

Then it hit her. She lived because she wanted better for herself. Throughout her life, she had been told she was worthless as a human and had always been used by those who claimed to care for her. When Rico saved her, he had cared for and protected her for no reason at all. He even said good things and tried to make her feel better about herself. This had made her feel special in a way she hadn't felt in a long time. Plus, he took care of her over the past days as well as he could. She at least owed it to Rico to pull through after what he did. He provided when she was at her worst. He kept her warm when she was cold. Kept her cool when she had hot flashes. Dried her off after a bout of sweats. Kept the vomit out of her hair and face. Even changed her underwear and replaced them with Depends.

Rico cared.

She'd never had a man show that much compassion before, not even her father.

Finding the strength for the first time in what felt like weeks, Angie sat up and leaned against the bathroom wall. Her lips were dry. Grabbing a water bottle from the floor, Angie chugged the entire thing in seconds. Her stomach churned and most of the water came right back up, splashing across the cold tile beside her. Maybe she still had a ways to go before all the withdrawal symptoms disappeared.

She wiped her mouth and decided she had to walk a little before she could run. Grabbing another bottle, she tried again, this time taking small sips. The water felt good as it traveled down her throat and stayed down.

She picked up a packet of cheese crackers and ate those, too. The process was slow. She didn't want to throw that up as well.

Once the crackers were gone, Angie leaned against the wall looking for the strength to stand. It was time to get out of that diaper, get cleaned up, and to step into a new direction in life.

She had done it.

The withdrawals hadn't killed her. There had been word of a few girls on the street trying to go cold turkey with the intent of getting out of the business. There was no telling how true the stories were, but Angie heard that none of those girls had been able to do it. Their bodies shut down, causing seizures, heat attacks, and strokes. Angie had survived. She felt victorious, like a mighty warrior queen. She just hoped she wasn't celebrating too early. That the victory song wasn't premature. She'd never done this before. What if it was possible for more withdrawals? The calm before the storm?

Angie frowned at the thought.

Lying there for a while, she waited for a new bout of cramps and aches to stir up. They never came. When she was confident they weren't coming back, she stood and turned the water on in the sink. First things first, and the first thing was to get out of the shit filled diaper.

Rico had been nice enough to place a few things on the floor next to the sink. Shampoo, conditioner, deodorant, a comb, toothpaste, a tooth brush, a bar of soap, a stack of dish rags, and a towel—all provided by the store, of course. Beside these things in a separate pile was a stack of clothes. A shirt that read 'I Heart Texas,' a pair of shorts, a pair of shoes and socks... and best of all, a clean pair of underwear. She just hoped the clothes fit. If they didn't, they would be better than the shit and piss covered junk she was wearing.

The battery operated lantern on the counter lit the small room adequately. Angie stripped down and looked at herself in the mirror. Completely naked and covered in her own filth, it wasn't a pretty sight.

Angie let the water run and soaped up a dishrag, determined to clean the best she could with what she had. It took several rags to get the job done, and she had one hell of a time washing all the shampoo out of her hair. It dawned on her that running water was a luxury she might soon have to live without.

***

The street teamed with the undead.

So much so that Rico knew his time was limited. It would be a matter of minutes before the horde of zombies in the street pressed past the unruly barricade blocking the entrance. After a quick glance out the left window near the front of the store, Rico calculated there had to be at least 60 walkers headed straight for him. It was as if they were drawn to each other from their cries and moans, because they gathered in a group before walking toward the store as a pack. For as slow as those things traveled, it still wouldn't take much time to close the distance.

A single zombie approached the perimeter of the barricade and bumped its way past the few remaining obstacles. It lost its footing as it stepped on dead bodies and fell to the floor. A number more of the ghoulish brethren followed in its footsteps—just a few yards away. He couldn't take them all on at once and expect to win.

Stress had taken him to a new level of fear he hadn't experience as of yet. His chest began to hurt, growing tighter by the second. The heart was a muscle, too. Had he pushed it to the point it would soon give out?

Sweat wet his palms. The grip of the baseball bat—an item he found underneath the checkout counter—felt slick. Rico quickly wiped his hands on his pants and prepared for the inevitable. The bat had proved to be a useful weapon in his war against the zombies. Not too heavy so as to slow him down, but dense enough to do major damage as long as the blow found a vital area. The gun snuggly rested between his belt and the small of his back, empty. The last wave of zombies ate the last of his bullets. Surely firing the weapon had to attract more undead. He was damned if he did and dead if he didn't.

Batter up, Rico thought, not waiting for the zombie to pull itself up. The bat's barrel went behind his head and came down in full swing. For this particular attack, he decided against using a batter's rotational, or linear swing—although it would have given him some momentary satisfaction to see its head fly through the air. He used more of an ax swing, imaging a log perched across the flat stump of a tree. When he was younger, he would chop wood for the fireplace. He'd bring the ax down hard, sending wood chips and splinters flying as the wood split in half. Chopping wood was one of the few things as a kid that made him feel like a man, but this wasn't wood, and he didn't have an ax.

The baseball bat came down fast, and Rico's aim proved true. Rather than splinters and chips of maple flying every which way, the gore of a dead man who wouldn't stay dead peppered the area.

The skull cracked with a loud pop. Not unlike a baseball thrown at 90 miles per hour meeting the bat just before launching through the air for a home run.

And that was it.

One hit.

That's all it took.

Rico heaved out a breath—bat in hand, eyes locked on the split skull. The zombie didn't get up.

Rico looked outside. He could fend off a few, maybe three or four at a time, if he could get them to scatter out in the store. He could run around the aisle like playing Pac-Man, knocking them off one by one. But not ten or twenty. By the looks of things, fate was about to test his skill level. Too bad, there wasn't any 'magic fruit' to eat to make him invincible.

Stepping away from the door, the former officer of the law readied the bat.

The only thing left to do was stand his ground.

Rico pushed every stray thought out of his mind and focused on the task at hand. His heavy breathing and the growing moans from the dead might be the last sounds to hear before meeting death.

A hand reached from behind and grabbed Rico's shoulder.

The unexpected attack caught him so off guard he spun around and haphazardly swung the bat.

Angie screamed and ducked just in time to miss getting her head bashed.

"What the … Angie! It's you. You're up," Rico said with relief in his voice.

"I whispered your name, but you didn't—Oh, my god." Angie turned her gaze outside through the window, and then down to the lifeless bodies strewn around on the floor.

"Yeah, it's been bad and about to get worse," Rico said, trying not to sound as hopeless as he felt. This wasn't the time to blow sunshine up Angie's ass, but he didn't want to freak her out either.

"Thank you," she said.

"For what?"

"For taking care of me."

"You're welcome and all, but I don't think now's the time for that sort of thing. We're going to die if we let our guard down." Rico turned and faced the barricade. Two zombies staggered into the store past the barricade and shambled in their direction. "Up for a fight?"

"Do I have a choice?"

Rico licked his lips and shook his head. He looked back at Angie. She had picked up a folding lawn chair and fitted her arm between the seat webbing, creating a makeshift shield. They both laughed at her choice of protection, but what else could she honestly use?

This was, after all, just a drug store.

As Rico raised his bat and ran toward the lead zombie, he thought about that. A drug addict in a drug store. Angie must have been serious about quitting. That was the only answer. He had seen her at her worst. From the time he was out, she could have had almost any type of drugs she wanted. Uppers. Downers. Loopers. You name it. But she didn't take the easy way out this time. She stuck it out.

Rico's bat collided with the zombie, sending a sharp pain that stabbed in his elbow. His chest wasn't as tight as before and he felt a slight surge of energy mask the fatigue. Maybe he had a soft spot in his heart for the little blonde lady. Maybe she was going to turn out to be okay after all.

A few zombies made it into the store, and Rico didn't waste any time disposing of them. Angie stood back with the chair held out in front for protection and watched. Probably more afraid of getting into his way than being unwilling to fight.

Beep... beep... beep...

Beep... beep... beep...

Beep... beep... beep...

A vehicle's horn grew louder from outside. It kept repeating the three short beeps in a row pattern. Rico and Angie rushed over to the window. A white unmarked van circled the parking lot, running over zombies that tried reaching for it.

Beep... beep... beep...

"At least we're not the only ones left alive." Angie leaned over Rico for a better look. "Do you think they know we're in here? You know, to rescue us?"

"I don't know," Rico said. "They may have heard me fire the gun. There are enough zombies out there heading this way to make them think something's up. This is a pharmacy, though. They may just be looking for drugs."

The side door to the van slid open as the van came to an abrupt stop. One man stepped out and hit the ground running. He was tall and wiry like a stalk of corn. Even from inside the store and all the way across the parking lot, the man looked tall enough to play in the NBA. His skin tone was dark black, and his hair was weaved into thin dreads pulled back in a ponytail that reached down just below his shoulders.

The shotgun in his right hand came up to his shoulder and spit fire, followed by a boom that rattled the windows. The undead in the line of fire fell backward.

"Is that guy crazy?" Angie gasped. "There are too many for him to take on by himself."

A zombie came into reaching distance of him and the shotgun went off again.

The zombie's head launched into the air and fell on the hood of a parked vehicle.

"Maybe." Rico smiled. "Maybe not. He at least has enough confidence to believe in himself."

The man didn't waste any more time blasting the undead army. He skirted his way around the larger group and found an opening leading a clear path to the store.

Rico quickly pulled a few dead zombies out of the way to aid the man's entry. After he snaked his way past the barricade into the store, the van's horn started blowing again.

Beep... beep... beep...

Beep... beep... beep...

Beep... beep... beep...

The van's side window rolled down about a quarter of the way and a loud bass thump blared over the radio. Zombies once interested in breaching the CVS now turned all attention to the van. As the undead gathered and scratched on glass and metal to get in, the van began to slowly drive away.

The black man turned his gaze down at Rico as he lifted his gaze up at him. "You guys looked like you needed some help."

"I'm glad somebody noticed. Thanks. What took you so long?" A smile of relief curled on Rico's lips as he reached out and shook the big man's hand.

The man smiled back, showing a row of gold on his bottom teeth.

"Where's the van going?" Angie pointed as the white vehicle slowly drove away, horn still blowing.

"Getting rid of the walkers."

"I can't believe it. Almost all of the undead are heading toward the van," Rico said.

Beep... beep... beep... The horn faded as the van moved farther away.

Rico rubbed the back of his neck and flexed his shoulders. "Okay, what's next?"

"Name's Quin, but most people call me Q."

"Damn fine to meet you, Q. My name's Rico, and the lady's name is Angie."

"Angie is a pretty name." Q tilted his head to the side and closed one eye, and sang an old Rolling Stones tune. "Angie. Aaaa-nnn-gie. Where will it lead us from here?"

Angie blushed.

Chapter 20

An uncomfortable silence fell over the three survivors after Q's short serenade. Angie took a few steps toward the window and looked out. Rico walked next to her and stood shoulder to shoulder.

"They *are* coming back, right?" Angie asked.

The number of zombies in view had diminished greatly. The van lured the zombies away like an ice cream truck chased by children on a hot summer afternoon. If gunshots and even their combined wails drew their attention, it made sense that something as simple as a blowing horn would, too.

The remaining zombies seemingly had forgotten all about the three of them inside. A few shifted from side to side on both feet, and the rest wandered around in irregular circles. What were they waiting for? Had they somehow forgotten about the three living beings inside the CVS? Once a zombie was drawn to a target, did it immediately forget any previous thought it had? If that were true, then it would be useful information to defend against the undead. The last thing they needed to do now was make any kind of noise that would test the theory.

"Just cool it, Bro," Q whispered. He had stepped up behind the two. He was nearly a head taller than Rico. When he whipped his thin dreads from side to side, they gracefully brushed against his shoulders. "No need to sweat. You feel?"

"So, they are coming back then?" Rico was a bit less trusting of the tall man after his overtly flirtatious reply to Angie's introduction. Even during a zombie apocalypse, women were going to complicate matters between men.

"Right as rain, my brotha. They ain't gonna leave one of their own behind. Just be cool."

Rico dropped his head and wearily rubbed his brow. Corpses along the floor mixed with disheveled items from the barricade. He found himself staring at the face of a woman dressed in a business suit. Blood stained the strand of pearls around her neck. It was hard to imagine her as a living person—a wife, a mother. The womanly features of her face had been twisted into a ghastly portrait painted by the likes of Jack Kevorkian.

Then he turned his head, looked at each of the undead, and tried to imagine what they had looked like while still alive, still human. Tears began to well in his eyes.

Q put a hand on his shoulder. "You know what you need, bro?" He reached into his pocket.

"A helicopter," Angie said, turning a smile at the tall newcomer. She fidgeted with her hands, seeming to be unsure where to put them.

Rico noticed her nervous gesture. Then watched her gaze at Q in a way he remembered once eyeing his ex-wife. There was no doubt she was infatuated with the man.

"A helicopter would be nice, but naw, yo." Q pulled something small and shiny from his front pocket. Handing it to Rico, he said, "Here you go, brotha."

Rico looked at it in his open palm. "A dime? What the fuck's this for?"

"Don't be like that, dawg." Q chuckled.

"It's for good luck," Angie chimed. A grin widened on her face.

"That's right my little sweet-thang." Q put his fist out and the two bumped knuckles.

"What the hell am I supposed to do with a dime?" Rico raised his eyebrows and felt like he had just become the butt of joke.

"Like the lady said, Mr. Porto Rico. It's for luck and shit." Q pulled a few shells from a pouch on his belt and began loading them in the shotgun. "You know, life and dimes. They say life can turn on a dime. It's all up to you, though."

"I don't get it," Rico said.

Q's gold teeth showed as he smiled. "You will, brotha. You will. Just keep that dime with you at all times. I got another one." Q patted his pocket. "I've had it with me for years. Got me through some tough times living in the streets. It's gonna get me through this zombie thang, too. One way or the other, it's going to get me through."

Rico nodded at the cryptic advice, pocketed the coin, and looked back out the window. Who was he to criticize the beliefs of another person? Hope was hope in any form it came. Hell, he noticed a Saint Christopher medal around one of the zombie's neck lying on the floor. A lot of good believing in God got him. "How long do you think it's going to be before they come back?"

"As long as it takes, my main squeeze. You feel?"

"Maybe," Rico said. "Let's just say I'll *feel* much better about the situation when we're at some place safe where we can relax."

Angie giggled, and Rico watched as she and the newcomer stared long and hard into one another's eyes. She dipped from side to side with one toe up as if in middle school vying for a young boy's attention.

"You kinda cute, girl." Q took her by the hand. "You ever partake, you know… in chocolate ice cream?"

Angie softened her eyes, and said, "Chocolate is my favorite."

"Look you two, we don't have time for this," Rico said, changing the subject. "Q, how did you and your friends know we were here?"

Q let go of Angie's hand and exchanged his 'come hither' expression for business casual. "We was already headed this direction. Drugs and shit at the drugstore. You feel?"

"Anything in particular you need?"

"We got a lady back at base that got sick. Diabetic or somethin'. I don't know. I ain't no doc. You feel?"

Rico nodded. "Yeah, diabetics are really bad off if they don't take their medicine."

Q continued. "Soon as we hit the street a few blocks down, we knew what was up. The street crawling with those things like that means they found something. And lucky for you, they found that something at the exact store we was aimin' for." Q raised his shotgun toward the pharmacy at the back of the store. "When the crew gets back, we gonna get some digs and split. You feel?"

"I do. The pharmacy has been untouched except for a few things we've taken. You know, for pain and stuff." Rico shifted his weight onto the other foot. "If you don't mind my asking, how many are with you in the van... and at the base?"

"Two in the van." Q said. "Me and one other dude. Some creepy Asian brotha that don't speak no English. Ain't that some shit? America, home of the brave and land of the no speak Ena...la...is."

Q laughed. And Angie seemed to laugh just because he did.

Rico didn't find stereotyping all that funny.

"Anyway, bro. That's all the posse that come up here."

"And the base? Where is it? Who all is in there?"

"Bro, you sure is the antsy type, you feel?"

Ignoring the comment, Rico said, "I was thinking of going to Fort Hood, north from here. It's close to where I live. I might find people I know. Maybe even my mother and father."

"I dig, I dig." Q put his fist out, and after a moment Rico knuckle bumped with him. "I wish I found my mamma. You feel? But we ain't no actual base, bro."

"Then what is it?" Angie asked.

"It's a sporting goods store."

"What, like Academy?"

"How'd you know?" Q put out his fist again.

Rico didn't bump it this time. Instead, Q waited a moment in awkward silence before dropping his hand back down.

"So, you're telling me that you and another group of survivors... along with a dying diabetic... are living in an Academy?"

"Yep." Q nodded. "Best place to be, the way I see it."

"How's that?"

"Everything we need in one place, you feel?"

"Except food and medicine."

"Whatever, bro. So what? You got me on a technicality. Shit is livid out there. You gots to represent if you aims to roll."

"Does everybody back at Academy have a lucky dime?" Rico said sarcastically.

Q shrugged.

"Leave him alone," Angie said, taking Q by the hand. "He's here to save us."

Q huddled next to Angie. "Yeah, bro. What gives?"

"Nothing," Rico said, looking down at Angie's hand, her fingers intertwined with Q's as if they had known each other a lifetime. "Since we don't know when the van is getting back, let's get ready. We just have to be real quiet so the zombies stay away. Does the van have a lot of room in it?"

Q nodded. "It's a cargo van. We can stack up a lot up in there."

"Okay, good. Obviously, we need something for the diabetic. Basic medications are going to be important, too. Let's gather up all the food, water, and essentials we can. We'll place them by the back door. That way when the van gets here we can load up rather quickly. I've got a Harley in the back that I'm not leaving. So, we'll need to let your Asian friend know I will be following you back. No crazy driving. Last thing I need is to get lost out there. I don't know my way around."

"I feel." Q nodded. "Goin' all commando and shit."

"He's a cop," Angie said.

"Oh yeah?"

"I was a cop back in Killeen. So, I have no jurisdiction here," Rico clarified.

"That's cool, bro." Q put out a fist, but dropped it down as soon as he realized Rico wasn't in the mood. "I can get behind the Five-O. Protect and serve. What, what!"

"You know, it amazes me how everybody remembers that line to 'protect and serve.' It doesn't mean I take orders from you."

Q spread his arms wide. "I feel you, bro."

"Let's just start gathering supplies. We don't know when the van will be back. And I want to be ready when it does decide to show up."

*

Rico worked behind the counter passing bottles of drugs to Angie. The drugs were arranged alphabetically with the generic substitutes next to them. He'd call out the names pronouncing them the best he could, and Angie would tell him what to get and what to leave. She filled plastic bags to capacity until having a plentiful supply of pain medication, antibiotics, diabetes meds, and various pills for high blood pressure.

Quin had found a moving cart and walked around gathering up miscellaneous supplies. He started on the drink aisle, stacking soft drinks and water. Cans of food went on next, and then where he could, he piled on the snack food. It didn't take long before the cart filled to capacity.

When Q pulled the cart to the back, Rico and Angie were waiting. A mound of plastic bags set to one side of the Harley. "Looks like you two scored big time. I don't guess they had any medical marijuana tucked away?"

"I wish," Angie said.

Rico shot her a laser stare. "This is Texas. That stuff's not legal here."

"It's all cool, bro. I got all the food and shit we can carry on the van. Too bad there's not room for more. I guess we can always come back. Still some shit I'd like to get."

"That looks like a pretty good haul to me," Angie said.

As impressed as Angie and Q seemed with things, Rico had his doubts. It looked like a lot of supplies, but if this Academy that Quin was talking about had a large number of survivors, then what they had wasn't going to last long at all.

***

"What wrong with your boy?" Q asked, as he removed snack food from the cart.

Angie shrugged, "With Rico? I don't know what's up with him."

"I ain't tryin' to cramp on his style, you feel?"

"I know," Angie said. "Rico … Rico's not like us. You know, streetwise. Even though he was a cop and dealt with people … like us, he doesn't know how to fit in. He tries, but he just doesn't get it." She helped Q unload the cart by the door. The heavier items on bottom would be the first to go into the van and they needed to load it as fast as possible.

Rico had left the two alone. He said he was going to the bathroom and going to get his bat he left at the pharmacy counter.

The smell of rotting corpses filled the air like dank fungus that burned at the nostrils.

"Then what's the dig? He should know he ain't like us by now and have come to grips with it. Is it just me? Is this personal?"

"I don't think so, honestly," Angie said. "Rico likes to be in charge, and you coming here changed everything. There's no doubt he's grateful you and your friend saved us. Now he has to deal with a new situation that's not in his control. The man's got some indecision issues, too. But for me, I'm glad you showed up. We would have died if you hadn't. That's a no brainer."

"For real, yo," Q said. "Although, by the body count out front, it looks like you guys did a good job holding your own."

"Thanks, Q." Angie hugged the tall black man.

Q embraced her. "For what?"

"For saving us." Angie started to cry.

"It wasn't nothin' but a thang, little sweet treat. I got yo' back. Rico does, too."

"I know," she said, looking into his eyes. "It's just been so hard. There are things you don't know about."

Q ran his fingers through her blonde hair. "I know. It's been hard on everybody." When he looked up, Rico glared at him from the hall leading into the back. "Uh..." Q cleared his throat and pushed Angie to arm's length before letting her go. "Let's finish up. The van should be here soon."

Chapter 21

The van briskly careened down a winding road lined with entrances to subdivisions. The Asian man at the wheel no doubt had traveled this way before. He weaved in and out of stationary vehicles like orange cones on an obstacle course.

As Rico had hoped, the van stayed off two lane roads—minimizing hazards along the way. They passed a welcoming sign to Bryan, Texas, a neighboring community. Urban sprawl had provided a bypass through once rural farmland connecting the two towns.

While loading supplies, Quin had told them how main roads leading in and out of the city were near impassable with congestion. Not only that, but the undead flocked to stalled vehicles in search for food.

This Quin guy, Rico had a thousand conflicting feelings toward him. Q dashed in to save them like Rambo. Had he done that because he was so brave, or because he was just that stupid? If Q was reckless, then he and the driver might be leading Rico and Angie to certain doom. Had Angie been on the back of the bike right now, he might have veered off and taken chances on their own. But Angie was in the van with Q and the Asian guy. Despite how Q made it sound by using words like 'they' and 'we,' there was only one other occupant in the van. Sending only two people out on a drug hunt seemed to be a bit irresponsible. There's safety in numbers. Then again, maybe they wanted to minimize their losses if things had gone badly.

Rico had asked multiple times how many survivors were at the sporting goods store. All the while, Q avoided giving him direct answers. Why did he want to keep it a mystery?

Loading the van didn't take long. It's amazing how fast a job can go while your life is threatened. Once the van was loaded down all the way, he realized how little it would amount to if there were a large number of people at home base. The goods probably wouldn't last 20 people more than a week.

A few of the zombies in the street had noticed the van make its stealthy approach to the back, but it wasn't anything a shotgun couldn't handle at the last moment. By the time the noise had attracted any unwanted attention, the goods were loaded and they were on their way.

The pistol stuck away in the small of his back had started to rub a blister on his skin. Surely, a sporting goods store would have a nice supply of holsters.

Rico did his best to keep from riding up the van's ass. There were a few times when he almost got snatched by a zombie hiding between vehicles when he lagged too far behind. It was better if he rode the van's bumper so it could act as a battering ram clearing the way. That was a bit tricky, as the van would hit the brakes unexpectedly from time to time. Once he became distracted while looking at a zombie eating a man by the side of the road, and the van weaved a hard right to avoid a turned over motorcycle. Rico almost didn't see the object in time to swerve and miss until he was almost on it. His heart raced. His knuckles were tight—his grip on the motorcycle firm.

Just when he thought he had enough of this shit, the sporting goods store came into view.

The Academy front parking lot was a treasure trove of walking corpses.

"You have got to be kidding me," Rico said, his mouth wide with disbelief.

***

"Oh, my God." Angie put her hand to her lips, leaning forward in her seat to get a better look out the front windshield of the van.

"It ain't as bad as it looks," Q said, putting his hand on the small of her back. "We been rollin' it tight at this joint long enough. If they was gonna get in, they woulda already. You feel?"

The Asian man looked back and nodded. He had slowed the van to a near crawl. Angie imagined so as to not call attention, but with Rico riding a Harley behind them, she didn't see what difference it would make at this point.

"Shouldn't we go faster? Rico's bike's going to have them coming for us," Angie said.

The driver must have thought so, too. The van immediately picked up speed and turned down a side street that led them away from the parking lot and main entrance.

"How the hell are we even supposed to get in there?" Angie gasped. "There's got to be a hundred of those things."

"More than that, sugar bear." Q ran his fingers over his dreads, clearly not fazed by the mob of corpses eager to get inside the store. "At least that's what this Sarah lady says. She's good with numbers, or some shit."

"Whatever." Angie exhaled loudly and shook her head. "That can't be good. What, those things outside outnumber those inside by how many? Ten to one? More than that? They'll overrun us."

"Don't sweat it, Angie." Q leaned forward and put his arm around her. He picked up a radio on the floorboard and keyed the microphone. "Hey, we're back. Let's get the party started." Q turned his attention back to Angie. "It's cool. Trust me. We got just about everything we need in that place. It's a freakin' fort. Locked down to the ground!"

"I don't know. You've only been there a few days. You don't really know what can happen. Wait—what's that noise? I hear horns!"

"That's part of the plan. The guys know we're here and they're using air horns to get them zombies' attention. Keep them distracted until we sneak our way in."

The driver pointed at something as they rounded the building to the backside of the store. He spoke, but his words weren't coherent enough to understand. At least not at first. Not until Angie saw what he pointed at. A man stood on the roof of the store with a two-way-radio in his hand.

The rear of the store had vehicles parked to form a wall protecting the large rollup door to the unloading dock. As the van drew closer, the man on the roof brought the radio up to his mouth.

A Chevy SUV near the corner of the wall moved out of the way, leaving enough space for the van to enter. A moment later the rollup door began to open. Another person, a black woman in a dirty sundress, stepped out onto the landing and waved the van over. She, too, had a radio in hand. She talked into it briefly and then handed it to a young white girl inside the building.

Once the van passed the wall of vehicles, the Chevy SUV quickly moved back in place to seal it shut.

"See, we got it on lock, just like I said." Q leaned back against his seat and grinned. "Nothin' to worry about. We got out. They wait for us to get back. Easy moneys, yo."

"What about *them*?"

"What, the dead out front?" Quin chuckled. "Those things are dumb as dirt. They're so worked up about that front door that they don't have time to even consider checking out the back. You might say we got some mannequins and shit in the windows to use as bait to keep the zombies there."

"But the doors up front—with that many zombies out there, won't they eventually break in?"

"Nah...." Q waved a dismissive hand. "If they get too rowdy, we can just trick 'em same as we did at the drug store. Use the van to lead 'em away. Then come back."

"Are you sure?"

"Yeah, most definitely," Q said. "We done it a time or two before."

"You have?"

"Yeah, why?"

"If you've done it a time or two before, then why the hell are there so many?"

"I don't know, ho. I ain't no big thinker. I guess 'cause we can't draw *all* of them away with the van. You saw how a few dead heads stuck around back at the drug store when Bruce Lee up there tricked 'em out."

"Yeah..."

"Well, *yeah* nothin'." Q tightened his lips into a tight O. "That's just how it works, you feel? We lead them out, but not all of them go. Since they got mad numbers on their side, no matter how slow the van goes to draw them away, there are a lot that linger around. After a while, they go back to the door. Moaning and whining like the little bitches they are. And thus the game begins again, you feel?"

"So, they just gather up again?"

"They… know," the Asian man said in piss-poor English.

"What?" Angie asked, the van coming to a stop at the open door.

The woman in the sundress stepped up to the van and opened the doubled doors at the back. Without even a concerned greeting, or a 'fuck you,' she began digging through the bags of drugs. Once she had her hands full, she was gone, disappearing back into the store. A young white man who moved the SUV chased after her.

"Bruce Lee is right." Q stretched his arms, preparing to step out the van. "They know we're in here. I don't know how they know, but they do. Somehow, after leading them away, they come back. It's like they can sense us inside."

"Really? They didn't act that way so much at the drug store. It's like they forgot about us after the van led them away."

"I don't know how them dead thing's minds work. Maybe if enough zombies gather in an area, other zombies can sense that and come looking for dinner. Maybe they like magnets, and as the magnet gets bigger, it has a stronger draw." Q unassed himself from the seat. "No more talking. We got shit to do, girl." He rudely climbed over her to get out of the van and didn't offer a hand to help her.

Angie stepped out of the van just as Rico dismounted the Harley.

***

Rico watched the Chevy SUV pull out from the wall of vehicles and followed slowly behind the van into the shade of the loading dock. A woman in a sundress immediately stepped over, opened the rear door of the van, and started scrounging through the goods. He parked the Harley to the side and hit the stop to kill the *thump thump* of the engine.

Welcoming committee of one, he thought. That could indicate that there weren't many survivors holed up in the store. Unless, of course, others hid somewhere with crosshairs of rifle scopes aimed at his chest. He set the Harley on the stand and looked around the large room for snipers.

The woman pulled out several bags from the van and gave him a nonchalant glance as she hurried inside the store. Rico was ready to introduce himself but watched in disbelief with his mouth opened. He wasn't expecting to be received with hugs and kisses, but the way she acted was downright rude. The guy who moved the SUV raced past him.

Q and Angie were having a discussion inside the van but he couldn't hear what about. Was Q hitting on Angie? Were they talking about him? Rico shook it off and told himself not to be so paranoid.

A door on the van opened. A long, black leg exited as the foot searched and found solid ground. Q eased himself out. He turned to face Rico with crossed arms and a shit-eating grin plastered across his face. Angie followed, wearing a none-too-pleased expression.

"Are you people out of your fucking mind?" Rico pointed toward the front of the building. "It's only a matter of time before those things find a way into this place."

"Leave it to the Five-O to stress, bro." Q rolled his eyes. "We cool!"

"No," Rico said. "We *are not* cool. Not with that many of those things out there just itching to get in!"

"Keep your voice down, bro. If you so worried about the situation, you sure don't act like it." Q stiffened his back.

"Angie?" Rico said in a softer voice, his eyebrows lifted.

Before Angie could say anything, Q put his arm around her and pulled her closely. "One big happy family, yo."

Angie turned her gaze to the ground, then back at Rico. "They did save our lives."

Rico pressed his lips together and held his mouth shut. This was no time to show his ass and make a bunch of enemies. He needed to stay in control and not call too much attention to himself.

The Asian man hopped out the driver side door and joined them. His arms were loaded down with supplies from the cab. He nodded toward the back of the van and muttered something in his native tongue.

"Yeah, yeah, Bruce Lee," Q said. "I hear ya." Looking to Rico, he said, "Look, bro. You just got here. After you spend a night or two, you'll see this place is legit. We could use an extra hand scavenging for gear on the outside. With all them dead heads you had scattered in the pharmacy, I know you got this bag. You feel?"

"I don't know," Rico said. "Most of those you saw were stragglers. I was able to win those battles, but you saw what happened when we got severely out numbered. This place is even worse."

"Come on, dawg." Q whipped his dreads back and forth, then ran his fingers over them. "Just a few nights. You look like hell. You could use some rest. Take advantage of our hospitality."

Rico sighed. As much as he hated to admit it, this much was true. He was exhausted.

"Okay, then." Q nodded. "Then it's settled. If you don't want to stay here, that's cool. Stick with us for a while and decide then. For now, get some rest. Do a few runs with Bruce Lee and me. Then you and your girlfriend can be on your way. You can even take what you can carry in supplies. We got guns and ammunition. You can even trade your bike for one of the cars in the parking lot if you want."

Rico thought of the empty gun pressing against the small of his back. If he did decide to leave, he needed to do it on good terms. They might not be as willing to share if they didn't like him.

"I'm not Rico's girlfriend. We're not even what you would call dating. I'm not anybody's girlfriend," Angie said.

The words slapped Rico like a lead weight—taken aback by the unexpected statement. He just hoped it hadn't showed. Why did she feel she needed to clarify this now? Sure, it was true. They weren't dating. Hell, they didn't even know each other. And what he knew of her wasn't that great. A prostitute junkie who admitted she couldn't be trusted. Suddenly that first night of mayhem seemed like lifetime ago. Still, Angie did have her moments where she proved herself. That had been what made Angie special. She showed signs of redemption. His sister Jennifer—who Angie reminded him of—never had.

Q showed his gold teeth. Not in a pleasant smile. His upturned mouth was slightly twisted, pure arrogance on display.

If Rico looked at him any longer, he was going to have to wipe that smile off his face with a closed fist. He turned his gaze down to his Harley and cleared his throat. "I *could* use some ammunition."

The big man unfolded his arms. "There's plenty enough to go around." Q turned and walked toward the door leading into the store.

Rico's hands ached when he let go of the handlebar grips. He had been squeezing them tightly the whole time since he arrived and hadn't noticed until now. His right leg came over the seat, and he stood on the hard concrete—waiting for Angie to make her move. She set her gaze to the floor and followed Q. Rico trailed behind her.

The Asian man went to the back of the van and grabbed a few more items. He muttered something under his breath. Rico could only imagine he was aggravated that none of the others came to his aid. Rico had thought about helping but decided it was best if he and Angie stayed together for now.

"So, is his name really Bruce Lee?" Angie asked.

"He answers to it, so I guess it don't really matter," Q said, placing his arm around Angie again as they walked into the store and down a wide hall. Various rooms lined the hall to either side. They passed a set of bathrooms and entered the store through double swinging doors.

Bruce Lee followed close behind rattling the goods in his arms with each step.

The woman wearing the sundress barreled down an aisle and stepped past everyone without saying a single word. She had a set of keys in one hand and a two-way-radio in the other.

"Let's wait here for a moment," Q said.

Rico heard the radio squawk as she headed down the hallway. The rollup door in the back cranked down with a mechanical whine. When she returned, she spoke into the radio, "All clear."

"Roger that," a faint voice crackled back.

The interior of the store looked like it was ready to receive customers just as any other workday. The power was on and the shopping area comfortably lit. The intercom played light, airy hits from the past at low level through speakers scattered across the store. The walls were lined with various mounted trophies. Deer heads. Boar heads. Tiger heads. Bear heads. Even an alligator head with gaping jaws open lined the walls. Shelves that displayed clothing also sported various taxidermy animals. Bobcats in attack positions. Ducks in flight. Foxes.

However, homages to slaughtered animals weren't what had snatched Rico's attention.

He found himself truly smiling for the first time in a long time.

The rows of locked case shelves at the back of the store were all loaded down with guns, guns, and more guns. And from the looks of it, Q had told the truth. There was plenty of ammunition to go around.

Chapter 22

By the time night arrived, Rico had settled down to a semblance of his old self. The feeling was odd considering the horde of eager corpses awaiting them right outside in the parking lot. Somehow, someway, he was able to let himself relax. Perhaps it was the mood brought on by the others in the group. Or maybe even overexertion finally had its toll on his body and mind. Chalking it up to a mixture of the two, the persistent pounding and moaning coming from the dead outside became a distant haze in the farthest reaches of his mind. Like the aftershock hum in the ears after a long night out at a loud concert—the noise was only noticeable when he focused on it.

So, rather than focus on it and keep dangers fresh, Rico did himself a favor.

He relaxed, tuned it out; there was nothing he could do about it anyway.

The outdoor furniture area provided a variety of comfortable chairs and loungers, along with a couch or two. Drew had arranged some chairs in a circle so they could all look at one another while they ate. Tonight's menu included vegetable soup and bread, chased down by water or soda. The soup had been warmed in a large pot on a camping stove. By Rico's estimation, there were enough cans of fuel to last the group for several weeks. Hopefully enough until help arrived.

The first thing that caught Rico's eye when handed the bowl of soup was the green peas floating on top. He avoided them when he shoved the spoon in and brought it to his mouth. The warmth of the soup slid all the way down to his stomach—bringing with it a feeling of security. It was as if the soup was the best thing he had ever eaten in his life. Rico didn't realize how hungry he truly was. Had one of the other survivors not told him to slow down, he would have slurped down all of his soup in a matter of seconds. He felt slightly embarrassed making a pig of himself and slowed down to savor the meal, which was a good move, because had he downed it too fast, it might not have stayed down.

Rico felt comfortable around the new group of strangers despite the fact that he had only met them a few hours before. He guessed he understood why Quin had avoided telling him the number of people taking refuge inside the store. There were only seven of them in total before he and Angie joined. Had he known there were so few, he may have opted out of following Quin. The group was too few in number to realistically put up a fight with the ghouls waiting to eat them outside. If there was one thing in evidence here, it was that the chaos of luck and fate was no stranger to race.

Quin told them why he preferred to be called 'Q.' He explained that his mother called his brother, Jake, 'J.' And his aunt Clare, 'C.' He had been called a single letter of the alphabet his entire life. Q boasted of being a big shot in the music industry. Rico wasn't much into rap music, but he knew a few of the bigger names. And the likelihood that Q had laid down some sweet beats with Ice T, Triple Six, and Snoop was near zero. Regardless, Q swore he had connections in the music industry. Said he got to know all those guys by, in his words, "Slingin' the green, you feel?" Rico, along with several of the others who had probably already heard this a time or two before, rolled his eyes. Angie, on the other hand, was on the edge of her seat, elbows in her lap, fist against her chin. Eyes wide with excitement. She seemed smitten with this tall, handsome black man. In Rico's opinion, he was just like most people trying to make it in the music business he had read about—full of shit.

Then there was Bruce Lee. Although his driver's license actually revealed him to be one Patrick R. Chang, just about everyone continued to call him Bruce Lee. He didn't speak much that afternoon. Instead, he took it upon himself to wash up the pot and heat up the cans of soup. When it was ready, he spooned out an equal portion in each bowl. Once everyone was seated, he delivered drinks before sitting down to eat with the group. After that, he slowly ate while watching others. Despite his poor

English, Rico got the impression Bruce Lee did get the gist of most conversations.

Every time Rico thought about Bruce Lee's real first name, he had to hold back a laugh. Apocalypse or not, an Asian named Patrick, but who only spoke broken English, seemed rather funny. Rico imagined Patrick trying to say, 'Kiss me, I'm Irish,' on St. Paddy's Day.

Rico wasn't the only one who found the name amusing, because just after dinner, Drew Finley brought up the same observation.

"Ever hear of someone from China named Patrick?" he said, laughing aloud, slapping Rico playfully on the back. Not caring if Patrick or anyone else heard him.

Nevertheless, that's the kind of person Drew Finley was. Like his wife, Sarah Finley, he was a little on the overbearing side. Obnoxious was a good way to describe the couple, but of course, Rico would never say that to either of their faces. Not in a million years. They might talk his ear right off the side of his head if he let something like that slip. Any time a welcomed moment of silence presented itself, Drew refuse to let silence exist. While another person took a turn to say their piece, Drew acted as if he didn't listen and spent the time planning what he was going to say next. In fact, that was what Drew did now. While everyone else was trying to eat while their food was still warm, Drew's mouth ran ninety to nothing. He obviously thought talking was more important than eating. Or maybe it was that he just preferred hearing his voice over eating.

Drew and Sarah Finley had both been Lieutenants with the Salvation Army. They seemed like good people. If half the stories they told about what they did in life before the chaos were true, they probably were. The stories included running a food bank, donating to shelters, and providing for the poor any way they could. The list went on and on, much like their mouths. Once he got used to them though, there was no doubt they were sweet people. Despite their spiritually strong views, Rico found it rather awe inspiring that neither of them talked much about God. The ex-cop just assumed the couple realized no one needed to hear the doom and gloom of God's wrath. Hell, they had all seen it firsthand anyway. It waited just outside the door to consume them.

Then there was Debra. She was a cute, petite girl nearing college age. Although her actual age had never come up, Rico guessed her to be about 17 or 18—definitely in the onset of adulthood. Her parents were none other than Mr. and Mrs. Finley. She was the opposite of her parents in demeanor. Debra kept to herself, much like Bruce Lee, and just watched as the grownups talked. When questioned or invited to join the conversation, she would shrug or sink back into her chair. She was obviously very shy, at least around a lot of people. She didn't act that way when Angie spoke to her. And you didn't have to look twice to know that Drew and Sarah weren't her birth parents. That was because Debra was white. Mr. and Mrs. Finley were from African-American heritage. Both were sensitive about being called anything other just plain old American. An interracial family wasn't something that bothered Rico one bit. In fact, Rico wondered, if humans survived the apocalypse, they might be so few in numbers that racism would disappear once and for all. Everyone would depend on each other for basic survival. There would be no time to pick sides and start fights. Is that what was happening now? Had things become so bad on Earth that the Universe had hit the reset button on mankind and would ultimately bring them together as one? That question was yet to be answered.

Rico did wonder how the Finleys came together as a unit. When he thought about it, he might be up for hearing his own voice as much as Drew's if he had as many good deeds to boast about. The Finleys were the quintessential all-American couple just doing things to make the world a better place.

Rico liked them.

Angie loved them. She especially was drawn to Debra. Rico watched them snickering together about this or that while the others ate their meals.

It warmed Rico's heart to see Angie in this light. A weak woman forced in the wrong place at the wrong time with the wrong people. But that was then. And this was now. And now, Angie had a second chance. A chance to be the person she chose to be. Not bound by drugs or men. Not bound by laws or selfish gain.

It felt good being a part of this group—despite how he had always preferred to be a loner. He liked seeing Angie genuinely happy. She was a new person. Second chances came in mysterious ways. And if anyone deserved a second chance, it was her.

"What are you grinning about?" Angie asked.

"Nothing," Rico said, and drank from his bottled water.

They stared at one another for a moment.

Quin cleared his throat. "So, ah… what's the word on the sickie?"

"Steven is checking on her," Sarah Finley said. "We have the medicine she needs, but none of us know how much to give her. Right before she passed out she said she was a diabetic and needed medicine."

"Yeah," Angie said. "It's pretty easy to overdose on that stuff."

Steven worked as cashier for Academy sporting goods. It just so happened, the night things fell apart he had pulled a double shift in order to work on price changes for the next day. He was the one who let everyone inside the store.

The young man was in his mid-twenties and had lived an ordinary life since high school. Working at a retail store was far from being his dream job, but he basically didn't qualify for any other line of work. Girlfriends took up too much time and money, so there was no love interest for him to worry over. Most of his free time was spent playing video games. Still, as average as he was, he did possess a unique quality. He had a magnetic level of compassion. His empathy made him seem instantly trustworthy. Steven didn't try to run the show—in fact, he really didn't talk all that much. But when he did have something to say, it was always meaningful, and everyone was quick to listen. It had been his prompting that had led Q and Bruce Lee to the CVS.

Rico made a mental note to thank Steven for technically saving their lives.

Malinda Garrett was 'the sickie' Q had referred to. No one really knew much about her. According to Drew Finley, the woman fell ill right after they all had arrived at Academy. At first, everyone thought she passed out from shock, but as she floated in and out of consciousness, she managed to say she was a diabetic. It wasn't until her symptoms worsened that Steven forced the issue to go out and find medicine.

Although everyone else was currently huddled together in the center of the store, surrounded by racks of hunting coats and camouflage jeans, Steven had gone to the break room to be with Malinda. Steven checked on her often and did his best to make the woman comfortable. When asked about Malinda's condition, Steven didn't seem very optimistic.

So, after that, Rico made it a point to quit asking. If Malinda took a turn for the worse—or better, for that matter—Steven was sure to let everyone know.

Rico turned his attention back to Angie. *Where will it lead us from here?* Ugh. Ever since Q sang a line from the song to her, the Rolling Stones tune had become an earworm playing over and over in his head.

Q's chair squeaked and he rose to his feet. He set the soup bowl on a table and stepped over to Angie, ignoring everyone else. He offered her his hand. "Hey, I got somethin' I wanna show ya, you feel?"

"Sure, okay." Angie placed her bowl on the floor, and then Q helped her up. "Where're we going?"

"It's a secret, yo." Q turned and led the way with Angie close behind holding on to his hand.

With that, the two walked away, leaving the others watching as they disappeared out of sight.

Rico almost yelled for Angie to stop. At the last second, he held himself in check and pushed on a piece of meat stuck between his teeth with his tongue. Now was not the time to show his hand.

"Why do you let Q do that?" Sarah asked, breaking the uncomfortable silence that had followed.

"Come again?" Rico looked at his bowl and scooped up the remains with his spoon.

"I see the way you look at her, Rico." Sarah lifted her eyebrows. She reached over and took Drew by the hand. "You can't keep hiding your feelings from her. If you do, someone like Quin will come along and snatch her away."

"Whatever," Rico shrugged and ate the last bite of soup. "We don't really know each other." He wiped his mouth with the back of his hand.

"So what?" Drew said, lifting his wife's hand to his lips and planting a kiss. "Excuse the terminology, but sometimes you just got to take life by the balls and slap them around. If you don't, they will slip right through your fingers."

Rico winced and shook his head. He wasn't in the mood to listen to a self-proclaimed Dr. Drew. "First of all, I don't intend to be doing any ball slapping. That kind of sounds uncomfortable." As pissed as he was, he decided to make it sound like he was joking.

Debra giggled. At least he fooled her. Rico wasn't so sure the others had bought it.

Bruce Lee jingled bowls and spoons as he gathered them up. Though his hands were full, he managed to carry empty drink bottles between his arms and chest. He took them to the back, toward the break room.

Mr. and Mrs. Finley continued with the touchy feely routine. What were they trying to do? Teach Rico how he should court Angie? What was next? Debra joining in and give him some dating tips? Fuck that. Rico found his cue to leave.

"I think I'll help Patrick with the dishes," he said, climbing out of his seat. "It'll give me a chance to check on Malinda and Steven. It would be good to know how she's doing."

As he walked away from the happy family, Rico heard Sarah whispering something to Drew. It involved the police force, or maybe the fact he had been a cop—something of that nature. This spiked his curiosity, but he didn't stick around to find out what it was all about. Instead, he picked up a few empty drink bottles and followed the quiet Asian man to the break room.

Bruce Lee turned as Rico neared, nodding his appreciation. The two men walked together toward the back of the store.

Drew Finley started up his persistent rambling. Fortunately, his voice faded at each steady clop of shoes against tile. What didn't fade was the buzzing noise coming from outside. As long as there were people inside, trapped like sardines in a can, the undead would stay put. Pounding and moaning. Moaning and pounding.

Rico sighed. He wondered how long it would take for that persistent concert hum to grow in the back of his head and to drive him insane.

When they reached the break room, Rico helped Bruce Lee place the dishes in the sink and dispose of the drink empties.

Steven sat by Malinda over in the corner. He was hunched over and slightly shaking.

Small sobs emerged and filled the dank break room.

Steven turned and looked up, all hope gone from his expression. Tears dripped down his cheeks.

Chapter 23

"Keep 'em closed," Q said.

Angie playfully giggled as Quin guided her through the store by the elbow. With both hands up to her eyes, she could have peeked through her fingers if she wanted. But why do that? She loved surprises. And after the last few days, she thought she would never experience joy again. Her heart raced with excitement.

The trek took long enough—probably seemed farther because of her slow pace after bumping into a display and at times brushing against merchandise. Finally, Quin brought her to a stop.

"Okay, yo. Open that mess!"

Angie pulled her hands away from her face and blinked her eyes into focus. She didn't really know what to expect. And realistically, she knew whatever Q had for her couldn't have been much. What was there in a sporting goods store, after a horde of zombies sent everyone in hiding, worth getting excited about? Nothing in particular came to mind. So the excitement was less about the proposition of gain and more over the thrill of the game. It had been a very long time since a man did something other than wave a handful of cash to vie for her attention. Quin wasn't taken in because of some slutty outfit that her pimp had forced her to wear. And he wasn't treating her to a surprise with the meager hopes of some reward in return. At least, that's what she hoped.

"For me?" She tilted her head to the side and smiled. "You shouldn't have."

"It was nothin', you feel?" Q grinned, revealing his gold teeth. "Anything to bring a smile to your sweet little face."

"Aw, thanks. The only thing that's missing is a white picket fence."

Before them was the surprise. Quin had taken the time to set up a tent. It was her own little spot to call home. The rapper want-to-be had set up house, complete with two folding chairs in the front facing a small, steel, wood burning fireplace. Beside the chairs were several bottles of water in an ice chest, a brand new pair of hiking boots that were clearly just pulled from the shelf, and a small mobile-DVD player.

"I wasn't sure what size boots to get you, so I got a 7."

"Close enough. I'll try them on later," Angie said.

"And we even got us a little somethin'-somethin' inside," Q said, unzipping the tent. He folded the tent flap back for her to inspect. "Got a queen size blow up mattress and battery fan."

"Wow," Angie nodded. "Fresh sheets and pillows, too. You didn't have to do this, Quin."

"Please," he said. "Just call me 'Q'."

"Okay, Q." She looked inside the tent again, then at the two chairs placed in front of the tent. "It's just that..."

"Don't worry, my peach." Q puffed out his chest. "We got a few DVDs to pick from. None of that hunting crap they got on the display by the register."

"Peach?"

"Did I say something wrong?"

Angie glared at him. She thought of the names she and her girlfriends used when hustling the streets for a quick buck.

"Don't call me that, okay?"

"What, peach? What's wrong with peach? I love peaches, you feel?"

"I don't care how you feel, Q. Just drop it with the fruit names, okay?"

Looking at the tent, the queen sized bed, the two chairs, it was all coming together. Quin was no different. He was just like every other guy. He just had his angle. They all did. His was just a little more subtle than walking up and asking how much it cost for a blowjob. This was just his way of staking out his territory.

Angie turned and walked away.

"Hey, wait a minute." Quin followed. "What's the big deal here? What'd I say?"

"Nothing, just forget it," Angie said, not looking back.

"Just give me a second," Quin caught up to her, grabbing her by the arm. He yanked hard and spun her around. She fell into his chest, her long blonde hair sliding down across her face. "What is the deal? I go off and make some shit and you just brush it to the side like it ain't nothin' but a thang. What gives?"

"You don't own me." Angie lowered her gaze. Things with Q had moved faster than she expected—faster than she wanted. And despite her flash of anger toward his aggression, she couldn't help but feel a sense of security while held in his arms.

Q closed his eyes and slowly shook his head. "Look, Angie. It ain't like that, you feel?" He lifted her chin but she refused to look at him. Once she finally gave in and met his gaze, he said, "We ain't in no rush for nothin'. I just want to be there for you, yo."

"I don't know." The last several days had changed her, allowed her to feel more independent and believe in herself. As proud as she was over the change, being responsible for herself brought with it a fear of the unknown. She was used to having a man around to tell her what to do. Even though relationships had always been abusive, she felt a strange sort of comfort just having someone—anyone—who cared.

"Hey, you let Rico look out for you, right?"

She nodded.

"Okay then, what makes me any different? I ain't gonna try nothin'." Q raised an eyebrow and slightly shook his head. "If we are in a tent, then you got somebody right there. Shit hits the grits, then boom. I'm in the slide before the slumps start jumpin'."

"What?"

Quin laughed. "Just let me be there to protect you, girl." He wrapped his arms around her even tighter.

Angie didn't refuse. In fact, she felt comfortable. Sighing, Angie let herself go. She leaned into him hard. It felt safe. It felt right. She could hear his heart pounding in his chest. It felt good to be wanted. It felt invigorating to know that someone cared.

"Okay," she finally said after a few moments in his embrace.

"Yeah, yeah!" Quin stepped back and stretched out his arms. "So, what you in the mood to watch? Might as well take our minds off the shit outside when we have a chance."

"What do we have to choose from?"

"We got the movie Friday After Next, Forest Gump, or Ghost Busters."

"What do you want to watch?" she asked, leading them back toward the tent.

"Friday After Next, yo. Figured we could use some mindless entertainment."

"I can get into that. My life's usually so hectic I never take the time to watch movies."

"Really? What was your life like before The Spook, part 2?"

"You know, Q. I've always been a private person—kept my business to myself. But now, with things away they are, I'm just going to let it all hang out and let the chips fall where they may. You want to know what I was doing the night the dead came back again? Hustling tricks and shooting heroin. Not much different from what I had been doing for the last few years. That's it. The girl you want to protect is just a street walking junkie. Or ex-junkie, I should say. Just went cold turkey with the junk. I don't ever want to get on that stuff again. And I don't want to sell my body anymore, either. If I survive this thing, I hope to do something with my life. I'm not sure what. I need to learn a trade, or maybe even go back to school and become an accountant. I used to be good at math back in school." Angie turned and noticed Q had fallen a few steps behind and had his gaze locked on her backside. She couldn't tell though if he was ogling her ass, or just mindlessly following while she told her story. "Am I rambling?"

"Not at all." Q flashed a reassuring smile.

When they arrived at the tent, Angie asked, "Where do you want to watch the movie? Out here, or in the tent?"

Q stepped over to the DVD player and picked it and a disc up. "Let's watch it in the tent. That way, if we get tired, we can just go to sleep."

Angie leaned over and entered the tent after kicking off her shoes. "Hey, once you're inside, the space looks bigger than it does from the outside." She nestled in on one side of the mattress. "Bed's really soft. It beats the hell out of sleeping on a tile floor in a bathroom."

Q entered the tent holding the DVD player by his thigh, right next to a large bulge in his pants. "Mmm hmm. Whatever you said, sugar pie. Whatever you said."

***

"Is she okay?"

"No, she stopped breathing." Steven looked up from Malinda still lying on her makeshift bed. His Academy nametag glistened, the overhead light shining down at him.

"What happened?" Rico asked, kneeling down beside them.

Malinda's eyes were open, vacant and fixed on a single position on the wall. Rico already knew. He had seen it enough before on the job. She was gone.

"I... I don't know," Steven said, his bottom lip quivered. "She needed her shot. Diabetics need their shots!"

Bruce Lee leaned in close over Rico's shoulder. He said something in his native tongue. Rico ignored him.

"How much insulin did you give her?"

"I don't know," Steven said. "I'm not a doctor. I'm just a cashier, remember?" He straightened his chest and pointed at his nametag as if to prove a point. "I was just trying to help!"

"Calm down. I'm not blaming you, but they told me you had some type of medical background," Rico said.

"I told everyone I had some first aid training back when I was a Boy Scout. You know, cuts and breaks, CPR, that sort of stuff."

"If she's not breathing, why aren't you doing CPR?" Rico felt for a pulse in her neck.

"I already did . . . It didn't work. She's dead."

The Asian spoke again, pointing at the woman. Rico thought he picked up the word 'no,' but it might have just been in his head.

Ignoring the man again, Rico focused on Steven. "Where's the needle you used?"

Steven lifted a bag of drugs the plastic syringe and insulin bottle had been shoved under. "I used this one. It was clean, I swear. Had to take it out of the plastic and everything."

"It's okay," Rico said, taking the syringe. "A dirty syringe wouldn't have killed her. That's a big syringe, though. I thought diabetics shot up with smaller amounts. How much drug did you give her?"

"I don't know, man." Steven ran his fingers through his hair, his eyes fixed on Malinda's unmoving eyes.

"How much, Steven?" Rico shook the cashier, pulling him out his haze.

"I don't know. The syringe took a lot to fill it up. I found two different types of insulin. One said it was rapid acting, so I used it. Malinda has been out for a long time, and I had to hurry and save her before she died."

The glass insulin bottle looked almost empty.

"Please tell me you didn't use all of that?"

"Not at first. I gave her one shot and she started to stir. Her eyes opened but it was like she wasn't awake and was fighting to gain consciousness. As she drifted back to sleep, I figured I didn't give her enough. After the second shot, she went into convulsions and stopped breathing."

"Steven, you shouldn't have gone at this alone. Why didn't you ask us to help?"

Steven rocked back and forth and shook his head. "I... I was only trying to help. I swear."

"It's okay," Rico stood to his feet, pulling Steven along with him. The three men paused for a minute in silence. "It's not your fault. Like you said... you were only trying to help."

Steven nodded.

"But right now, I need you to go get us some blankets to cover her with."

Steven nodded again, gave one last glance at Malinda's corpse, and walked away.

Rico needed the young man to leave for what was going to come next. He turned to Bruce Lee and pointed at the empty drug bottle. The poor woman had died of an overdose.

Despite the langue barrier, Bruce Lee understood Rico's point. He grimaced and shook his head. "No good."

"That's right," Rico said. "No good at all." Death wasn't the only fear now. The rising of the dead had to be dealt with. This was no time to get others involved to discuss the 'proper disposal' of a potential zombie. There was no way to know how soon she would turn.

Rico covered Malinda's head with a pillow so blood wouldn't splatter. He pulled the new 9mm from its holster and aimed.

"Better safe than sorry, my ex-wife used to say."

Bruce Lee nodded his approval.

***

Steven was past the center of the store where the grill and supplies were stored. With a blanket in his hand, he turned, making his way back to the break room.

When the gun shot went off, its report echoed across the store, ringing like the shrill call of a bat deep in a dark cavern.

Chapter 24

Angie had drifted off into a slight doze when the abrupt noise jerked her awake. Q was still by her side and looked as surprised as she felt. "That was a gunshot!"

"Some shit must have gone down, yo."

"You don't think zombies got in, do you?" Angie gasped.

"I doubt that, plum." Quin put his hand on Angie's thigh.

Shoving his hand away, she got to her knees and started crawling toward the tent flap. Did Q ever get excited over anything? Perhaps he was too cool for his own good.

"Hate to see you go, but love to watch you leave," Quin muttered under his breath.

"What?" Angie looked back.

"Nothin'," he said, setting the portable DVD player aside. "Let's go see what's going on, you feel?"

"Whatever," she rolled her eyes and stepped out of the tent.

Quin smirked, licked his lips, and grabbed at the bulge in his pants. When he was out of the tent, Angie was putting on her new shoes.

"Well, at least we know the zombies didn't get in."

"How do you know that?" Angie asked, looking up to see Quin trying terribly to sneak a peek down her shirt.

She pulled up the neck of the shirt with one hand.

Quin looked away. "Because, yo. Ain't none of the other muthafuckas running amok all screamin' and shit, you feel? If the undead did get in, it wouldn't be this quiet. People would be shouting and firing guns and whatnot."

"You have a point." She stood to her feet and looked down. "Lucky guess on the size."

"Thanks."

"Now, let's go see what the hell that was all about. I hope no one shot himself."

Quin nodded. "You lead the way."

"Why, so you can stare at my ass the whole way there?"

"No… and even so, what's the harm in looking, yo? You got the goods to make a man sweat."

"What's that supposed to mean?" She knew what it meant. And even though he was acting inappropriately, she couldn't help but feel flattered.

Quin didn't reply. Instead, he just smiled.

Angie blushed, which only made Quin smile even more. She turned her gaze to the floor and started walking.

It didn't take long for them to make their way across the store. When they reached the commotion, Drew Finley and his daughter were standing next to Steven. Sarah tightly hugged on the young man.

Steven was in near hysterics—in full blown breakdown mode—crying his guts out. He shook and sobbed. All the while, Sarah Finley patted him on the back and let the tears soak her shoulder.

"What happened?" Angie asked.

Before anyone said anything, Rico and the Asian man stepped out of the break room and started toward the group.

"The school teacher didn't make it," Rico said, coming to a stop just a few feet from Steven and Sarah. He put his hand on Steven's back. "We need to do something with the body."

"It was all my fault," Steven cried out in a gurgling release of sorrow.

The emotional flood ran anew. Sarah didn't seem to mind. She softly spoke words into Steven's ear and gave Rico a displeased glance.

Rico stepped back and looked to Quin and Angie. "Where have you guys been?"

"We was watchin' a movie, yo. You ain't the law in here. No need to keep no tabs on me."

"I didn't mean it like that," Rico said.

"And where was you?" Quin puffed out his chest. "What the hell happened? Who fired off a round up in this joint?"

Rico sighed, his gaze dropping to the floor. "I had to do what needed to be done."

Steven cried harder. "I… I was only… trying to… help!"

"We know, dear." Sarah patted his back. "We know."

"What the hell you mean you did what had to be done? That bitch didn't turn, did she?"

"Watch your language around my daughter," Drew said.

Quin looked to Debra and nodded.

"We just had to be sure," Rico continued. "She died peacefully. There was nothing we could do. We were just too late getting her the medicine she needed."

Patrick pointed at Steven and said some words no one else seemed to understand.

Steven burst out into violent sobs. "I murdered her. I'm… a… murderer."

"No you're not, honey," Sarah assured.

It was obvious Steven wasn't listening. He was too busy crying.

Rico gave Drew a concerned glance.

Drew nodded.

"Look," Drew said. "Maybe it would be better if Steven took a walk. Took some time to cool down and clear his head. We can talk about what to do with Malinda after that."

"Sounds like a good idea," Angie said, stepping over toward Sarah to help. "Let us ladies handle this."

No one disagreed. Angie, Sarah, and her daughter Debra joined Steven in one big group embrace. After the hug was over, the three women led the grief stricken cashier away.

"Hey, Angie," Rico called out.

She turned back, leaving the two other women as they continued on with Steven.

"Can you give him something to calm down?"

"Yeah." She nodded with closed eyes. "We got plenty of downers from the CVS."

"Good. Make that happen."

"The man needs to rest. Maybe he'll wake up with a clear head tomorrow," Drew said.

Q put his hands on his hips. "Hell, we all need some rest, yo. Give me some of what he's havin'."

"Not a good idea, Q," Drew said. "We need to have our wits about us. The world is an unmistakable danger. Like a mirror we can't see through quite cle—"

"Yeah, yeah, preacher man." Quin tossed up a hand. "No drugs. I get it."

With that, Angie turned away and jogged to catch up with Steven and the other girls.

"So, what are we going to do with the body?" Rico kept his voice low. He was tired and didn't want to draw this out any longer than he had to.

"Did you seriously have to shoot her in the store?" Drew asked.

"What would you have rather I did?" Rico grumbled. "I didn't want to take any risks with her waking up. I've already taken too many chances since everything folded. Besides, what's done is done. So let's get past that and talk about this corpse in the break room. I don't know about you, but I don't intend to wait for Steven to come back around. He might start a scene. If Angie gives him a strong dose of drugs, and I think she will, he'll be knocked completely out until tomorrow. By then, the body will start to smell. So, we need to do it now, while he's away, and get the body out before things get nasty."

"No good," Bruce Lee said.

"Yeah, what he said," Rico said.

"You have a point," Drew agreed.

"For real, yo. I don't want no stinky bitch near my digs."

"I feel," Rico said, not caring if Q thought he was mocking him.

"So then, what do you have in mind?" Drew asked.

"I say we move her now," Rico said

"Where to?" Drew asked.

"What kind of question is that?" Quin threw up his arms. "Anywhere but in the store."

Rico nodded. "Think it's safe to sneak her out back?"

"Now?" Drew asked.

"Yes, now."

"I don't see why not."

"Good," Rico said. "Between the four of us, it shouldn't take long. She didn't seem like a heavy woman to begin with, but the extra hands will get it done quickly. The blankets and stuff that she was using in the break room are good enough to wrap her up in. We can use that to take her outside."

"Then what?"

"As much as I want to be holy—no offense, Drew," Rico shrugged.

"None taken," Drew said.

Rico continued, "I don't see that we have the time or resources for a funeral. I'm not going out there and digging a hole when we have an entire parking lot of undead just on the other side of the building. I want to spend as little time outside as humanly possible."

"For real, yo."

Bruce Lee nodded.

"Okay then," Drew said. "So you want to wrap her up, tote her outside, and just leave her in the grass?"

"Well, I think we'd be better off if we just tossed the body in the dumpster out back," Rico said. "I know it sounds like crap when I say it that way, but what else are we going to do? Did any of you really know the woman? Did Steven even know her? It's probably 50 yards from the back lot to the grass area. There'll be stragglers for sure and there's no need to risk our lives over a dead body."

Drew and Quin nodded. Bruce Lee just stood there, clearly trying to make heads or tails of everything. From what Rico could tell, the man was picking up on what mattered. Move the body. Be quick about it.

"Then what are we waiting for?" Drew said. "Let's get this over with before Debra comes back. I don't want my little girl seeing this."

Rico motioned for them to follow him to the break room. Malinda's excretory muscles had loosened and wet the makeshift bed. Bodily gases floated in the air, encouraging everyone to work faster in removing the body.

"That's some funky shit already up in here." Q coughed a little and spit in the sink.

"Drew, gather the sheets at top—help me wrap her up." The two had her wrapped tight like a mummy in little time. "All right, Q, you help Drew at the top and lead the way. Ready? Okay then, lift." Rico lifted the legs and followed the two from the break room.

Bruce Lee led them toward the back and eased the door open. With a quick glance outside and a sweep with his gun, he looked back in and waved the men to move. They were outside and had the body in the dumpster in a matter of moments. The breeze was light and felt good against Rico's skin. It made him wonder how long it would be before they could come out of hiding and enjoy the world once again like before.

As they ran back toward Bruce Lee and the open door, Rico glanced to the sky. He wondered for a moment about dying himself. About becoming a corpse. About roaming the wastelands of America forever. About the pain. About what it must feel like to feel yourself rotting away. He thought of the galaxy. Of the space dust that caused all of this. Of what things out there might be far worse. He didn't like being outside. It was starting to get to him. As soon as he found himself rushing past Bruce Lee and stepped back into the store he felt better. Secure.

"Let's go ahead and remove anything in the break room that will remind Steven that Malinda was in there."

Everyone nodded, and the four men made their way back to the room.

"I have a feeling it doesn't matter what we do," Drew Finley said. "Steven was pretty shaken up. Come tomorrow, we are going to have a lot to deal with on our hands."

"I know," Rico said. "I know." He turned from the hall into the break room and saw the three girls standing by Steven, who was sleeping in his bed. "What the...?"

"You took care of Malinda?" Sarah asked.

"We took her outside. Don't worry about her. She's at peace."

Q poked his head over Rico's shoulder. "Why you bring him back here?"

"Right after I gave him some pills, he insisted he wanted to go back and be with Malinda. We told him the plan to move Malinda out of the store. That didn't seem to bother him too much, but then he said her spirit still lingered in the room and he wanted to be there with her. The guy wouldn't take no for an answer. We barely got him back here before the drugs kicked in. He's down for the count," Angie said.

"You know, I'm too tired to give a rat's ass about any of this now. I need sleep. We all need rest. Tomorrow will come and we'll deal with it then." Rico pushed his way past Q and headed into the store.

Drew called out, "Good night."

Rico threw a dismissive wave into the air and immediately felt like a heel for storming out the way he did. Everyone in the group had basically been nice to him and they were concerned over Malinda and Steven. Tomorrow, he would make it a point to apologize to everyone. Blame it on fatigue. They'll understand.

He heard the doors opening into the store from the hall. Q led Angie by the hand toward their tent.

Q saw Rico staring and winked. "Good night. Don't let the zombies bite." His laugh faded as they strode away.

"Yeah, fuck you too, asshole," Rico said, only loud enough for him to hear.

Chapter 25

Rico slept until around noon. He woke and found the others pretty much just keeping to themselves in their own tents. This did seem a bit odd, but he guessed it was none of his business how others spent their time. Still, with 'no one minding the store,' so to say, the group was vulnerable to the unexpected. There really was no one in charge and no one held accountable to keep current of the situation. What of the storefront? The barricade still in place holding tightly? Any other possible entrances they had to worry about? How about food? He knew there was a supply, but he had never taken inventory.

Steven was still sacked out in his bed in the break room. He didn't even stir when Rico heated a can of ravioli and ate his lunch.

After he ate, Rico made a quick inside perimeter check and verified all was well. He avoided spending much time at the front, and spent even less time when he neared Q's tent. Fortunately, there was no activity inside to set his imagination into action.

***

When darkness fell, there was a feeling in the air totally different from the night before, despite the fact it all looked the same. Everyone was out and about. Dinner had become the social hour. They sat around in the center of the store, each in their own lawn chair. Patrick, aka Bruce Lee, stood by the grill making everyone grilled cheese sandwiches with the last of the bread. Everyone sipped on drinks and made small talk while the food was being cooked. The groans and moans of the dead outside lingered in the air like a thin mist. The noise threatened to become thick fog and engulf everything in the store. The zombies wanted more than anything to get inside, but they couldn't, so the mist would just have to remain as it was.

He wasn't sure what was up, but something felt different.

And he didn't like it.

The only person missing from the group was Steven.

"I don't think it's a good idea to let Steven wake up in the break room," Sarah Finley said. "He's going to be lying right where Malinda had been. That can't be good."

"She has a point," her husband agreed.

"But he wanted to be there," Rico said. "You have to consider that not everyone grieves the same way. If you isolate him from what he thinks he needs to fix himself, then you're only adding to the problem. Since you guys have been here, that break room has been his home. He chose that room to take care of Malinda because it had running water and a kitchen. Waking up to the realization that woman is gone will happen no matter what. It will happen if he woke up in a tent, in the bathroom, or yes, even in the room where she died. It just doesn't matter. Steven will just have to learn to deal with the past. But the past is not what I'm worried about."

"You're not worried about Steven's past?" Debra asked.

Her mother glared at her. This caused the young girl to sink back into her chair and sip on her water. When her mother returned her attention back to Rico, she seemed to relax. Rico found that odd, but let it go.

"No, I'm not so much talking about Steven's past," Rico said. "If anything, Steven has one of the biggest hearts I've ever seen. His empathy for others is exemplary. It's us as a group I am worried about. I'm worried about our future. Our future and the undead outside. We have to come up with a plan to secure our future, and we have to do it soon. We can't just stay here forever. Either that or—"

"Well then," Quin chimed in. "Since you seem to have it all figured out, yo. What you got?"

"Hey, I never said I had it all figured out. But look at it this way. You guys have been out looting, right?"

Everyone nodded.

"Okay, so... who is to say someone doesn't come sticking their noses in our business? This place is a perfect target for looters."

"Man, we ain't got no food up in here!"

"That may be true, Q." Rico patted the pistol on his hip. "But we have guns and ammo. And lots of it."

"I see where this is going," Drew Finley said.

"I can't believe I'm hearing this," Sarah gritted her teeth and crossed her arms. She looked so red in the face that she might explode at any moment.

"You okay?" Rico asked.

"I'll tell you when I'm not okay, okay?" Sarah stood from her chair and stomped angrily away.

Rico threw up his arms with confusion. "What did I say?"

"Nothing, you said nothing," Drew assured.

"She's crazy," Debra said.

"Debra!" her father scolded.

She shrank into herself.

"My wife... she isn't angry. She's sick."

"What do you mean?" Rico asked.

"She crazy, yo!"

Debra giggled. Her father glared at her. This made her quit laughing.

"Let me explain," Drew said. "My wife needs medication. Medication that we ran out of two days ago. She's bipolar. Without the meds, she'll get worse. Her emotions are going to be amplified. Like a rollercoaster. Highs and lows. Only, without what she needs... her highs are going to be very high. She'll make you think she's on drugs, she's so happy."

"And her lows?" Angie asked.

Drew sighed. "Her lows are bad. Any little thing will trigger it. She can't control it."

"Then what did I say to upset her?" Rico asked.

"It could have been a number of things," Drew said. "But if I had to pinpoint it on any one thing—it was suggesting we aren't safe here. No one wants to hear that. No matter how true it may be. And like the highs of a rollercoaster, her lows are very low. Like I said, any little thing can trigger it. She will be rainbows and sunshine one minute and Hell's wrath the next. I have learned to live with it. I love her. As long as she has the medication that she needs, for the most part it stays in check."

"That's not a problem, yo." Quin nodded. "We can get that shit. We need to do another raid anyway. You feel?"

"That would be good, since it was my fault for not telling you all about this earlier. I was hoping we would be rescued before she started going downhill," Drew said. "In the meanwhile, everyone please just give her some space. Above all, realize that she isn't upset. She just needs to feel safe."

"Well, if that's what she needs—this isn't the place," Rico said. "I agree. We can do another raid. Get some more supplies. We are running low on some of the food items already, but staying here is a big mistake."

"What do you have in mind?" Drew asked.

Before Rico could explain, Bruce Lee walked around handing out grilled cheese sandwiches. When the Asian handed out the last one, he turned off the grill, sat down beside Debra, and began eating. Rico watched as Debra batted her eyes and smiled at the young man. When Rico looked to her father, he didn't appear to have noticed.

"What do you have in mind?" Drew asked again.

"Oh, right." Rico nodded, taking his gaze away from Debra and Patrick, who were both sharing playful glances at one another. "I... um. I think that it would be best to move camp. I don't expect to do it overnight, but we can't stay here. I think that once we have the supplies we need, along with the medication for Sarah, and when Steven comes back around—it will be time to leave. It's not safe here for two reasons. One is obvious." He pointed toward the front of the store. "The dead outside clearly want in. As each day passes, more and more of them gather. Before we know it, they will be spilling out into the street. And that's saying a lot considering how large the parking lot is out there. I don't know about you, but I find it hard to sleep at night knowing that we could be overrun at any moment. All it takes is one single crack in the glass for the dead to come crawling in. And no amount of ammo is going to take care of that. We need to find somewhere safe. Somewhere secluded. Somewhere less populated."

"I like that idea," Debra said, still casting playful glances at Patrick.

The Asian man didn't seem to mind. He played right back.

"What made you decide against going to a military base? I thought you wanted to go to Fort Hood?" Angie said.

Rico took a deep breath and puffed it out. "

Yeah, I know. I'm conflicted. I think what had me change my mind is the fact that the undead tend to gather in once place. As the numbers grow, more and more seem attracted. The radio instructed everyone who could flee to head to a military base. Well, if a large number of humans gather in one place, then don't you suppose the undead can't be far from sniffing them out? Then the undead numbers will grow until either the military kills them all, or gets overrun by zombies. Either way, our best bet is to be where there are the least amount of zombies for us to have to defend against."

"But where would we go?" Angie asked.

"I don't have that figured out yet," Rico said. "But my bet is north. When we do our next outing, we can try to pick up a road map or something. We can pick out a destination on the map as a group."

"You said something about others trying to raid this place," Drew said.

"Yes." Rico nodded. "Right now, I don't think the undead outside are all that much to worry about. Yes, their numbers are growing, but realistically, they would have already gotten in if they were going to. What worries me the most is people like us. We can't be the only survivors. If you think we are, then you're only fooling yourself. This place," Rico waved a hand around, "is exactly the type of store I would raid. Food and medicine aren't the only things people need. Guns and ammunition are essential for survival. In our current situation, protection is at the top of the list. It's only a matter of time before someone else gets the idea and comes busting down the doors to steal from us. If having a horde of ghouls in the parking lot doesn't give away the fact that we're in here, then finding us during the raid will. It plays out one of two ways in my head. One, they get in and play nice. Everyone wins. We all team up."

"Safety in numbers," Drew Finley said.

"Right," Rico agreed. "But then there is the second potential outcome. The outcome that I feel is a hell of a lot more likely." He took a deep breath, and said, "Outcome number two has us at a disadvantage. If others come and try to raid this place, they either must have a lot of manpower, or are totally insane. With the amount of undead outside, you would need either an army, or think you are God, to get in here. So, if someone does break in, then we are in for a rude awakening. Whoever breaks in is not going to want to play nice."

"Man, I bust up a nigga if he try any shit!"

"That's all well and good. And impressive sounding, too. But if I can help it, I would rather just avoid the situation all together," Rico said. "We already have the van. If we can, I think it would be smart to get a second one. Load each van with guns, gear, and food. Split up the people that ride in each van into two teams. If something happens to either team, the other one still has what they need to keep going. And that's exactly what I want to do—go."

"Go where?" Debra asked.

"The country. Out in the sticks. Some place near running water, and a place where wild game is plentiful. As far away from other humans as possible."

There were a few minutes of silence while everyone finished their food and sipped on drinks.

Drew Finley cleared his throat. "I agree. Steven should be coming around soon. I'm surprised he's still asleep now. Once we know he's going to be okay, we can plan another raid. Get another van, medication for my wife, and a road map."

Rico nodded.

For the first time since they all started eating, Drew's eyes went wide as he looked over at his daughter. He stood to his feet, set his plate in his chair, and grabbed Debra by the arm. "Get up."

"What? I didn't do anything. I'm still eating."

"You're done eating when I say you're done eating. Now get up, young lady."

She grumbled and did as her father said. Rico and the others watched as Drew dragged his daughter by the elbow away from the dining area.

"She's a little young for you, don't you think," Angie asked, glaring at Bruce Lee.

The Asian shrugged, a sheepish grin plastered across his face.

"That's my boy, yo!" Quin leaned up in his chair, fist-bumping Patrick.

Patrick blushed and went back to finishing his food. He may not have spoken much English, but it was obvious he knew what had just happened. Why Quin had gotten all excited. Why Drew had suddenly grown angry.

Everyone finished their food in silence. When they were all done, Quin took Angie by the hand and led her back toward the tent they shared. Rico watched them leave, vulgar images of flesh against flesh flashing in his mind. The thought made him boil with rage on the inside. Patrick began picking up the mess left behind. After he had all the plates together and double-checked that the grill was off, he made his way toward the break room to wash the dishes. Rico didn't follow him this time. Wasn't in the mood to help. His mind was on other things. Angie things. Quin wasn't good for her. And he didn't see why she was attracted to him.

However, that wasn't the only thing he didn't see.

Had he gone with Patrick to the break room, he would have seen that Steven wasn't in his bed. He would have seen that Steven was gone.

Chapter 26

Steven felt the clouds underneath his feet as he walked on air. It wasn't the first time he had ever felt this way. He was drowsy while being wide awake—floating above his own skin. Above everything. The drugs took the edge off reality.

Before, when he stood at the storefront window of his previous place of employment, it made him sick to look at the droves of undead outside. Made his stomach churn to see the rotting corpses up close. The festering decay. Maggots writhing in and out of eye sockets and beneath serrated skin. The black flies buzzing overhead. Bones jutting from elbows and jaws. Skin torn from muscle. But most of all, those eyes. The milky white glare. Before, he couldn't bring himself to look them in the eyes.

What he did to Malinda had made him feel less than human. Made him feel ashamed. Unworthy. Coupled with the emotional distress he knew he was going through—like any sane person would—the drugs they forced on him to sleep helped quell the internal carnage.

In a moment where he should have felt sickness and despair, he felt alive. Energized. Untouchable.

"I should feel sorry for what I did to you, Malinda," he muttered under his breath, making his way toward the double doors. "But I don't. You're free now."

He had a better full frontal view of the zombies outside from this position. Bodies lined the doorway looking in. Packed tightly, shoulder to shoulder, the creatures pounded against the door moaning with excitement at the fact that they could see him. The drugs numbed the sounds they made to a dull throb.

It was as if he was watching a movie on a large screen TV.

Steven grabbed the door handle. The steel was cold to his touch.

In the parking lot, the moonlight cast an eerie glow on the ravenous horde. Bodies shifted in the darkness in an unholy dance. With his hand still on the door handle, he looked directly at the zombie before him, pressed against the thick glass. Its face was a distortion of decay, dried blood, and mashed skin as the ghoul was forced against the door by the mob behind it. The creature still managed to snarl and chomp its teeth at Steven, clearly eager to break free of the invisible barrier. Touch his living skin. Feel his warm body. And yes, taste his meaty substance.

What would it feel like to be eaten alive? In his state of transcendence, would he even feel it? Would he somehow mesh with the cannibal corpse and become part of its consciousness?

He stood there for a long time watching the dead, wondering what it felt like to rot. Decay. With a grin on his face, he continued his stare. The zombies stared back, their eyes fixed on him with raw hunger. Steven looked past the twisted Earthly façades in hopes of seeing something remaining of their lost humanity. As he did, he noticed something familiar. It all made sense now. It was his job to open the store. These were customers. There were so many of them because it was Black Friday. Academy was having the biggest sale of the year. He'd seen it before. Getting to work at 7:30AM even though the store didn't open until 10:30 that morning. There were already hundreds of people out front. Some of them were sitting in chairs at the front door waiting to be let in. First dibs on the sales. Others were camping in tents, still not awake yet, but they would be soon. Steven had to force his way through the crowd to get to the front door. Once he got inside, he thought the crowd would force their way in. Somehow, someway, they hadn't. He got in and managed to lock the door behind him.

"We're no different than you, you know?" he said, looking at a ghoul slobbering against the glass. "Once I did open the doors to let all those shoppers in, they were nothing but a bunch of animals. Hmm, that's all we are. Animals. You want me to let you in, don't you? So you can go shopping. Is that what you want?"

The zombies groaned, pounding against the glass.

Reality shifted in Steven's head. It felt like a locomotive sped through his mind and faded into the distance with debris following in its wake. His spirit returned from above and into its suit of flesh. Steven's jaw dropped as the flood of emotions threatened to drown him.

"I did a bad thing," Steven continued, taking his hand away from the door handle. "I... I killed a woman. I didn't mean to. I've never killed anyone before. I didn't mean it. It was an accident.

You understand, don't you? Of course you do. You don't want to eat people. You didn't ask for this. You didn't ask for that space dust to infect you. It wasn't your fault. It was an accident. Just like what I did was an accident. I understand now. You're not the bad guys here. You're the victims. And that makes us the bad guys. Because… because we let this happen. We let it happen again. We should have fixed this. Should have had a plan. But we didn't. Why? Why didn't we have a plan?"

Steven pounded his fist against the glass. The zombies became even more excited.

"I can give you what you want." Steven produced a revolver from his back pocket and pointed it at the glass. At the zombies behind it. "I can end this for you. I can end this for everyone. I can end your pain, but is that what you really want? Or is what you want more selfish? Like the rest of the world. You want only what's good for you. You want to eat me, don't you? You want to come into my store and eat me and my friends. You want to eat me because I killed a woman. It was an accident. I'm not a doctor. How was I supposed to know how much insulin to give her? I was only trying to help. I didn't know. I didn't know."

Steven sighed and lowered the gun. He stared out at the moon for a long time. The zombies shuffled about in the parking lot like waves in the ocean. The ghouls before him at the door pressed their bodies against it in hopes they could be all that much closer. His grip tightened on the butt of the gun.

A single tear fell from Steven's right eye. The drugs in his system were no longer strong enough to push all the pain away. Knowing that made him angry. Knowing that he would feel even worse come tomorrow when the drugs wore completely off made his stomach feel like it was in his throat.

He swallowed dry and hard.

The gun rose to his temple as tears began to fall.

***

A tent wasn't much protection from anyone or anything wanting to get inside, but the four walls and roof brought isolation Angie so desperately needed. At least with the rest of the world blocked away, she could relax and pretend. Tonight was an ordinary night like when she was just a kid. Nothing better to do than relax with a friend by her side while mindlessly watching Ghostbusters on a DVD player. The only thing missing was popcorn and Cokes.

It wasn't long into the movie when Quin slowly brought his hand up and caressed her back. His touch cracked the illusion of the innocent past and reminded her of what and who she was today. With each stroke, his fingers moved lower and lower down her body.

A part of her wanted to slap his hand away and tell him to lay off, but the other part of her craved the attention. Wanted him to keep going. Keep going until it went all the way. She needed it. Spent her entire life feeding off the attention of men. She hated herself, but it was true. She was never going to get away from her old lifestyle. Once a prostitute, always a prostitute. Just because she wouldn't be exchanging money or drugs this time around didn't mean she wouldn't be exchanging something else. The sense of protection was a high commodity at the end of the world, and protection always came at a price. Sadly, when it came to men like Quin, she knew what that price was. Even sadder than that, she felt comfortable paying that price. There was a certain need that could only be fulfilled by giving control of her body away to a man who knew how to take it.

Q's hand went lower.

She didn't stop him.

***

"I can't stand it, Drew." Sarah's arms crossed her chest as she rocked back and forth.

"It's okay, honey." Drew reached over and ran his fingers through his wife's hair. They sat in their tent across from each other. "I explained it to the group. Everything will be fine. They're planning to go back out soon. We can get you your medicine then, I promise."

"You told them?"

"I had to. I should have said something earlier when they went out for the insulin. I was hoping we'd be back home before you started having problems again. I . . . I thought maybe God might keep you from going over the edge—"

"Well, He didn't, and now everyone's going to think I'm some crazy person."

"Being bipolar is nothing to be ashamed about. You were just built different. That's all. Everyone has some medical issue in life. There wouldn't be so many of those drug commercials on TV if it wasn't true."

"I just wish the zombies outside weren't so loud." Sarah's eyes moistened and her voice cracked into a sob.

Drew lowered his hand to her shoulder and gave it a squeeze. "They're outside. We're safe in here. Don't let them bother you. Hopefully the Army will arrive in a few days and get us out."

"But I can hear them . . . hear what they're thinking. They're in pain. I don't know how to describe it. They need me. They need us. They want us to become part of them by eating us."

"Honey, it's just your imagination. You're scared and it's running wild. I'm sure all of that will go away when you start taking your meds again."

"I know, I know, but it seems so real." She put her palms to her face. "I just feel so exhausted," she whimpered. "It's like I have no control of my mind. It keeps shifting from one thing to the next."

"I know, honey. I know." He held her tightly.

Drew Finley was used to dealing with his wife's emotional turmoil, but right now, her internal problems were the least of his worries. Although he was next to her doing all that he could to bring comfort, his mind was elsewhere. He kept thinking of his daughter and the growing connection with that Asian man. Aside from his name, the group knew little to nothing about him. Now he was watching his little girl start to grow fond of him. This wasn't the time or place for crushes—especially not with a man more than ten years her age that didn't speak near a lick of English. He wanted to tell his wife. Get her opinion on the matter. Maybe she would tell him not to worry and that he was just being over protective. Now wasn't the time for such things. Telling her now would only upset her even more. He thought to have a talk with Patrick, but wasn't sure that would honestly do him much good. The man wouldn't understand him one bit.

***

Rico sat by his tent propped up in the gun and ammo department. As safe as everyone else felt in this place, he didn't feel safe at all. That's why he was busy preparing for the worst. He had pulled a backpack off of the shelf in the hiking department, and right now, he was loading it with gear. It wasn't that he planned on leaving anytime soon, but if for some reason he had to jump ship at a moment's notice, he wanted to be ready. He stuffed 4 bottles of water and packs of crackers into the backpack, wishing he had a few MREs to stick in there, too.

Rico had a 9mm Beretta 92FS pistol on his hip. Out of all the guns available, he chose the Beretta because of its historical military sentimentality. The 92FS replaced the legendary 1911A1 Colt 45 sometime in the 80s. The grip fit his hand perfectly, and the magazine held twice the capacity of the Colt. Too bad Academy didn't have a Tommy gun with a 100 round drum. It would have been the perfect zombie gun. He still had to make up his mind to go with a shotgun, or an AR15 style rifle, when it came to choosing a long gun.

A small .22 revolver caught his eye, so he grabbed it and placed it in his front pocket. Next came all the ammunition he thought practical enough to carry and four extra clips for the 9mm. As much as he liked the Beretta, the .22 would probably be easier to find ammunition for if the need were ever to arise. He packed an extra shirt off the clearance rack along with a six pack of socks.

Once he was finished, he set the backpack next to the tent flap and crawled inside to rest. The blowup mattress was comfortable enough, but try as he might, he just couldn't manage to drift off to sleep. His mind raced with all things present, past, and future.

What about Angie and Quin? How far had things gone between them? Did he really have feelings for Angie? Hell, by now he thought he'd have been able to sort that shit out. What about the advice the Finley family had tried to give him? He wouldn't be chasing his tail over Angie had he taken their advice.

Then there was the trip back to CVS to consider. Would they be able to find a suitable van like the one they had when it came time to leave Academy? He knew he told them he wanted to head out in the country somewhere, but maybe Fort Hood, or one of the other bases would be a better safe zone? If only the emergency message over the radio would update, he'd feel better about going there. Going back home made him think about Pop and about his possible horrible fate. His mother and father—his own flesh and blood—were in Killeen. When it all came down to it, he thought about Mary Etta, his ex-wife. Despite the trouble in their marriage, he hoped that she was okay. That she was faring better than he was.

He thought about the undead out in the parking lot, and about Sarah needing medication. How it all made sense now. She didn't seem wound too tight emotionally. Happy one minute and sad the next. Or zoned-out like the first time he met her in the back when they arrived at Academy. Was being with someone like that in the group safe? She potentially could get them all killed.

Above all things, he was thinking about getting Angie and fleeing into the night while they still had a chance. While they still had a choice. At least he'd be in total control of their fate. It was the most selfish action he could take. He wondered if he could live with himself if he and Angie did up and abandon the others. But what if Angie refused to come with him? Would he still want to leave? It was a question he couldn't answer. His indecision frustrated him to the point that he decided he was going to look for something at CVS to help get his ADD straight again.

His thoughts faded into the darkness, and he finally started to nod off.

"Rico! Up! Up!" Patrick shouted from outside the tent in broken English, and then sputtered out a bunch of words in his native tongue.

The only word that Rico made out besides his own name was 'Steven.' Rico didn't speak Asian or Chinese, or whatever it was Patrick spoke. One thing that did translate well with the universal tongue of any language was tone, and right now, Patrick sounded panicked.

"Steven!" Patrick said.

Rico sat up and crawled out of the tent. "What is it?" By the time he stood to his feet, the noise echoed across the store.

The gun's report reverberated off the Academy walls like an opera singer in a narrow hall made of glass.

Chapter 27

Rico and Patrick ran down the center aisle past racks of hunting jackets and hiking gear toward the sound of the shot. Rico's bare feet *slapped* the cold tile with each frantic step forward as he tightened the belt on the holster across his waist. Patrick turned down a narrow lane, briskly running between the women's workout clothing and the bathing suits. Rico followed, with one arm closing the distance between him and Patrick. The other hand reached for the gun.

Once they stepped past the women's wear, the two came to a halt before the registers and the front doors just beyond. The undead were there to greet them as usual—banging and eager, the shatterproof glass preventing their entry.

It was a sight Rico thought he'd never get used to seeing. All he could imagine was the glass exploding inward and a flood of zombies pouring in like an angry swarm of ants. He shook it off and motioned for Patrick to stay put while he eased around the service counter to see what lay just beyond.

A few steps later, two legs lying on the ground came into view near the doors. Rico looked over at Patrick, closed his eyes, and bit his lip.

Patrick gingerly stepped over to Rico's side. "Steven."

"Steven," Rico said. He put the gun in the holster and continued around the counter, reluctant to get any closer to the doors.

But he had to.

Steven was lying on his side, his body sprawled out like a drunk who passed out on the floor rather than the couch, but this was no frat party. This wasn't a domestic disturbance call because some punk kids were playing their music too loud and drinking too much. No, this was real life. As Rico looked down at the body—

the hole in the side of Steven's head—the blood still dripping out—he couldn't help but think back on his time as a police officer. At how mundane and trivial so many of the call outs had been. Domestic disputes. Noise ordinances. Bar fights. Drunk drivers. Prostitutes. All of those people, the ones he dealt with every day. The ones that made his city seem so terrible. They were just living their lives. Living their lives the way they wanted to. None of it compared to this. This pressure everyone was under. The relentless lack of hope. The awareness of what the future may never be like again. As Rico watched the blood pool on the cold tile around Steven's head, he felt ashamed at ever believing his job as a police officer was really that hard. This—their new life—it was hard. And honestly, he didn't blame Steven one bit for what he did. At least now, the young man was free. He was free from the terror of waking up every day to that buzzing drone of moans and pain. Free from the fear of getting eaten alive and knowing that it was only a matter of time before one of them sank its teeth into you.

Rico envied Steven in a flood of emotions he had never felt before.

Suddenly, the pistol holstered on his hip felt much heavier.

It was obvious there was nothing he could do to help Steven at this point. Still, Rico knelt next to the body and felt for a pulse on Steven's neck. He hoped like hell he wouldn't detect one, knowing he'd be the one to end any prolonged suffering.

The roar from the undead outside increased. Rico looked up at the deteriorated flesh on the ghastly faces and felt an icy tingle on the back of his neck. Something touched his shoulder, and he jumped.

Patrick came to his side to offer a hand of comfort. "Bad . . . very bad."

Rico cleared his throat and rubbed his hand across his mouth. "Yeah, man. Not good at all. He, uh, he didn't need to go out this way." He leaned over and picked up the gun. The barrel wafted the perfume of a spent casing. He put the gun in his back pocket as shoes hitting the floor approached.

Drew walked into view with his arms wildly swinging from his side. He abruptly stopped and placed one hand on a counter.

After momentarily rocking back and forth as if he was on a boat, he steadied himself. "Is he dead?"

"Yeah, Steven's gone now." Rico rose and placed a hand on the butt of his pistol.

"Lordy, Lordy. That poor man. I wish he had come and talked to me first. I could have given him hope. There's always hope."

"Where are Sarah and Debra?" Rick asked.

Drew waved a hand. "I told them to stay in their tents. I gave Debra a gun. She knows how to use it."

Rico nodded.

"Do you know what happened? You didn't see him . . ."

"No, no. The drugs must have worn off. We didn't get here until afterward." Rico sighed. "I guess everything that went down was just too much to handle. Took the easy way out."

Rico's palms began to sweat, thinking about it. *You can take the easy way out, too, Rico. Do it.*

"Well, we can't leave him here," Drew said. "How do you want to do this?"

Rico mulled it over a bit. "We should wait till morning to move the body. Maybe dump it in the trash bin before we head out to the CVS. We can—"

"No," Drew interrupted. "I don't want my wife or my baby girl to see this mess. We do it tonight. Just the thought of a dead body in the store will drive Sarah crazy." Drew quickly raised a hand. "Uh, not crazy, crazy. I meant upset."

"I knew what you meant. Okay then, let's do it like before and get Quin to help us," Rico said. "Since it's night time we need to be extra careful. I know that none of the zombies have crossed the vehicle wall yet, but I always worry about that every time we open that door. We need to move as fast as last time."

Patrick and Drew nodded.

"Where is Q anyway?" Rico asked. "Surely, he and Angie heard the gun go off."

"I'll go get him if you and Patrick want to get a blanket or a rug to wrap Steven in."

Rico grabbed Drew by the arm just as he started to walk off. "No, I'll go. Angie's my friend." Rico hesitated. "I, uh, I want her to be reassured everything's okay and talk to her a bit." The words carried slight desperation.

Drew nodded and looked like he was about to say something. About to comment on the concerned look most likely plastered across Rico's face.

However, before he could say anything, Rico tried to save as much dignity as he could by turning and walking away.

***

Drew led the way toward camping supplies with Patrick lagging slightly behind him. The last thing he wanted to do was tell Sarah about Steven committing suicide. Learning of his death was sure to send her off on another emotional cliff. As much as he tried to protect Debra from things, he knew her to be strong. If nothing else, the zombie apocalypse had matured her in a positive way. Instead of becoming clinging and needy, Debra joined right in with the rest of the adults and pulled her weight. His little girl was growing up and becoming a woman, which unfortunately, opened another can of worms. Maturity also brought along with it some negatives. Since he and Patrick were alone, now seemed to be the best time to see if he could make his concerns known. Drew came to a stop in front of a shelf containing sleeping bags.

"All right, Patrick. I want to talk to you about something, and I'll do my best to let you know how I feel." Drew waited for Patrick's expression to show some sign of understanding, but gave up after a few seconds. "I've seen the way my daughter looks at you."

Patrick's eyes widened for a split second.

"Good, you do understand me, don't you? At least a little." Drew glared. "I've seen the way she looks at you, and I've seen the way you look back at her. In fact, there's been more than one occasion where she's volunteered to help you do some things around here. I didn't think much about it at first, but now . . . Okay, I'm rambling and that's wasting time and doing us no good." Drew slowly raised his hand and pointed a finger right at Patrick's nose. "You're too old for Debra. She's just starting to grow into a woman. Her life's screwed up enough right now with those things outside. This isn't the time or place for her to get her heart fluttering over a boy. You'll only end up hurting her, and we've already been through enough pain. We've already lost enough." Drew sighed and turned away, grabbing a sleeping bag from the shelf. Had he just wasted two minutes of his life he would never get back?

"Debra?"

Drew shook his head. "You don't understand a word I'm saying, do you?" Frustrated, his hand began to shake. "Just stay away from my little girl. Got it?" He poked Patrick in the chest with his finger with the demand.

Patrick brought his arm up and knocked Drew's arm to the side. "She's not a little girl any more, Drew. She can make her own decisions now."

"What the fuck? You speak English? You could understand us this whole time. What the hell?"

"Yes, I speak English just fine. And apparently Mr. Holy Roller knows how to cuss. I was born in America, Drew. My parents named me Patrick, for the love of God. Of course I speak English."

"But all this time... Why did you pretend you didn't?"

"I have my reasons," Patrick said, taking the sleeping bag from Drew. "Some of my classes in college dealt with behavior modification. I've always had a fascination with people. How they think and react to situations. I knew if I pretended to understand only a little of what was being said, eventually I'd be treated like I wasn't in the room. People would start saying what they really thought in front of me—show their true self. I like to hold my cards close to my vest and surprise people when I play them."

"But this isn't some stupid game. It's life and death. You shouldn't have acted that way. It, it's deceiving. How can we trust you from now on?"

Patrick giggled and shook his head. "We can talk about trust later. Let's get back on what I've observed. You people spend most of your time talking about pointless things. The 'what ifs' and the 'maybes.' You're too afraid to take control and are waiting for Superman to come save us. That's weak, and we need to be strong. The situation is too dangerous for us to hide like this. It's more than that. We're in a prison just waiting to become victims. We should go back into the real world and try to live as normal of a life as we can. Those things out there don't change anything. Pioneers had to deal with wild animals and American Indians. We'll have to deal with zombies. Your daughter likes me because she sees it that way, too. She thinks it's foolish of us to hide and worry. The police guy's idea about going north. Living out in the sticks away from everything. We should have done that the day after we met up here—before that army of undead gathered outside."

"But we couldn't. We had Malinda and—"

"And nothing. We could have brought her with us, and if she died, then she died. We risked everyone's life by trying to save her. What did that get us? Steven's death and Malinda dead anyway. We should leave now. No reason to wait. No reason to gather more supplies first. We'll take what we have and get whatever we need along the way. This place... those things outside. They're killing us. Just look at Steven. They're tearing us down, and we don't even see it. We need to leave. Telling me to back away from Debra won't save her. Us working together will. You worried about Debra and Sarah's safety? Then take them away from this place. I'll be right there with you."

"I'll do no such thing." Drew balled his hands into fists.

"Mr. Holy Roller has a temper, too." Patrick ignored the threat. "You talked about trust earlier. That's really funny because I know all about you."

"All about what?" The tone in Patrick's voice made Drew's heart skip.

"Debra, she told me about her past." Patrick clutched the sleeping bag tighter. "I've seen plenty of white people adopt black kids, but I'd never seen a black couple adopt a white kid. So I asked how that came to be and she told me."

Drew's shoulders sagged, his fists falling loose.

"That's right," Patrick said. "She told me all about her abusive mother and the kind of environment she grew up in. How her mother *entertained* men in her apartment for money. You were one of her mother's clients. Sarah, your wife, still to this day knows nothing about it."

Drew lowered his gaze to the floor. "Because . . . because of Sarah's issues we had some problems. I'm guilty of allowing the sins of the flesh to get the best of me. I'm not proud of what I did."

"Debra also told me when she was old enough that her mother sold her to other men for even bigger money."

Drew's head snapped up. "I never laid a hand on Deb—"

"I know," Patrick cut him off. "She told me that, too. And how she watched one of her mother's John's beat her to death while she hid in a closet. When you found out, you came to her rescue."

"I knew her mother had a daughter, but I never knew she was prostituting Debra. When I read the story in the paper, I learned that there weren't any relatives for Debra to live with. She was going to end up in an institution. I . . . I felt like God told me it was my responsibility—"

"Oh, please, man. Again with the God stuff?"

"Let me finish. I'm not preaching, damn it. I'm speaking my heart. I'm not perfect, but I do feel like God works through me sometimes. God presented an opportunity after my sin to do something good. Debra needed a family, and Sarah and I were in the perfect position to take care of her. We worked things out with the state, and after a couple of years, Debra became ours. Sarah and I love her very much and will do anything to keep her safe."

"Yeah, Debra told me how hard you had to work for the adoption to go through. You guys went to therapy with her every week for that two year period. She genuinely loves both of you. Debra said that even if her mother hadn't sold her to men, she would still rather have you and Sarah as parents."

"She said that?" Drew's words cracked.

"She did. She loves you. And I love her. She loves me, too."

"But she's sixteen!"

"And in a little more than a year she'll be eighteen. Look, life's been hard on Debra and she's a lot more mature than most sixteen year olds. She can make her own decisions right now. How you react to her decisions will affect how she feels about you. So if you don't want to ruin what you have with Debra, then you'll let her come to me."

"I... is that a threat?"

"You can call it whatever you want, Drew, but I will say this." Patrick stuffed the sleeping bag under his arm. "I have seen how your wife looks at Debra when she talks with Angie. Pulling your daughter away when you need to let her grow is—"

"No one tells me how to raise my baby girl."

"That's just it, Drew. She isn't a baby girl any more. She's a young woman."

"I know. I see her growing right before my eyes. I just can't force myself to let go."

"You can't protect Debra for her whole life. Take Angie, for instance. She and Debra have a similar past. It's good for Angie to be around because they can relate, but Sarah keeps them apart. You and everyone else need to get your heads out of your fear-filled asses. We need to start building our lives again. Otherwise, we'll all end up like Steven, letting fear become our master."

"I... I don't know what to say."

"Then don't say anything. Let's just get back and clean up before Rico and Quin return."

Drew nodded and wiped his eyes with his hand. He stepped off toward the storefront.

"Oh, and Drew."

"Yeah?"

"Your secret is safe with me so long as my secret is safe with you."

Drew didn't know why Patrick wanted to continue to play silly games, but right now, he was in no mood to discuss it. "Whatever."

***

The barrel of Steven's gun poked Rico in the ass with each step to remind him it was still in his back pocket. The gun had been used just minutes before to take a life. He wondered why the thought of that didn't bother him more.

As Rico walked toward the tent, he kept thinking about what Drew and Sarah had said about love. How he needed to make a move on Angie before someone else like Quin made it first. He guessed the reason why he was so hesitant about it was because he wasn't sure how he felt about Angie. Did he have feelings for her simply because they had survived for so long with one another as support? Or was it more than that?

However, before Rico really had the chance to ponder the concept of his true emotions, he was standing in front of the tent. What he heard coming from inside answered all of those questions for him.

The back of the tent bent and pulsed with the throbbing vibrations indicating what was happening inside.

Angie moaned, calling out Quin's name. Only, this wasn't a moan like that of the dead outside. This was a moan of pleasure laced with unbridled lust.

Rico didn't know what to do. He just stood there. Anger filled him. The more he watched. The more he listened. It just rose up inside. He imagined himself ripping open the tent flap and shoving his pistol in the back of Quin's head. He imagined seeing the look on Angie's face, her body bare glistening with sweat. How she would be relieved to find Rico there to rescue her from her violent rapist. The gun would go off, splattering Angie across the face and chest with Quin's blood and chunks of pink and red brain. The tall black man's dreads flopping about as he fell limp to his death in the tent.

'Thank you,' Angie would say.

However, Angie wasn't saying thank you. She was calling out Quin's name between gasping breaths of pleasure. A cry of passion no one could mistake for rape. Angie wanted it. She begged for it.

Quin was inside of her, and she loved it.

Rico bit his lip so hard that he tasted blood. Whatever he felt for Angie—or whatever he *thought* he felt for her—died in some way.

The two were so engrossed in lovemaking they ignored the gun shot. Then Rico remembered seeing both Q and Angie with MP3 players and earbuds stuck in their ears. They were probably jamming to music while Q jammed it to Angie.

He turned around and walked away before doing something stupid.

It didn't take long before he found himself with Patrick and Drew at the front of the store.

"Where's Quin?" Drew asked.

"It doesn't matter." Rico brought a hand up and rubbed his forehead. "Let's just do this so I can go to bed."

Drew looked over at Patrick. Patrick dropped to his knees and zipped up the sleeping bag with Steven inside. The two lifted the dead man from the front, and Rico grabbed the legs as he had done before with Malinda.

The walk back to the dumpster had Rico thinking who was going to be next. If he had his way, Steven would be the last.

*

The entire time Rico lay in bed, unable to fall asleep, all he could think about was how Steven was the lucky one.

Rico's gun still felt heavy on his hip, even though it lay inches away by his side.

Chapter 28

The next morning, Rico was the last to arrive at the dining area. Patrick dutifully stirred a large pot on the side burner of the grill. Debra wrote in a notebook. Drew devoted his full attention to Sarah, who sat glassy eyed, staring into space. Quin sat next to Angie. He had a pocketknife out, scraping under his long fingernails. Angie had her arms crossed with her eyes closed while leaning on Q's shoulder, earbuds in listening to her MP3 player. No one looked Rico's way.

Well, this is awkward, he thought. So much for a crisis bringing everyone together. Steven's death had caused everyone to withdraw into themselves.

Without any fanfare, Rico left for the break room. He took out six bottles of water from the refrigerator and put them in a bag. Why did the store still have power? There was no way to know, but he couldn't imagine staying there for another five minutes if it didn't. The experience in the CVS had taught him that. Rico had never been claustrophobic until the zombies had him and Angie boxed in with the power out.

When he made his way back to the group, Patrick was dishing out oatmeal into bowls. Rico went about handing out water and giving a customary good morning with each delivery. Drew gave him a smile and a nod, Debra said thank you, Q lifted his nose in the air and took two, acting as if he did Rico a favor. Angie didn't stir.

Patrick passed out the bowls of oatmeal and joined Rico over by the grill where both stood and ate without exchanging words.

Spoons hit against plastic bowls with occasional scraping noises. Bottles rose to lips with gulps of satisfaction. Everyone ate in silence, focused on their own little world. It just might as well have been a group of strangers randomly eating at a restaurant.

Rico thought of a hundred ways to break the silence. From using humor, to giving a heartfelt speech, to giving a good ass chewing like he got in the military.

Debra beat him to it.

She cleared her throat, setting down her empty bowl. "Sure was good. Thanks, Patrick. Could have used a little dash of sugar, but I liked it." She picked up her notebook and started writing again.

Patrick kept his gaze straight ahead and acted as if he didn't hear Debra mention his name. The Asian was one strange bird. Rico sensed something was just not quite right about him, but couldn't put his finger on it.

It was obvious the elephant in the room wasn't going to eat itself. It was time to take a knife and fork to it. Rico put his bowl down and chugged the rest of his water. "Thanks for making breakfast, Patrick."

The Asian turned to him and gave a slight nod.

"It's really too bad Steven's not here to share it with us." There, he did it. Rico looked about to gauge reactions.

Angie stopped eating—her mouth still open. Q set his bowl down and burped. Sarah didn't flinch, and Drew looked up with sad, glistening eyes. Debra darted her gaze up from the notebook for a second but continued writing.

"Guys, we can't hide from what happened last night. Steven took his own life. I wish he had talked it out before making such a final decision. He didn't, so there's no second chance. I know he blamed himself for Malinda, but she would have died anyway had he done nothing. I don't know if the drugs we gave him to sleep put him in a state of mind to kill himself. He was by the front of the store watching the zombies when he pulled the trigger. Steven took the easy way out." Still not having everyone's attention, Rico shouted, "Bam!"

All eyes turned to his direction. Angie pulled out the earbuds.

"In a split second, it was over. How about it, guys? You tired of all this shit, too? Ready to give up? I'm going to come clean and tell you I gave it some serious thought last night."

Angie gasped. Q chuckled.

"Why do you think I had those thoughts? Because I spent my time worrying about the *what if's* of the situation. Fear kept growing the monster sleeping under my bed to where the only way out seemed to be pulling the trigger and joining Steven and Malinda in the dumpster." Rico reached down and pulled the pistol from the holster. "My gun was right there next to my bed last night. I took it in my hand and brought the barrel under my chin." He lifted the gun and placed it under his chin. "All I had to do was pull the trigger—just like Steven. It'd be over in an instant. Bam! Dead. No more worries. No more anything." He let his words hang in the air for several seconds.

"But you know what? I was able to separate the *what if's* from reality. What if the zombies get in? We die, right? What if we get bit? We turn into one of them. What if we run out of food and can't get anymore? We starve. When I focused on the *what if's,* I lost hope. But when I held the gun to my head, I had a grasp on reality. There were no *what if's* concerning pulling the trigger. My death would have been certain. At that moment, I felt ashamed of myself. I felt ashamed for giving the power of my reality over to my fears. I put the gun down and slept with a clearer head than I have in a while. I want to live. I choose life." Rico put the gun back in the holster. "And I'm going to fight believing I can win from this point on. If we hope to survive as a group, we all have to think the same way. Does anyone else feel differently? Let's get it out in the open now."

Drew Finley looked back at Q and Angie. When they didn't say anything, he turned to Rico. "I think it's safe to say we're all upset over Steven's death. And we'd be fooling ourselves if we didn't say our fears have a way of controlling our actions. I do like the way you addressed our situation head on. It does put it in better perspective and helps us think things more clearly. It's time to focus. All we need is a plan."

"All right, let's plan to move out tomorrow at daybreak. We'll spend the rest of the day coming up with a plan we can all agree on," Rico said.

"I have one request," Drew said. "Right now, Sarah's having a hard time keeping things together. It's going to make the move more difficult. Can we at least get her some medicine so she can have her wits about her during the escape?"

"You know, that's probably best. There are only seven of us now, and we're all going to have to give one hundred percent if we hope to make it. We can go out this afternoon. Shouldn't take but just a few hours. I . . . we owe Sarah that much if we expect her to help us."

Drew put his arm around his wife. "See, honey? You're going to get your medicine today." He leaned over and kissed her forehead.

"It doesn't matter," she said, eyes locked on her breakfast. "We're all going to die in here."

Rico went to Sarah's side and patted her shoulder. "No, we're not. We're going to work together and make it out. I promise."

"Okay, so, I was talking with Patrick last night and," Drew cleared his throat, "Well, I mean, I was talking at Patrick... and I think the idea of going someplace secluded is a good idea. Do you think we can get a map and another van today?"

"I don't know about the van, might have to take that SUV out in the back. It won't hold as much as a cargo van, but it's right there and we have the keys for it," Rico said.

"Sounds good."

"Since Quin and Patrick have gone out together before, I say we just keep it that way. Drew, you can stay here and watch over the ladies. I'll tag along with them to help out."

"I want to go," Angie said.

"No," Rico firmly said.

"Yeah, peach," Quin said, pecking her on the cheek. "You'll be better off here, you feel?"

She bit on her little finger. "Okay."

"Then it's settled, yo." Quin glared at Rico.

"Don't leave right now," Debra said, stepping forward and taking Patrick by the hand.

Drew went to say something but put himself in check.

"We can wait, but the sooner the better," Rico said. We need as much daylight as we can get. I say we go back to the CVS. It wasn't that far away and I think I remember seeing some road maps by the counter."

"Hell, we got maps at the counter here, yo."

"I know, Quin," Rico said, trying to act more civil to the man than he felt toward him. "I've already looked through them. All of those maps are gaming maps. Shows the layout of local lakes and hiking trails. Nothing that will be of much use to us. Trust me."

"Whatever, yo."

"Then I say we leave in a couple of hours. That gives each of us time to prepare." Rico patted the gun on his hip. "I think I might break the pistol down and give it a good cleaning." He turned to Q. "Do you know how much gas the van has right now? Wouldn't want to get out there and find ourselves stranded."

"I don't know, yo. I ain't never checked. Bruce Lee is the one who normally drives."

"Gas... how much? Fuel? Petrol?" Rico said slowly to Patrick, using his hands to gesture pumping gas.

Patrick made a face as if trying to understand and then gave a thumbs up. "Good."

"Okay, good then. We'll be able to rock."

Debra smiled and led Patrick away holding his hand. Angie and Quin headed back toward their tent, which left Drew and his wife alone by the grill.

"Is Sarah going to be okay?" Rico asked.

"You don't have to talk about me like I'm not here, okay?" Sarah said. "I'll be fine. I just need my medicine. You don't know what it's like. Feeling this way. You think I don't realize that my life is a rollercoaster? Well, it is, and it makes my head hurt just thinking about it."

"I'm sorry," Rico said, not sure what he should say—if anything at all.

"Here." Drew pulled a piece of paper from his pocket. "I figured we would be doing another run for supplies soon, so I wrote down what she needs."

Rico took the paper, studied it for a moment, and then stuffed it into his pocket.

***

"I wish you didn't have to go on a run before we pack up and leave this place," Debra said, a gust of wind blowing her blonde hair in front of her eyes. She quickly pulled it away and faced the breeze. The roof was her favorite place to sneak off to.

Patrick stepped up behind her and wrapped his arms across her chest. "I wish we didn't, either. I know it's selfish, but I wish you and me could just up and leave on our own."

"Then why don't we?"

"You don't really mean that, do you? You could go off and leave your parents behind?" Patrick asked.

"Part of me wants to. Not that I want to leave them. It's just that I know they'll flip out when they find out about us. It'd just be easier not to deal with it."

Patrick let her go and scratched the back of his head. "Don't worry about your parents. You just let me handle things. Your dad knows you're growing up—it scares him. I think I'll bring him around eventually. Once that happens, he'll convince your mom everything is okay."

"Maybe, but what if he freaks and you two get into a fight or something?"

"Honestly, it's the chance we're going to have to take. As romantic as it sounds for us to leave and live a life together, we need to stay as a group. It's really our best chance for survival. One day though, when all this is over," Patrick waved a hand toward the mass of zombies below, "we'll move away and have a place of our own."

Debra walked to the edge of the roof and looked down. "You know, when we talk about starting a life together, I get all happy inside. Then, when I turn and face reality, our future seems to be a dream that will never come true. How can we hope to ever live in peace when monsters like that are everywhere?"

"Look at them though." Patrick came to her side. "There's a bunch of them but they're stupid. They're driven by one instinct, to satisfy hunger. It shouldn't take long for us to outsmart these things and do away with them once and for all. I'm sure the government just needs a little time to regroup before putting a plan in action. If we escape to a remote location where we can wait it out, then the dream will become a reality."

"Do you really believe that, or are you saying it just to make me feel safe?"

"I'm saying it because I believe it. History is filled with stories where groups of people are faced with insurmountable odds and they survive. In this case, all of mankind finds themselves fighting for the same side. There's no way this alien zombie menace will wipe out Mother Nature's greatest creation."

Debra grabbed Patrick's hand. "When you say it that way, it makes it sound like we're at war unlike any war before."

"It is a war. And there can only be one victor."

***

Two hours latter Rico, Quin, and Patrick climbed into the van at the back of the sporting goods store. With the engine cranked and the van rolling, Rico watched in the side mirror as they drove past his motorcycle. He longed to feel its power—its freedom—again. Wanted more than anything for things to be the way they were in the beginning and grab Angie and leave. Never look back. They were better off before all of this. Before the group. Having more people around only complicated things.

The van turned the corner and headed out toward the road.

"You mentioned you led some of the dead away from the store a time or two in the past. I think it would be a good idea to do that now, don't you?" Rico pointed toward the Academy parking lot.

The parking lot didn't have a single yard of pavement in view. It was nothing but shambling bodies. Rico imagined that parking lot was what it must have looked like at Woodstock back in the day. Just bodies as far as the eye could see.

"We'll do it later," Quin said, his upper lip rose as if he smelled something bad. "Don't want them dead creeps following us to the CVS. That wouldn't be good at all, you feel?"

"Right," Rico nodded, turning his attention away from the sporting good store's parking lot and toward the road ahead.

The van passed a number of zombies milling aimlessly about, but nothing like what was at the sports store.

Once Academy was out of sight, Quin cleared his throat. "I know you was outside my tent last night, yo."

Rico felt like he had just gotten slapped across the face. Was Q in the mood to pick a fight? He watched Patrick turn his gaze to the back of the van.

Quin laughed. "Don't worry about that sushi chompin' muthafucka. He don't understand us no how."

Rico's lips mashed together, and his cheek began to twitch.

"You was standing outside my tent when I was fuckin' your girl. You like watchin' us or somethin'?"

Your girl, he thought. *He's trying to make it personal.* "Excuse me?" Rico resisted taking the bait.

"What, did I stutter? I asked you if you got a thing for watchin' people fuck?"

"Hey, man," Rico stopped himself and took a breath, then raised a hand. "What Angie does is none of my business."

"Then why you been makin' it your business? I know how you feel about that bitch. I seen the way you been lookin' at her. She don't want you and your little Mexican burrito. She wants a real man. A man that knows how to stuff that shit."

"Don't you dare talk about her like that!"

"Or what, Rico?" Quin grinned, showing his gold teeth. "You gonna arrest me? Get over it, yo. She don't want you. So quit dreamin' and quit hoverin' over my tent. You know, I squirted in that bitch's face and she loved it. Licked it right up. That bitch is nasty. The only kinds of sluts that run that game been runnin' the train, you feel?"

The bastard wanted a fight, and Rico was about to make his wish come true. "Shut the fuck up before I—"

"Before you what, Rico?"

Rico reached for his gun.

"Don't even think about it, pussy."

The van rocked as it clipped something on the right side and then came to a violent stop. Not having his seatbelt on, Quin tumbled forward. Rico reached out and caught Q—mainly to keep him from smashing hard against him. The airbag burst from the steering wheel, and the horn blared a continuous bleat as smoke bellowed out from under the van's hood.

Quin grabbed at his head and flopped down on the floor.

Rico unbuckled his seat belt and leaned up to get a better look at Patrick, who was pulling himself away from the steering wheel. Patrick's eye was already swollen shut, his bottom lip busted. Blood ran down his chin.

"You okay?" Rico shouted over the horn's wail.

Patrick reached up and touched his eye. He winced in pain. When his mouth opened, Rico saw blood stained teeth.

"What the fuck, yo? You didn't see that fucking car or what?"

"Now isn't the time," Rico shouted. "You okay?"

Quin nodded, still holding a hand to his head.

"We need to leave. The noise will attract the undead."

"No shit," Quin said, and then groaned.

"Think you can move?" Rico asked, trying to help Patrick.

"Yeah." Patrick grimaced. "I'm a little shaken up, but I think I'll be okay."

"What the hell? That muthafucka speaks English?"

"Not now, Quin!" Rico looked to Patrick. "Can you sit up?"

Patrick nodded.

As much as Rico was surprised to find out the Asian could, in fact, speak English, now wasn't the time to have Patrick explain. He would have time to do plenty of that when they got back to the sporting goods store.

"Fuck seein' if Bruce Lee can move. See if the van'll start."

"I highly doubt it's going to start," Rico said, pointing toward the hood past the shattered windshield. "The front bumper is folded into the hood pretty good, and that steam coming out means the radiator's busted."

"Well, what about taking one of these cars?" Quin shouted, just as the horn finally gasped like a dying goose and went silent.

Moans rose in the distance.

Chapter 29

"We need to move." Rico reached around and unbuckled Patrick's seat belt. "Think you can walk?"

"I think so. My legs feel okay, but my chest and face . . ." Patrick's words faded into a cough.

Rico scrounged around the floorboard and found the three radios. He gave one to Quin and clipped the other two on his belt.

"Are you out of your fuckin' mind, yo? That would be suicide goin' out there on foot! We need some wheels. The store must be like five miles away," Quin said.

"More like two miles." Rico glared at Quin, unholstering the pistol from his hip and chambering a round. He jammed it home and looked back up at both men. "I don't think we have much of a choice. We're as good as dead if we sit here and do nothing. If you can hear them, then you know they're close by."

"He's right," Patrick said between pursed lips and gritting teeth.

"Fuck, yo." Quin threw his hands up.

"The store is only about two miles back. That's not all that bad. Could be worse. Could be twenty miles back. But it's not. So let's go before it's too late."

Rico nodded at Patrick. Patrick nodded back.

"Okay," Rico said, opening the van passenger door and stepping out into the street. "Patrick's in bad shape. I'll be the lead. Patrick stays in the middle, and Quin, you cover us at the rear. And don't shoot unless you absolutely have to. These things are attracted by sound. We can handle them at close range without our weapons so long as it's only a few. Firing a gun will only attract more. And then... well, then we're fucked."

"Fucked? No, I'm fucked," Quin said, helping Patrick out of the van and then stepping down onto the street behind him. "You just want me at the rear so I can get eat up by those fuckers. Hell no. You follow up at the rear. I'll lead."

"We don't have time to argue," Rico said, and then sighed. "Whatever, just start leading the way."

"My pleasure," Quin said, turning back to the wrecked van and pulling his shotgun from the floorboard. "Let's go!"

"Just take it easy and don't get too far ahead of us."

The three men stepped away from the van, scanning the street. There were no zombies lumbering toward them, at least, not yet. The air carried putrescent aroma and undead moans which echoed off of the buildings around them.

Rico walked at a brisk pace with a hand on Patrick's back— practically pushing him forward. Quin took the lead and never once looked back. The tall black man's dreads bobbed and swayed back and forth with each pounding step on the concrete. He didn't come to a stop until he reached the end of a building. Quin poked his head around the corner.

"We clear?" Patrick asked, blood dripping from his mouth and down his hand to his elbow.

Quin didn't reply. Probably didn't hear the man's weak voice. He kept his gaze fixed down the street.

Rico glanced toward the van. It was now at the end of the block, but still in view. That was when he saw them. The undead emerged from behind buildings and around corners. With each step forward, the moans grew louder.

"I'm gonna try that car," Quin pointed.

"We don't have time for that. Let's just stay low and keep moving."

However, it was useless. Quin dashed toward a green Saturn parked on the side of the road.

By the time Rico and Patrick caught up, Q had already tried the passenger door and had moved over to the driver's side.

"You're wasting time. We've got to keep moving," Rico said.

"Man, shut up." Quin yanked on the door handle. "You ain't in charge of nothin'!"

"Keep your voice down."

"We've got company." Patrick pointed back toward the van.

Rico didn't even bother to look at what he already knew was happening down the street.

"Shit, it's locked."

"Of course it's locked. It's parked on the side of the street," Rico said. "You could break out the glass, but what are the chances of the keys being in a parked car? We'll check out the next abandoned one we come to. Let's get the hell out of here."

"Suit yourself, dipshit," Quin said. "But when I get a ride, I'm leaving your ass behind. Go back to the store and slide my dick back in that blonde bitch of yours."

"You motherfu—" Rico charged forward, slamming into Quin.

Quin fell back and bounced off the Saturn. He dropped his shotgun in an attempt to block Rico's punch. It didn't work. Rico's fist met square with the tall dread-head's jaw. The connecting blow *cracked* like the sound of a lion tamer's whip. The impact of the punch sent Quin to his knees.

Holding his mouth, Quin spat blood on Rico's boot. "You hit like a girl."

"Guys, please!"

Ignoring Patrick, Rico said, "Soon as we get back, I'm out. Fuck you. And fuck the rest of the group. I'm gathering my gear and taking Angie with me. I'm taking her as far away from you as I can. You stupid prick. You're a bad influence. She deserves better than you!"

Quin laughed.

"Guys!" Patrick shouted again.

"What's so funny?" Rico asked.

"Better than me, yo?" Quin grabbed his shotgun and stood to his feet. Still holding his jaw, he said, "That bitch ain't never gonna change. She's been turnin' tricks for so long that's all she know how to do. And she'll keep doing it, too. You know how I know, Rico? Because she tricked you!"

Quin broke out in laughter and then turned and walked away.

"Where are you going?" Rico called.

"Back to the store. You two dipshits can find your own way back, you feel?"

Quin's laugh faded as he picked up his pace and began jogging down the side street.

***

The situation didn't go quite as Quin had planned. He thought he could get Rico to back down and let him lead the group. The cop had less bitch in him than Quin gave him credit for. He at least thought Rico would submit to his authority just to preserve the peace in the group. Especially since Angie had come on over to his side.

If that dumb muthafucka thinks he's gonna take Angie from me, he's got another think comin', Quin thought, heading toward the store.

And what was the deal with that Bruce Lee, muthafuckin' Patrick? That son-of-a-bitch spoke English better than he did. What's up with that? What else was that prick hiding?

Now with Rico in enemy mode and Patrick a potential adversary, Quin's clout in the group had dropped dramatically. He felt he could bully his way with Drew when it came right down to it. Drew had to deal with his wife's shit and wouldn't have the stamina to take him on head to head for leadership.

Fortunately, Quin recognized the area and knew the quickest route back to Academy. If he was lucky enough to make it back, he was determined to show them who was boss, once and for all.

***

"We need to stay focused on what's in front of us, not what's behind us," Rico said. "They're too slow to catch up with us from the van."

Patrick nodded, watching the undead leak into the streets in droves. There had to be at least twenty of them now—some of them closing the distance to the van at a faster pace than others.

"Think you got it in you to do a little running?" Rico hesitated to ask because Patrick looked like death warmed over.

"I can at least try to run for a little ways. I feel like dog shit." Patrick pulled out his revolver and held it close to his chest. "Damn, I wish we at least had a bicycle."

Rico gazed toward the path Quin took and realized he had no fucking clue where he was, or how to get back to the store. "You really could speak English all this time?"

"Yes, English is my first language. I didn't learn Mandarin until I went to college."

"Why would you pretend you didn't understand? I wasted a lot of fucking time over-explaining things hoping you'd pick up on the gist of the conversation. Others did, too."

"I had my reasons," Patrick said. "Trust issues, mainly."

Rico nodded and left it at that. If they didn't make it back to the store, it wouldn't matter anyway. Rico went from thinking Patrick might have a little of the crazy going on in his head to considering maybe the young man was 'crazy like a fox.' Quin had just now showed all his true colors to Rico. He'd bet Quin showed his ass a lot sooner in front of Patrick when he thought the Asian couldn't understand him.

"All right, let's go. We take the same way Quin went?" Rico asked.

"Yeah."

"Stay low and avoid any undead, if possible. They're slow, so I hope we can just outrun them."

Patrick turned and started off in a slow jog. Rico wished they could have moved faster, but considering everything, they were lucky Patrick could walk at all. After a few blocks, Patrick had them turning lefts and rights—snaking in between houses and buildings in an area where residential and business converged. At least one of them knew where they were and where they were going. Otherwise, Rico was sure he would have gotten lost. So far, they had been lucky. No run-ins with the undead yet.

The two continued the journey for what felt like thirty minutes. Above all, staying alive. Keeping their eyes open.

As they ran, their breathing getting heavier as they went, Rico felt his muscles burning. He thought back on when he used to be nothing more than an out of shape, overweight cop with a wife who hated him. A loser. He couldn't help but smile as they ran despite their situation. The burn of the run, the ache in his muscles, the heat of sweat beading down his brow, it all reminded him of who he used to be. The shell of a man who spent most nights lounging around at Pop's old bar. For a moment, he thought about what he and Angie would do if and when they got out of all of this. How he would give her as much space as she need and let time and circumstance determine where their relationship might go. Then, just as the first zombie shuffled out from behind a tree half a block ahead of them, Rico remembered.

The monster he thought he had put away came back. The crippling feeling of fear and defeat poured into him, making his gun once again feel heavy—the bullets inside calling, longing for him to end it all right then and there. One slight pull of the finger and he would be gone. Away from this hell on earth.

The zombie saw them approaching. It snarled and hissed as its eyes went wide. Its mouth dropped open, drool and matted blood dropping from its chin. With both arms raised toward Rico and Patrick, it slightly picked up its pace, eager to meet them. To give them a big hug. And embrace them with gnashing teeth and clawing hands.

"Oh no," Patrick gasped, stopping to aim his revolver.

"Shhh." Rico stopped, using his hand to lower the Asian man's weapon. "It will only draw out more. We can take it."

Although hesitant, Patrick complied.

The zombie lumbered forward. From the looks of it, the undead man in all his splendor and putrid glory had been a postman. The outfit was a dead giveaway. Not to mention the blue mailer's tote bag slung over one shoulder. The man was covered in dirt and brown muck that couldn't be anything other than dried blood. The skin below his right eye sagged and flopped with each step.

Rico walked toward it and put the gun in its holster.

"What the hell are you doing?" Patrick asked.

"I'm going to take care of it."

"Let's just go," Patrick whispered. "We can take a short detour."

"No," Rico said. "It might find a way to call others. I'm not sure how these things communicate yet, and I don't want to take any chances. It'll just take a sec."

As he stepped toward the approaching zombie, Rico knelt down, picking up an ornamental brick lining a flowerbed.

"Dude, I don't want to see this."

"So don't." Rico looked back.

Patrick tightly closed his eyes.

The undead postman started to open its mouth even wider. Just as it began to moan, Rico lunged forward with the brick up over his head. The rock came down on the creature's skull with a splattering effect that Rico didn't anticipate. The zombie's skull caved in as if no bone had been present under the scalp. With a dull splat, the zombie fell limp, blood and pink chunks of gore gushed from under the rock and mashed skull.

"Is it over?" Patrick asked.

"Yep," Rico said, staring down at the unmoving creature. When he turned back around to face Patrick, the Asian man still had his eyes closed. There was no time to warn him. "Patrick!"

A zombie had stepped out onto the sidewalk behind Patrick and was on him before he had time to react. The obese female fell onto his back with teeth snapping, tearing out chunks of flesh.

Patrick shouted out as he tried to get away.

"No!" Rico yelled, and dashed over to save his friend.

Patrick fell to the pavement, thrashing under the creature that must have outweighed him by 150 pounds.

The zombie clawed and bit, sinking its teeth deep into his right shoulder. Blood spurted forth as the zombie tore away loose fabric, skin, and muscle. Patrick's shirt instantly soaked with crimson.

The ghoul gulped flesh like a bird choking down a whole fish and went back for more.

Rico charged forward with his gun at the ready. At point blank, barrel jammed against the undead woman's skull, the former policeman pulled the trigger. Pus and matted chunks of dead flesh flew in every direction.

Patrick screamed.

The zombie fell limp.

Rico holstered his gun and pulled the woman off Patrick. The wounds on his back looked nasty. There was no time to do anything about that now. "Come on, man. Get up." He grabbed him under his arms and helped lift him up. "You can't stay here. We've got to move."

Patrick didn't say anything other than a few grunts and indecipherable curses. He was in obvious shock and in automatic mode when Rico pulled him along.

Blood gushed from Patrick's shoulder as they escaped. Zombies exited the open doors of homes, stepped out from the corners of streets, and out from behind abandoned cars.

Rico didn't stop this time. The cat was already out of the bag. With all the strength he could muster, he pulled Patrick along.

Rico wouldn't be able to make it to Academy unless Patrick stayed alive long enough to guide them there.

Chapter 30

Sweat streamed down Quin's face as he raced closer to Academy. Zombie activity had been light so far. He was able to smash a few skulls along the way with the butt of his shotgun and didn't have to resort to gunning them down.

For a minute or two, he heard an engine running in the distance. He did consider heading toward it, but the noise faded away. There was no doubt other people were alive. From the looks of things, most of them had to be in hiding. If that were the case, the passing of time would bring them out in the open. Quin imagined food in the typical household would last maybe a week at best. Desperation would put them on the hunt for food. Desperate people do desperate things. The living would become just as dangerous as the undead; no, the living would be more dangerous.

The store was still several blocks away when he keyed up the radio and called for help. No one responded. He wasn't in range just yet.

When he did get back, he'd have to immediately put his plan in action. Patrick would slow Rico down to buy him enough time to grab Angie and escape.

By now, he could see the blue Academy sign down the street. A mass of zombies swarmed out in front. Q continued running parallel to the side of the store until he passed it and ended up in the sparsely wooded, undeveloped strip that ran all the way behind Academy.

Two zombies wandered from behind a tree to give Q a big welcome. He brought the butt of the shotgun up, smashed the lead under the chin, and knocked it down. A well placed foot to the solar plexus laid out number two. Before either could get up, the shotgun butt mashed heads into the ground. After wiping brain goo on the grass, he keyed up the radio again.

"Hey, get them air horns blowing out front and unlock the back door." He waited a few seconds and called again. "Wake up, muthafuckas. We had to come back. Let us in."

The speaker beeped. "Q? Where are you?" It was Drew's voice.

"I'm out behind the store. Call the zombies to the front and unlock the back door."

"That was quick. Did you get Sarah's medicine?"

"I'll tell you the story when I get in. Get yo ass in gear before I end up a ten piece dark meat snack for a bunch of zombies!"

"All right, Debra's heading to the front to turn on the air horns. Sarah had an anxiety attack so I gave her some sleeping pills. I'll come to the back and move the SUV so you can drive the van in."

"Negatory, my brotha. There ain't no van."

The air horns wailed in the front. The few zombies between Quin and the wall of cars turned and shuffled off toward the noise.

"What happened to the van?"

"I ain't got time to talk. Get back here and unlock the door."

A minute later, Drew called. "It's unlocked."

Quin clipped the radio on his belt and ran the fifty yards or so to the wall of cars. He put one hand on the hood of a sedan and jumped, sliding his ass over the hood with the shotgun held high in the other hand. His feet hit the concrete as he slid off. *Just like in the movies*, he thought, giving his ego a boost that he could accomplish anything.

He made it to the door and turned the knob. Once inside, Drew was there with his gun pointing to the floor.

"Q? Where are Rico and Patrick?"

Quin wiped the sweat off his upper lip and waved his hand. "They didn't make it. Where's Angie?"

"Didn't make it? How—" All expression faded from Drew's face as the dread set in.

"Ain't got time to explain. Where's Angie?"

"In your tent, I think, but—"

"I want you to go turn off the horns and wait for me in the front."

"But—"

"Not now. Do what I said, and I'll be right there in a minute." Quin wasted no more time in the back, running down the hall and into the store.

He emerged near shelves of off season sales merchandise and dashed two aisles over to their tent. There was no time to make up some long, bullshit story. He was going to give the orders, and Angie was simply going to have to do what she was told. Where they would go was beside the point. He would have time to figure that one out once they were on their way.

"Angie, get your skinny ass out here," Quin said after arriving at the tent.

She grunted and poked her head from the tent opening. "What—oh, my God. What happened to you?" Angie stepped out of the tent and took Quin in her arms.

"That bitch cop friend of yours socked me in the mouth and left me for dead. That's what!"

"That doesn't make any sense. Why would he do that?"

"He's jealous and shit. Come on, we gotta go."

"You mean go now? Did you get the medicine, and are we all packed up?" Angie pulled away from him. "Where are Rico and Bruce Lee? What happened? We can't leave without them."

"I don't have time to explain," he said, stepping past her and crawling into the tent. "We need to leave."

The air horns in front stopped.

"Q, you're scaring me," Angie said. "Please... what happened? Where's Rico? You didn't kill—"

"Fuck Rico, and no, I didn't kill him, though I should have." He stuck his head out of the tent. "That wetback did this to me." He pointed at his lip. "He was the one with killing on his mind."

"Something had to have happened for him to have hit you. What did he say? What did you say?"

"I didn't say shit," he said, crawling back out of the tent. He flung a backpack over his shoulder, and said, "Rico's crazy. Lost his marbles, you feel? We ain't safe no more around that fool."

"I don't believe it," she said. "And until you tell me exactly what happened, I'm not going anywhere with you. Rico is my friend. He saved my life. He was there for me when no one else was."

"Hmm." Quin rolled his eyes and yanked Angie by the arm. "I said we ain't got time, and you just need to shut the fuck up and come with me."

"Hey, let go of me!" Angie struggled to pull from Quin's embrace.

"What's going on here?"

Quin turned and saw Drew with his hands planted firmly on his hips.

"I told you to stay in front. There ain't nothin' going on here you need to be concerned about."

"I got two eyes. I'd say there's a lot for me to be concerned about," Drew said, staring down at Quin's tight grip around Angie's arm. "Why don't you calm down? Let Angie go, and tell me what the hell is going on. I want to hear the whole story of what happened out there."

"I don't gotta explain nothin' to you, yo. You a disgrace to all us other brothas. Thinkin' you white and shit."

"Excuse me?" Drew said, stepping forward. "I believe you have it backwards, *'brotha'*!" He accented the remark using quotation fingers. "Working hard for a living and volunteering time to help make the community stronger doesn't make me white. I'm not trying to be white. I'm trying to be a man. Color makes no difference. As for you, all you've done is leech off of the system. Use every excuse in the book to get what others have worked for. Hard working people like myself. If either of us is the disgrace, it sure as hell isn't me. *'You feel'?'*" He used finger quotations again. "Now, let her arm go and start talking. No one is going anywhere until we get this over with."

"Man, fuck you." Quin let go of Angie and shoved her to the side. That was so he could hold the shotgun with both hands.

He pulled the trigger.

The shotgun blast reverberated like a cannon exploding in a Catholic cathedral.

Angie snapped her head back and swooned.

Drew gasped—his eyes and mouth agape with shock as he held his belly. He looked at Quin for a moment and then down at his bleeding abdomen. His body sagged, and his knees buckled. He fell, and blood splattered to either side as his stomach hit the floor.

Quin was busy congratulating himself when Angie turned on her heels and ran off. "Fuck that bitch," he said, kneeling down beside Drew. "I didn't need her anyway."

Drew struggled for breath, blood gurgling around his mouth. "Why...?"

"Why?" Quin chuckled. "Because people are like fish. After a few days, they get old and start to stink. We had a good thing going at first. Everybody was trying hard to get along. I got the proper respect. Then Steven had to turn into a head case. At least he had the decency to take himself out so we wouldn't have to put up with his shit. Patrick and that stupid slut daughter of yours was busy playing stink finger. That was going to lead to nowhere good. You and your wife thought you was Jesus and the Holy Mother. Saw the world only through your eyes. You didn't know how to keep it real. And Rico... well, I didn't like him much, but he knew what was going on. Had a level head. He was too much competition—maybe we was too much alike in some ways. But how was I supposed to get rid of him and keep Angie on my side? I done decided it don't matter much now. Seeing as how I kind of screwed up my relationship with Angie, what with shootin' you. But, shit, yo. I got a plan now. I don't need none of you. Time to smoke this joint." He laughed even harder now. "Heck, I made a funny." He patted his pocket and pulled out a lighter. "Won't have to share my weed with that blonde bitch anymore, either."

Quin stood to his feet, pulled a rolled joint from his backpack, and put it in his mouth. While he lit it, Drew grabbed him by the ankle. The dying man's grip was weak, but Quin had to give it to the man. At least he had some spunk.

He took a deep draw from the joint and held it in. After exhaling, he kicked Drew's hand away and started toward the front of the store. There was no turning back now. The only thing that mattered was him.

He sucked on the joint. The end burned while the smoke rolled down his throat. He held it in for a long time before exhaling.

***

Angie arrived at the Finley's tent and saw Debra frantically trying to wake Sarah. How was she going to tell them? What was Q going to do? She was scared for everyone's life now.

"Debra, uh, your mother. Is she okay?" Angie asked.

"What was that gun shot? Where's Dad?" Debra looked up with sad puppy dog eyes.

Angie bit her lip. "We need to get your mother up." She dropped to Sarah's side and began to shake her. "Sarah, wake up. We have to leave. Sarah."

Sarah's eyes blinked a few times before remaining open. She wiped her mouth and sat up. "What is it? What's going on?"

Angie rose and helped Sarah up and out of the tent. "We've got to hide until Rico gets back."

"Hide? Why? Where's Drew?" Sarah looked glassy eyed about.

"We don't have time. Come on, let's go someplace with a lock. The bathroom. We'll go to the bathroom and wait for Rico." Angie pulled Sarah along. "Come on, Debra."

"I'm not going without Drew. Where's Drew?" Sarah asked.

"I'll tell you when we get to the bathroom."

Sarah jerked her hand away and stopped in her tracks. "No, tell me now."

Angie's shoulders slumped. After a long pause, Angie said, "Drew's dead."

"What... what are you talking about?"

"Q shot Drew . . . he's dead."

***

Quin stood at the front doors to Academy contemplating how things could have been if Angie would have just listened in the beginning. Why did she have to ask questions? Make things so damn difficult? Now Quin was going to be without a for sure supply of pussy. How long would it be before he found a new squeeze? Hopefully not long. In just a few minutes, he'd have the cop's Harley underneath him and he'd be off to start a new life. Find a new place to call home—at least for a little while. Losing Angie would be hard on him. He really did have a soft spot for her in his heart, but he'd get over it. There were more bitches in the sea that would make him quickly forget about her. If he were lucky, maybe he could come across a greenhouse stocked to the brim with weed plants. He was imagining it now while he stared blankly out the glass doors toward the horde of undead eager to get in.

At his feet, the tile was stained red with the blood of Steven's brains. No matter how hard they had scrubbed, some of it just wouldn't come up. The dead gnashed and thrashed against the glass. Quin's presence antagonized them with the eager hope of sustenance sliding down their undead gullets.

Quin wasn't concentrating on the undead, not at all. He was imagining what his new life was going to be like. Now that he wasn't going to be tied down to a group, he could go anywhere he wanted. Do anything he wanted. He would go out into the country like Rico had suggested. Only, he would find himself a nice little house, far away from everything. Self-sustaining with a riverbed and windmill for power. The greenhouse in the backyard filled with full grown marijuana plants and ready for the plucking. The woman that would greet him at the door would be hot. It didn't matter what color she was. He wasn't picky. White, yellow, black, it didn't matter. Because she would be super model hot with big tits and a bodacious booty. Smoke all day and fuck all night. Yeah, it was out there. This wasn't just wishful thinking. He knew he would find her. Find his plants. He just had to get away. Be given the chance to look.

Quin wasn't about to share, not with any of these pricks. They were all stuck up. Rico and Angie. Patrick and Debra. Sarah and Drew. They were all just a bunch of trouble. And to make sure that he would have his prize to himself, he had to make sure that none of them had the chance to follow him. He had to take care of them now while he had the opportunity.

Quin smiled, took another drag from his joint, and held it in for a long while. When he couldn't hold it in any longer, he stepped up to the glass doors and blew out smoke. The smoke bellowed out of his mouth in a plume of gray that pressed against the glass in a spread of fog. Once the smoke cleared, Quin found himself staring one of the undead right in the eyes. His face was only inches away from the zombie. The only thing between them was glass.

"I bet it smells to high heaven in that parking lot." Quin chuckled. He took another hit and put the joint out, making sure to save it for the road.

With the buzz firmly kicked in, Quin stepped away from the glass and raised his shotgun. The plan was simple. Let them in the front door and make his way to the back. He would be out before Sarah and any of the others knew what the hell was happening.

As Quin lifted the gun, picking out which of the undead ghouls to aim at, he knew that his plan was sound. But he also knew he was a little too fucked up and not thinking everything through. He was too close to blow out the glass. He'd have to hightail it to the back, and he just wasn't in the mood to move that quickly. So he started down the aisle with the intent of getting as far away as possible before blowing the doors wide open.

Chapter 31

"How you holding up, buddy?" Rico asked, looking back at Patrick.

Patrick's face had red and whitish splotches over it. His eyes looked empty, like he'd been staring at the sun.

"Patrick?" Rico stopped.

Patrick stopped, too. Then he collapsed to the ground, gasping for air like a fish out of water.

The journey had finally come to an end for the young man. It was going to be hard telling the others what happened. No one had a chance to say goodbye. Debra would be devastated. He wished there was some way he could bring him back to the store, but that wasn't practical. They had managed to make it this far without much contact from the undead. There was no way Rico had any chance of eluding zombies while carrying Patrick on his back.

There was still one last thing to do. He had to make sure Patrick didn't rise from the dead and become part of the problem. The thought of smashing his head in with a brick like he'd done earlier brought frightful images to his mind. There was no way he could do that. A gunshot would be quick, but that would make too much noise.

Patrick heaved out a final breath. All went silent.

Rico felt for a pulse and came away with what he already knew. Patrick was gone.

He wanted to roll Patrick on his stomach so he wouldn't have to see his face while he laid him to final rest. Unfortunately, his plan wouldn't work if he did. Rico pulled out a six-inch hunting knife from Academy and placed it against Patrick's throat. The blade bit cleanly as it severed flesh.

Rico immediately remembered seeing the video of the journalist who was captured in 2002 by terrorists, and beheaded on film. The poor man was alive as the knife sawed into his neck. The video contained the audio of the journalist's cries. Time slowed, cementing each instant of torment in Rico's mind. The haunting memories of suffering such torture continued until his grisly job was complete.

"Goodbye, Patrick. Maybe you'll get some answers to some questions we all have." Rico regretted leaving the man on the street, but the dead would just have to bury the dead. He had to hurry back while he had a chance.

There was no way to know if Patrick had been leading them in the right direction. A block away, he saw a most wonderful sight. Academy was just down the street, minutes away.

*

Two zombies lay with their heads crushed on the way to Academy's back entrance. It was impossible to know, but Rico suspected Q was responsible. That son-of-a-bitch probably had made it to the store a good hour before him. What was that prick up too? Rico expected him to be pissed for taking a punch. Q might be in there right now making up some cockamamie story, trying to make himself look like a hero.

It looked like there was a battle coming up to pick a leader from what was left of the group. If Angie and the others decided to follow Q, well, he wished them luck. He was out of there, and there would be no turning back or time for regrets.

Rico unclipped the radio from his belt. "Hey, it's Rico. Unlock the door so I can come in." He waited for a reply and tried again. Nothing.

"Guys? Anyone? Drew, Angie? Q, if you can hear me, let me in. We can work any problems we have out." Rico felt like he spoke into empty air and clipped the radio back to his belt.

Maybe this was a sign that he should leave. Fuck 'em. Fuck 'em all. It'd be a tough go without more ammo and some basic supplies. He'd have to find a vehicle, too. He almost left, but then his thoughts returned to Drew and all the good the man did. It'd be wrong just to leave without at least saying goodbye. He needed to break the news of Patrick's death, too. He'd just have to figure out how to find a way in.

There were a few downspouts from the gutter that led from the roof to the ground that he might be able to climb. Even if the screws held, pulling himself up probably was a lot harder than it looked. The dumpster set against the back, not far from the door. It looked like it was high enough for him to get on top and grab onto the roof.

There was only one way to know for sure. He waited for a zombie dragging its leg to pass before he made the mad dash to the wall of vehicles. Once over the barricade, he stepped over to the dumpster. He momentarily thought of banging on the door, but realized that unless someone was in the back room, no one would hear, except for the zombies, of course. Though the vehicle wall had done a good job keeping the undead away, there was no need to call attention if he didn't need to.

An old pair of gloves lying to the side caught his attention. He picked them up and put them on. The leather fingers were stiff but softened with each finger flex.

Rico found a handhold on the green painted metal and began the climb. The smell emanating from the dumpster was beyond description. Decaying flesh of Steven and Malinda mixed with whatever else fermented in the bottom.

Black flies buzzed around as Rico pulled up. There were two doors on the top. One was open. The other door was closed. Right at the back, the top had about a two foot flat area. From there, it slanted at an angle. He carefully stepped on the flat part and positioned himself under the roof.

Rico raised his arms and came up short. He turned and looked behind him, realizing if he jumped and missed—and if his footing didn't come down right—he'd slip and hit the concrete pretty hard. That was just the chance he'd have to take. After a few slight knee bends and deep breaths, he made the leap of faith.

The gloves clenched around the metal roofing, and Rico pulled himself up. It wasn't an easy task, but fear had kicked in a few extra endorphins to ensure success. Good thing for him he spent all that time in the gym after The Spook, or he'd have never made it.

There was a consequence to his actions. His old rib injury throbbed when he walked away. Tough. No time to worry about that now.

Rico headed to the A/C unit on top that had a door and ladder that led to the inside of the store. Drew had painted a large S.O.S on the white metal roof in hopes someone flying by would spot it and call for help. Rico hadn't heard an aircraft of any type in days.

Once inside the store near the back, something just didn't feel right. The store was large and no one was expecting him. He almost called out but stopped himself. If something was going on, it might be better if he snuck around until he found out. That would help limit any surprises that might await him. He had his gun out and ready while stealthily moving in search.

He heard some steps and saw Quin with a backpack on his shoulder and the shotgun in his hand. Q stopped and turned around, lifting the gun up like he was about to shoot toward the front.

"Q, what the hell are you doing?" Rico called out.

Quin froze instantly.

"Put down the shotgun and let's talk."

The shotgun barrel lowered to the floor. Quin flashed his gold teeth, turned, and faced Rico. "Rico the burrito."

"What's going on? Where are the others?" Rico held his pistol in both hands pointed to the side.

"They's around. Where's that Bruce Lee muthafucka?"

"Patrick didn't make it, no thanks to you. Zombie bit him, and he died."

"You and me made it. That's all that's important, right?"

"Damn, Q! Don't you care for anyone else but yourself?" Rico fumed.

"Well, when you put it like that, no, I don't." Quin lifted the shotgun and pulled the trigger. The shotgun blasted out its report.

Rico dove for the floor and heard lead shot peppering objects behind him. He felt like a sitting duck and decided to use the chaos of the moment to his advantage. Rather than run, he rolled back in Q's line of fire and squeezed off two rounds. He didn't have a clear shot, but he fired anyway. His gun kicked twice, both bullets missed the target. Two additional rolls had him behind a display and on his feet.

"I'm gonna kill you just like I liked that white wannabe Drew!" Quin cycled the shotgun.

Rico bounded from the display he hid behind to the next. Quin fired and missed again. Rico's heart pounded, and he opened his mouth to suck in more air.

"Where's Angie?" Rico shouted.

"That stupid bitch ain't worth my time!"

"What have you done, Quin? Where's Angie?"

"You know what I done!" Quin shouted over the dead silence. "Come on out and face me like a man, yo!"

"Why, so you can shoot me?"

Quin laughed.

"I never did like you much, copper."

"The feeling's mutual," Rico said, ducking out from behind the rack and taking a blind shot.

The shot must have been close to its target, because Quin shouted and ran out from behind cover. By the time Rico thought he had a clear shot, the tall back man was down and out of sight behind a shelf stacked with fishing hats. At least Rico knew where he was now.

"Give up, Quin!" Rico called out.

"Or what, you gonna arrest me, yo?"

"Let's call a truce. It doesn't have to end this way. Where are the others?"

"I don't know. They all ran off after I killed Drew." Quin lifted his shotgun, but before he could fire again, a handgun discharged. The bullet nicked him across the left shoulder.

"You killed my husband!" Sarah ran onto the scene with a revolver pointed in the air.

Quin dropped the shotgun as his right hand instinctually grabbed his left shoulder.

Sarah fired two more times and missed. Q turned and slipped to the floor. Before he could get up, Sarah shoved the hat display on top of him.

"Get this bitch off of me," Quin shouted, "before I kill her too."

"Sarah, put the gun down and get out of the way." Rico stepped forward with his gun raised.

"I'm going to kill him for what he did to my Drew!" Sarah's gaze turned to the shotgun. She dropped the revolver and picked it up.

By this time, Quin was out from under the flimsy hat display and on his feet. "Give me my gun back, bitch!"

Sarah lifted the long gun and closed her eyes. Quin ran to the side right before the mighty blast.

The icy noise of shattering glass rang from the front of the store.

Sarah opened her eyes, her mouth opened wide when she realized what she had done.

Quin disappeared as Rico joined Sarah by her side. He blinked twice and watched the end unfold. The undead were in the store. One by one, they leaked in like water pouring in from a hole in a dam.

Moans reverberated off the walls along with the pungent aroma of decay. Zombies were shoulder to shoulder as they shambled into the front.

"Holy shit," was the only thing Rico was able to mutter as he watched more and more of them stream in through the doorway. Before long, the entire building would be filled with the sea of ghouls that waited outside.

Things looked hopeless, but he wasn't dead yet. "Sarah, where's Angie and Debra? Are they okay?"

Sarah slowly turned her head. "They're safe. Locked up in the public bathroom."

"We've got to get them and get the hell out of here!" He grabbed her arm and pulled her along.

"I'm not going anywhere," Sarah said, jerking away from Rico's grasp. "I need to be with my husband." She turned and ran.

There was literally no time for Rico to go after her. The undead were closing in—some of them now no more than twenty feet away, struggling down narrow aisles and past clothing racks. "Sarah, meet us in the bathroom," he called back as he ran.

"Drew? Drew? I'm coming for you."

If Angie and Debra weren't in the bathroom, there would be no time to look for them. Rico would just head to the back and fight his way out the best he could. He reached the bathroom door inside the shopping area and pounded on it. The undead moans seemed to increase when he did.

"Angie! It's me, Rico. Please... open the door!" He rapped on it a few more times and thought if the door didn't open in the next few seconds, he'd have to leave. "Angie!"

The dead drew closer.

"Angie!"

The bathroom door swung open. Rico looked in at Angie. Her eyes were dark from crying, her face laden with fear.

"Move," Rico said, shoving past Angie as he pulled the door closed. He locked it just as the first zombie stepped up to the door.

Now it was the undead that wanted in.

***

Sarah Finley shed large tears over the face of her dead husband. She held his blood covered hand and prayed, oblivious to the undead closing in around her.

They had been together for so long. It would be impossible for her to go on in life without him. She thought about how they had first met at a church home group. About how he had kept looking over at her during the Bible study—making sweet eyes and cute grins. And how, despite the fact that she expected him to talk to her that night, he didn't. When she least expected it, Drew showed up at her doorstep with flowers, introducing himself for the first official time. He had always been the romantic type. Taking her out to quiet spots for intimate dinners and talks. Walking in the deep woods of a well-lit park at night. Hands held together tight. That tender kiss on the cheek. Then, when he asked for her hand in marriage—pretending like the car had a flat so he could kneel down to fix the tire. The real reason he dropped to his knees was to pop the question.

Her tears turned from sadness to joy as she thought about their life together. About meeting their daughter, Debra. About how hurt she was when she found out how Drew came to know of the young girl. But love was deeper than mere lusts of the flesh, and she forgave him. And to this day, Drew was unaware she knew of his cheating ways, and knew nothing of her forgiveness. Her mind flashed to a time when all three of them went to Six Flags. How they rode the fast rides and ate lots of popcorn, but Drew was the only one to get an upset stomach. How she and Debra gave him a hard time all that weekend. But those days were over. Drew was gone, and all that remained was the walking dead.

When the zombies finally reached Sarah in her grief and started eating her, she tried to ignore the pain. Tried to stay in a peaceful place where music played, children laughed, and happiness electrified the air.

However, it didn't take long for the pain to become unbearable. Sarah Finley was jerked from her memories by the assault that tore through her entire body. Zombies ripped at her clothing. At her flesh. At her muscles. They bit, swallowed, and gnashed.

Sarah screamed out in agony.

Just before a zombie at her feet yanked on her calf bone, breaking it free from her leg, Sarah saw the last thing she would have ever wanted to see.

Drew Finley rose to join the feast.

***

Quin zipped across the aisle until he hit a wall and turned, heading for the back. Right now, shooting the front doors open seemed to be a bad idea. He didn't realize how fast the undead could flood the store. The damned weed made him bulletproof and ten feet tall. He should have prepared his escape better before smoking the joint.

At least he managed to grab his backpack. It contained some food, water, and ammo—enough to get him by for several days. That wouldn't matter if he didn't get his ass out in a hurry.

He passed through the doors leading to the back and hit the button on the rollup door. The mechanical clank told him it was opening, so he wrapped the backpack straps on the Harley's seat.

He swung a leg over, turned the key, and hit the start button. The machine roared to life.

Quin slowly let off on the throttle and stopped in front of the wall of cars. Only one zombie was near. It just so happened that the undead was approaching the SUV they moved to make an opening in the wall.

The Harley idled while resting on the stand. Q hopped in the SUV and started it. Once in drive, he mashed the gas and slammed into the zombie in front of it. When he felt the back wheel roll over the zombie, he hit the brake and killed the engine.

No time to worry about anything now but escape. A quick dash had him back on the bike and heading away from Academy.

The *thump, thump* of the cycle's engine mixed with the dull roar kicked up by excited zombies inundating the sports store. Q could only imagine what was happening inside.

Rico probably went all Rambo and met the zombies head on. *That stupid sucka must have got his flesh stripped like a hungry man eatin' a chicken leg.* He laughed.

That bitch Sarah probably fainted—didn't even know it when the time came.

Debra, hell, he had forgotten about the girl. Too bad about her. She never did or said anything bad to him. Well, it was pointless to worry about Debra now.

As for Angie, he hoped that bitch was trapped somewhere, sweating it out. Maybe she got to watch Rico served up for dinner. That would be the shit! He wanted Angie to pay for fucking up his plan.

That'll teach her. The whole time she'll be crying, I'll be laughing.

Q pointed the bike north and never looked back.

Chapter 32

Rico wasn't sure how long it had been since they locked themselves in the bathroom. They had periodically taken long naps, which made him feel that maybe it was already starting to lead into the next morning of the second day. He was normally starving by the time breakfast rolled around and had felt that way after the last three separate naps.

He leaned against the bathroom wall, the sink to his right. Under his left arm, Angie was asleep, her head against his chest. Debra also appeared to be asleep, her head lying against Angie's thigh—her thin body stretched out across the cold bathroom floor.

The bathroom door shook on its hinges, more so now than ever before.

The dead outside were persistent bastards. Since the moment, he had entered the bathroom after Angie, the dead outside pounded against the doors. Moaning and groaning.

They did so even now.

Rico tried to think of what he was going to do. What was there that he could do to save them?

Nothing came to mind.

In truth, he didn't blame himself for not coming up with anything, either. They were cornered. Trapped. There hadn't been enough time to take Angie and Debra to the roof after Sarah blew the doors open. He could have saved himself, but at the time, he never considered that an option.

Picking up the pistol off the bathroom floor, he held it gently in hand, not wanting to wake the girls. It felt heavy again… like before. He sighed, studying the gun. Its weight. The safety, which he clicked to the off position. The narrow barrel. The hole at the end. He glared down into the barrel as if trying to find some truth inside. Some glimpse into why this had all happened. Why Pop had to die. Why any of them had to die. And, of all things, why he hadn't been killed yet. He was tired, emotionally and mentally.

Easing his left arm free of Angie's head without waking her, Rico ejected the clip. He fingered the round hole of the hollow point bullet on top. At least he knew if he decided to end it, he had enough ammunition to do the job on all three of them. Too bad it wasn't enough to deal with the dead outside. If it had only been two or three of those putrid things out there, he would have already opened the door and let them in, picked them off one by one and been on his merry little way.

He knew there was more out there than that. He had seen it with his own eyes. By now, there had to be over a hundred or more zombies standing outside that bathroom door, waiting, longing to get in.

The more he thought about it, he knew what had to be done.

Now, while the girls were asleep... that was the time to do it. When they didn't see it coming. Take them out of their misery so that he could hurry up and do the same for himself. He thought of Steven, the cashier, and longed for that kind of freedom.

He shoved the clip back into place.

It *clicked* once. It was locked in.

Angie shifted. "What're you doing?"

"Nothing," Rico said. "Nothing..."

When she looked away, he started to point the gun at her head. He'd shoot her first. Hopefully Debra wouldn't wake in time to realize what happened before the next bullet reached her brain. But when Angie looked back, Rico still had the gun pointed to the ceiling.

"What are we going to do, Rico?"

"I don't know," he said, watching the bathroom door shake against the hinges. "I don't think the door is going to hold much longer."

"I don't either," she said. "We're not going to make it, are we?"

"I don't know," Rico said again, his voice low. "We still have electricity and water. Maybe it's a fluke. Maybe, though, there are people out there able to keep it going. Maybe help isn't as far away as we fear. I just don't know. Here, let me up. I've got to pee."

Which was true. He'd had to pee for a long time now but didn't want to wake the girls. So, instead, he waited. Now that Angie was awake, he was able to relieve himself. She slid off of him while keeping her legs still so as to not wake up Debra.

Rico got to his feet and stepped over the young lady toward the urinals. Once inside, he closed the bathroom stall door and lifted the lid. With his pants unzipped and his Johnson out, it came instantly. The pressure relieved itself as the yellow substance streamed loudly into the water filled bowl. He thought of it waking Debra, but it was too late now. He had been holding it for a while. As he stood there going, his junk in one hand and his gun in the other, Rico looked down and saw a small round shape at the base of his jean pocket. Curiosity peaked; he set his pistol down on the toilet paper rack and dug into his pocket. Once he saw it, he remembered.

After he was done, he zipped up and stepped out into the bathroom, the small round object in his open palm.

"What you got?" Angie asked, now standing and looking at herself in the mirror.

Debra was still asleep. Her notebook carefully placed on the counter by the sink.

"A coin. The dime Q gave me back at the CVS," Rico said, and smiled.

"So much for good luck."

"Maybe the dime has nothing to do with luck."

Angie turned around. "You know, I've wanted to ask you about something you said to me—back at the trailer while I was jonesing for a hit. You said I was, 'just like Jennifer.' Who's Jennifer?"

Rico held on to the coin between his thumb and forefinger. "Jennifer was my older sister. She, too had a problem with drugs—with heroin. I was young. Around eight years old. I didn't understand her problem, mainly because my parents never explained it to me. They told me she was sick. I didn't find out until later—after she died—that she had been in and out of treatment to get off the stuff. She supported her habit by hooking, too. She never could break clean. My father loved her more than his own life. He blamed me for her death."

"You? What could you have possibly done for him to do that?"

"Jennifer was at home recovering from an ass beating her pimp put on her. She was bed ridden, and I stayed with her while Mom and Dad went to work. Jennifer had me go to a friend's house to get her some *medicine*." The words hung in Rico's throat. He sighed, and continued. "I was a kid. I didn't know. She was so happy when I gave her the bag. Of course, I didn't look in the bag, didn't know what was in it. Later I . . . I heard her scream out and went into the room. She thrashed around a bit. A belt was tied around her arm and the syringe was still in. I didn't know what to do to help her, but I did call 911. They were too late to help." Rico closed his eyes.

"I'm so sorry that happened to you," Angie said in a soft voice. "Your father blamed you for her death because you brought Jennifer the stuff?"

"Yep, he sure did. He's treated me like crap ever since then, too—never failing to remind me I brought the dope home that killed his daughter. I blamed myself for her death, too—for years, I blamed myself. It wasn't until after I left home and joined the Coast Guard that I had time to sort things out and realize it wasn't all my fault. Still, I have memories that haunt me from that day. How if I had stayed home, or called my parents first, Jennifer would still be alive."

"So that's why I reminded you of your sister. She was hooked on drugs and used you to get them for her. When I needed drugs, you didn't want to be any part of that—because you were afraid I might OD and you'd be partially responsible again."

Rico thought a moment. "Yeah, yeah, I guess that's pretty much it."

"And that's also the reason why you took such a special interest in a junkie whore to begin with? You thought of me as your older sister that you might be able to save."

"Yes and no. I mean, yes I did feel responsible for keeping you away from drugs. That maybe I could help right a wrong of the past in some way. But at some point, I wasn't sure if I had other feelings for you or not."

Angie leaned against the counter. "I know what you mean. The way you were concerned about me, how you protected me, no other man has ever acted that way. It touched me. It really made me feel special. You are special, Rico."

"Well, not so much. I'm just doing what any decent person should do."

"No, you really are special. You made me believe that I could be someone that I'm not. Gave me hope that I could be something better. At least I lived the fairytale for a little while."

Rico reached out and gently grabbed her shoulders. "It wasn't a fairytale. You could have been that person. You could have become whatever you put your mind to."

She moved his hands away. "No, that was all just some pie in the sky bullshit. When Q showed up at the CVS, what did I do? I went back to being the same person I was. Repeating the same mistakes. A dog returning to its own vomit. I know better than to act that way, but it feels comfortable. It's who I am. I'm destined to be a worthless piece of trash and there's no getting around it. I can tell you right now, if I ever get a chance to shoot up again, then I'm going to do it."

He held out the dime and looked at it. "They say life can turn on a dime. One day, we think we know where the world's heading, the next it becomes something we never expected. One day, we don't want to live, then the next day we do, and then the next day we don't." Rico shook his head. "It's a fucked up world we live in, isn't it?" The dime went back in his pocket.

"It is, and I'm tired of it."

At least Rico now understood his feelings for Angie had been misplaced. The image of whom and what she could become was just a fantasy he created in his own mind. Saving Angie wouldn't have made up for the past with Jennifer anyway.

"I'm tired too, Angie."

"What are you saying?"

"I'm saying that door isn't going to hold out forever. It's sooner rather than later before it gives. I can bring the end quicker." Rico stiffened his back, praying he had the resolve to keep the commitment.

Angie turned her gaze toward Debra. "I don't want to die by your hand. That would be wrong—and I'm too chicken-shit to kill myself. As stupid as it may sound, I want to die fighting. I want to take as many zombies with me out there as I can. But Debra . . . Rico, she's still asleep. Save her from what's on the other side of the door."

He reached in the pocket with the small .22 caliber revolver and pulled it out. The gun fit in the palm of his hand.

"Is that thing real?" Angie asked.

"Yes, it'll do the job without making a huge mess." He squatted next to Debra. She slumbered on. Perhaps it was from exhaustion, perhaps her body shut down because of the hopelessness of the situation, or maybe there was a God up there, mercifully keeping her asleep until he could complete the task.

Rico gazed up at Angie. She nodded and closed her eyes, turning her back to them.

Bam!

Debra's body jerked, and then remained still. Blood trickled to the floor by her head.

He rose and pulled out the Beretta. Instantly, his pistol felt lighter. He wasn't going to use the gun to take Angie's life or his. The burden of despair lifted from its cold steel.

This was the end. They could give up or fight to the death. They at least had each other and wouldn't die alone. That was worth something.

Just as Rico handed Angie the 22 revolver, the bathroom door fell open, the hinges busting loose. The horde of undead waiting to get in groaned with pleasure. From where Rico stood, he could see nothing but corpse after undead corpse. The store was packed with bodies.

Reflexes kicked in.

Euphoria flooded his entire being.

When life begins at birth, it's a violent event. Why should death be any different? If he came into the world screaming and crying, then it seemed fit to go out the same way. If life was glorious, then death would be glorious, too.

Rico pulled the trigger—firing into the crowd. He wanted to die fighting, leaving one last mark on the Earth.

You never know when, but life can turn on a dime.

Chapter 33

The ride down the old rural highway made Quin think of the few times he got to visit his grandpa before he passed away. The old man lived down a farm-to-market road on a few acres next to a pond.

Paw Paw T, the T short for Terrance, was a retired widower who kept busy by living off the land. Corn, peas, and a variety of other vegetables grew in the garden. The chicken coop housed a number of hens, and there was always at least one rooster around, strutting his stuff.

Q liked to feed the chickens and was amazed they would eat practically anything you threw to them. He also liked to go by the bank of the pond and catfish with a cane pole. Paw Paw T would keep the bait fresh on the hook while smoking hand-rolled cigarettes and occasionally taking a pull from a flask filled with homemade shine.

He was probably near the age of five when Paw Paw T had a stroke and died less than a week later. Q remembered the funeral. Everyone dressed in their Sunday best. The men all in flashy suits. The woman with bright makeup and wearing black dresses, large, flowery hats on their beauty shop hair.

When Q built up enough nerve to view the body, he was shocked to see Paw Paw T wearing his overalls and red checkered shirt. Of course, he had never seen the man wear any other clothing on the times he visited him. Q asked his mother why Paw Paw T wasn't buried in a suit. His mother said her father made his mind known he wanted to wear his overalls and work shirt to the grave—and he'd come back and haunt 'whoever' put him in a suit.

That's the kind of place Q wanted to find. Someplace where he could fish, have some chickens, grow some food, and lots and lots of weed.

He was surprised he had a want to live off the land. All the years living the urban life style was a direct clash from his grandpa's time. Maybe it was genetic. Maybe it was in his blood to be a farmer.

A school bus lay on its side just up ahead. It partially blocked his lane. He downshifted and slowed as he passed.

The bike traveled a mere 30 miles an hour when a zombie lurched out from behind the bus right into Q's path.

The undead was no match for the mighty machine. The living corpse took full impact and was knocked several feet backward—twisting and tumbling along the road.

Unfortunately for Q, the handlebars wrestled from his control, flipping him headfirst over the bike. Man and machine skidded along the rough asphalt highway, sometimes connecting in a brutal dance.

When Q's mangled body came to a rest, the Harley's engine coughed out its last breath. He was injured, but he didn't think he was too bad off. Some road rash on his left arm, but nothing else seemed to hurt right then.

The sunlight filtered through the trees that lined both sides of the road, and a breeze ruffled the leaves. Q took a deep breath and pushed himself up on his elbows. He had to blink twice to believe his eyes.

His left leg was broken at the knee and twisted to where he could look directly at the sole of his shoe. The other leg was a shredded, bloody mess. This was bad. Real bad.

The shock slowly started to wear off and searing pain from the injuries began to grow.

Something scraped across the pavement nearby.

Q slowly turned his head and focused through the pain to see what it was.

The zombie that took him down crawled toward him on hands and knees.

He reached to his side for his gun, but it was gone. The backpack was still attached to the bike, but between him and the zombie. Q had nothing to fight back with.

The zombie edged closer—lifting its chest from the ground as the move of each hand brought it closer. A gold chain around its neck connected to large gold letters that spelled MARCUS.

Q screamed as he rolled on his stomach. He had to get away. Had to pull himself to freedom so he could live out in the country like his grandpa. He wanted to live. He wanted to grow weed and stay high every day of his life. He wanted—

Marcus's reanimated corpse reached out and grabbed Q by the dreads. It pulled the tall man's head around until the two looked eye to eye.

Quin rolled back over and with flailing arms tried to keep the zombie at bay, but Marcus was too hungry and strong for a dying man.

The first bite tore off a few fingers from the right hand. Blood gushed down Q's arm and splattered his face. The next bite took off a thumb and a good chunk of the palm.

The world spun in Q's mind, and he threw up.

Marcus ate on.

Quin had felt pain before, but this time it was unique. He wished he could have had one last smoke before it ended like this. But no amount of pot could ever extinguish the agonizing pain of being eaten alive.

He saw bits of his own flesh between the teeth of the ravenous zombie. Blood dripped from its chin on to the large gold letters on the chain.

A soft voice in his mind's eye called Quin's name. Darkness faded in.

Epilogue

Three months later

The blades of the Black Hawk helicopter cut through the air above Academy Sports in Bryan, Texas. Four soldiers were strapped to their seats inside, waiting for the pilot to bring them in.

"Andy, it doesn't do any good to close your eyes. You're still up in the air the whole time," Steve Rogan said.

"I don't care what you say. I'm *skeerd* of heights." Andy had latched his thumbs around the shoulder straps to either side and held on for dear life. "I didn't sign up to be no paratrooper. They drafted my ass for this."

"Well, there aren't as many of *us* around as there used to be. You've got to suck it up and do it for your country. Besides, we're not jumping out of here with a parachute."

"It don't matter. I don't like hangin' my ass off no ladder."

A voice broke over the radio. "Not much activity on the ground. Don't know what's inside. In position now. Good luck, guys. Keep your eyes peeled."

Rogan and two others unsnapped the seat belts and rose.

"Andy, this is ridiculous. Come on." Rogan tossed the ladder off the side. It fell toward the roof that had a large S.O.S painted across it.

"Oh, all right." Andy Wells fumbled his way out of the seat belt and put his rifle over his shoulder. Rogan waited with an open hand to help him. The other two troops had already made the descent to the roof.

"Come, on. Piece of cake."

Andy turned his gaze down. "Hmm, looks a whole lot better when yer only twenty feet from the ground."

Rogan raised a thumb and followed Andy down the ladder onto the roof.

It was dark inside the store. Everyone had night vision goggles on and carefully stepped down the aisles.

"Collins, you and Horwitz go that way and look for survivors. Stay in touch on the radio. Expect the unexpected. Wells and I will see if there are any guns and ammo left."

Both men raised a fist. Collins led the way toward the front of the store.

"This place sure is creepy." Andy pointed to the mounted animal heads on the wall.

Rogan shrugged it off and headed toward the glass counter along the back. Today was the second day they had been off base to search for more supplies. It had taken three months to secure enough infrastructure and regroup to have the resources to go out on missions again. Conditions hadn't improved enough to go out on pure search and rescue missions to find others alive. The military was still too thin to do that. But if they came upon survivors needing help, they would do the best they could to bring them back.

Broken glass crunched underneath Rogan's boots. The glass cases had been pilfered of all handguns. The racks along the wall holding long guns were empty as well. No ammo of any kind remained on the shelf.

"Jackpot!" Andy called out.

Well, if there are any zombies in the store, they're sure to find us now, Rogan thought.

Andy delightfully giggled.

Rogan turned the corner and saw Andy with a stack of caps in his hand.

"Lookie here, lookie here. The official NFL Dallas Cowboys 2017 Super Bowl Champion cap. I always wanted me one of them."

"Andy, I . . ." Rogan took a deep breath. "Never mind."

Collins and Horwitz double timed down the main aisle and approached Rogan. Horwitz held something in his hand.

"Store's empty. No zombies, and no one left alive," Collins said.

"So there were people here at one time?" Rogan asked.

"Yeah. Found the remains of one by a tent. Over in front of a bathroom, we found a bunch of zombies killed by headshots. Looks like there were three inside the bathroom that didn't make it. The door was ajar so I guess the zombies eventually broke down the door and overwhelmed them."

Rogan turned his gaze to the floor and then looked up at Horwitz. "What are you holding on to?"

"It's a notebook. Looks like a girl named Debra used it for a diary." Horwitz handed the notebook to Rogan.

The front of the notebook had hearts drawn all over it. Inside each heart, a name was written. 'Drew,' 'Sarah,' 'Steven,' 'Malinda,' 'Q,' 'Rico,' and 'Angie.' There were two hearts intersected with one another; 'Debra' was written in one heart and 'Patrick in the other. He opened the notebook and flipped through the pages.

"I guess it tells the story of the group until the end," Horwitz said.

"I guess so." Rogan closed the notebook. "I can't imagine how many different stories of these dark times will be recorded before this war is over."

The End

SEVERED**PRESS**

f facebook.com/severedpress
y twitter.com/severedpress

CHECK OUT OTHER GREAT ZOMBIE NOVELS

Z BURBIA
by Jake Bible

Whispering Pines is a classic, quiet, private American subdivision on the edge of Asheville, NC, set in the pristine Blue Ridge Mountains. Which is good since the zombie apocalypse has come to Western North Carolina and really put suburban living to the test!

Surrounded by a sea of the undead, the residents of Whispering Pines have adapted their bucolic life of block parties to scavenging parties, common area groundskeeping to immediate area warfare, neighborhood beautification to neighborhood fortification.

But, even in the best of times, suburban living has its ups and downs what with nosy neighbors, a strict Home Owners' Association, and a property management company that believes the words "strict interpretation" are holy words when applied to the HOA covenants. Now with the zombie apocalypse upon them even those innocuous, daily irritations quickly become dramatic struggles for personal identity, family security, and straight up survival.

ZOMBIE RULES
by David Achord

Zach Gunderson's life sucked and then the zombie apocalypse began.

Rick, an aging Vietnam veteran, alcoholic, and prepper, convinces Zach that the apocalypse is on the horizon. The two of them take refuge at a remote farm. As the zombie plague rages, they face a terrifying fight for survival.

They soon learn however that the walking dead are not the only monsters.

SEVEREDPRESS

 facebook.com/severedpress

 twitter.com/severedpress

CHECK OUT OTHER GREAT ZOMBIE NOVELS

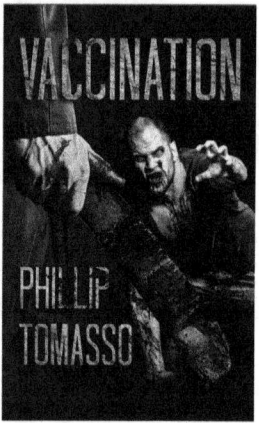

VACCINATION
by Phillip Tomasso

What if the H7N9 vaccination wasn't just a preventative measure against swine flu?

It seemed like the flu came out of nowhere and yet, in no time at all the government manufactured a vaccination. Were lab workers diligent, or could the virus itself have been man-made? Chase McKinney works as a dispatcher at 9-1-1. Taking emergency calls, it becomes immediately obvious that the entire city is infected with the walking dead. His first goal is to reach and save his two children.

Could the walls built by the U.S.A. to keep out illegal aliens, and the fact the Mexican government could not afford to vaccinate their citizens against the flu, make the southern border the only plausible destination for safety?

ZOMBIE, INC
by Chris Dougherty

"WELCOME! To Zombie, Inc. The United Five State Republic's leading manufacturer of zombie defense systems! In business since 2027, Zombie, Inc. puts YOU first. YOUR safety is our MAIN GOAL! Our many home defense options - from Ze Fence® to Ze Popper® to Ze Shed® - fit every need and every budget. Use Scan Code "TELL ME MORE!" for your FREE, in-home*, no obligation consultation! *Schedule your appointment with the confidence that you will NEVER HAVE TO LEAVE YOUR HOME! It isn't safe out there and we know it better than most! Our sales staff is FULLY TRAINED to handle any and all adversarial encounters with the living and the undead". Twenty-five years after the deadly plague, the United Five State Republic's most successful company, Zombie, Inc., is in trouble. Will a simple case of dwindling supply and lessening demand be the end of them or will Zombie, Inc. find a way, however unpalatable, to survive?

 SEVERED**PRESS**

facebook.com/severedpress
twitter.com/severedpress

CHECK OUT OTHER GREAT ZOMBIE NOVELS

900 MILES
by S. Johnathan Davis

John is a killer, but that wasn't his day job before the Apocalypse.

In a harrowing 900 mile race against time to get to his wife just as the dead begin to rise, John, a business man trapped in New York, soon learns that the zombies are the least of his worries, as he sees first-hand the horror of what man is capable of with no rules, no consequences and death at every turn.

Teaming up with an ex-army pilot named Kyle, they escape New York only to stumble across a man who says that he has the key to a rumored underground stronghold called Avalon..... Will they find safety? Will they make it to Johns wife before it's too late?

Get ready to follow John and Kyle in this fast paced thriller that mixes zombie horror with gladiator style arena action!

WHITE FLAG OF THE DEAD
by Joseph Talluto

Millions died when the Enillo Virus swept the earth. Millions more were lost when the victims of the plague refused to stay dead, instead rising to slaughter and feed on those left alive. For survivors like John Talon and his son Jake, they are faced with a choice: Do they submit to the dead, raising the white flag of surrender? Or do they find the will to fight, to try and hang on to the last shreds or humanity?

www.ingramcontent.com/pod-product-compliance
Lightning Source LLC
Chambersburg PA
CBHW070813180626
46818CB00001B/248